THE ZION CABLE

THE ZION CABLE

RON HELLSTERN

Editorial work by Eschler Editing

Cover design by Jason Robinson

Interior print design and layout by Caroline Bliss Larsen

Production services facilitated by Scrivener Books

RED ROCK CANYON
PUBLISHING COMPANY

Published by Red Rock Canyon

978-1-949165-26-5

This book is dedicated to David Flanigan, who built the actual cable system back around 1900 in what is now Zion National Park. I intentionally wanted my characters (and the love, murder, and mystery) to be lightly associated with Flanigan, but it should be noted that they and all the events, other than the cable itself, are strictly fiction.

1

Red Rock Country

Four-Ghost Canyon, Southern Utah, 1885

L ISTEN," SHE WHISPERED. "It sounds like someone is calling for help . . . or dying." The slender Paiute woman put her hand up to her ear, which signaled the teenage boy to hold still.

He listened for a full minute before he shook his head. "Star, it's just the wind. Relax."

"I have never heard the wind sound like moaning," she said. "Someone is dying. I told you I did *not* want to come into this canyon. This is an evil sign."

"It's the wind."

"Something in here frightens me."

"I think you're scaring yourself. There's nothing here to harm you, and *I'm* here to protect you."

She raised one eyebrow at his bravado but continued walking.

The summer heat made fifteen-year-old Colton Grey take a drink from his canteen. He took off his hat, wiped the sweat from his forehead, and ruffled his blonde hair to cool off.

"Do not tell me you are tired, Colton. I am nearly twice your age." She smiled despite her nervousness.

He fanned his face with his hat. "I'm not tired Star," he sighed, "but I hate this hot, desert country. That's why I like it here in the shady, narrow canyons." He walked over to the canyon wall and pressed his face against it. "You can lean against the cool stone and sometimes you can almost smell water locked deep inside the sandstone."

There was no perspiration on his stepmother's face. Her long, black hair remained in a perfect braid. "It is cooler here," she admitted, her smile beginning to fade. "And I do love the red color of the stone. Look at the red canyon walls stretching right up to that perfect blue sky. Don't you love that color?"

He glanced upward at the walls of the narrow sandstone canyon. Shades of red, copper, and tan were textured in layers and garnished with ferns and flowers along the base. The stone was smooth and wavy for a thousand feet skyward, as though Michelangelo had begun some of his finest sculptures there.

"Yeah, it's a nice color. But *everything* here is red . . . and dusty. We need more green, like that Manzanita bush. I'm tired of choking on desert dust, and I'm tired of red, red, red." He spun around and stirred up more dust from the dry canyon floor, "Oh, I didn't mean red *skin* Pootseev," he said quickly. He only used her Paiute name for *Star* when he was upset.

She smiled. "I know." But she looked toward the ground, long lashes covering her eyes.

"I like red skin. Wish mine was red . . . but not sunburn red. That's another problem with living in a desert," he grumbled.

"You look like your father, and you should be proud of that."

He kicked a rock. "Maybe *he* should be proud of me. He's always mad at me, unless I'm working." The word *working* echoed off the canyon walls. It embarrassed him to complain in front of her. She never complained about anything... except coming into this canyon.

"You work hard, and he knows that. He loves you very much. He just has a hard time showing it."

"He's mean. He blames me for my mom dying when I was born, and anything else that ever goes wrong on our ranch. Sometimes I wonder why you married him and took up raising me."

"Because I fell in love with both of you," she said, brushing her hand against his cheek. "We make a great family, red and white. And I have felt that way ever since I first saw you as a little boy playing down by the river."

"Yeah, well, he fell in love with you because you're beautiful and kind to everyone. But he also needed someone to take care of me."

"Colton, stop," she said softly while placing her hand on his shoulder.

She continued walking on to a sandbar where the canyon was nearly fifty feet wide. There she knelt near the base of the stone and picked a colorful mix of yellow columbines and violet shooting stars. Smiling, she touched them to her nose and inhaled. A sweet scent enveloped her face as she stood and closed her eyes to savor the aroma. She tiptoed behind Colton and placed several flowers in his shirt pocket. "Do you remember when you were a little boy and I would bring flowers to your bedside at night, scatter them on your pillow, and sing you to sleep? That was to make sure you had only pleasant dreams. And I loved it when you would say, 'Good night, Mother, I love you.'"

"I remember." He smiled. "I remember that you would also bring them to our table for every meal. And you pressed and dried some for the winter season. It's a wonder we still have flowers growing anywhere around here," he said with a grin.

She looked downward and was about to apologize, but his smile showed he was teasing.

"I thought you were the greatest mother a boy could have. And all the kids at school felt the same way about you. I would feel happy and sad when I heard some of them say they wished you were their mother. Since my own mother died when I was born, I . . . I . . ."

"Colton Grey, come here." She stepped forward and gave him a brief, gentle embrace. "Let us just talk about my grandfather's cave. You picked a beautiful day to lead me into this frightful place. If others in the village knew I had come into any slot canyon, they would be very upset." She stared into his eyes, put her hands on his shoulders, and spoke softly. "And I am not happy you have been exploring canyons all by yourself."

"Sometimes I like being alone. It's safe and quiet here."

"Safe?" she asked, her eyes darting around the canyon walls, looking for danger.

He remained silent.

Her eyes narrowed. "Colton, someone told me Ethan Morley and his friends were giving you trouble at school. Is that true? Is that why you come into the canyons?"

"Who told you that?" he snapped as he glared into her eyes. "I'm not running away from Ethan!" He spoke boldly, but it was that same boldness that betrayed the truth behind his words; Ethan was the town's bully, and Colton was his favorite target.

"It does not matter who told me. I just want you to always be safe and happy. What do they do to you at school?"

He looked away and mumbled, "I can take care of myself."

"I know that, but if there's a problem—"

"It's mostly just teasing about my name. It isn't a big problem."

"What do you mean about your name?"

"When I was eight years old and went to school for the first time here, the teacher asked us to tell our names and where we lived. She just wanted to be able to attach names to faces."

"That is a good idea."

"Unless you have a strange name like mine. Nobody had ever heard of a Colton before.

I explained to the teacher how my father worked in a coal town in England and wanted a name that connected me to his past and how it was also my mother's maiden name, but everyone just thinks it's weird. It's been seven years, and Ethan still won't let me forget it," he grumbled as he threw a stone up the canyon. "But, like I said, it isn't a big problem."

"Children can be cruel, like some adults. Sometimes when you were late coming home, I thought you might be out riding your horse with Tavaci or visiting Amber Duncan, not running away from anyone."

Taking a sudden interest in his boots, he stepped back and mumbled, "I don't go off to visit Amber."

"Of course you don't." She smiled. "Why would you want to go visit the most beautiful girl in the world?"

His face brightened. "You think she is too? I . . . I mean, she's pretty enough . . . I guess."

"I am sorry. I have embarrassed you. Let's keep walking. What makes you think this canyon is the right one?"

"Because I've explored every other canyon for miles around. So far I haven't found any markings or carvings anywhere. This is the only one I haven't been in very far. It has to be this one . . . I hope."

"If you are right, the signs should not be hard to find. My grandfather said he marked the cave entrance by carving images of himself, grandmother, and my parents sitting in a line, with baskets on their backs. After he told the people in the village about the cave, the four of them left one night and were never seen again. The village elders then forbade everyone from going into the canyons."

"So wouldn't the name Four-Ghost Canyon be a hint that this might be it?"

"The people called *all* the narrow canyons Four-Ghost because they don't know which one they went into, and they did not want to lose anyone else." Her eyes began to moisten as she lowered her voice. "But now you are old enough to help me, and I want to know what happened to my family."

He touched her arm to console her. "Now *I'm* your family. Well, me and Tavaci. We could have used his humor these past few miles. Why didn't we bring him along?"

"There's no reason to get him into trouble with the elders, and my younger brother does not keep secrets at his age."

"Wait a minute. He's as old as I am."

"I know." She frowned. "That's exactly what I mean."

He was about to protest, but Star was staring past him, her mouth dropped open, to where the canyon narrowed to only eight feet across and the red stone walls became a chocolate-brown color.

"That must be Ioogoon," she whispered, "the arrow quiver." She stepped back and clasped her hands by her heart. "I heard stories about this when I was a child. It is the place of Wainopits and Kinesava, the evil ones." Her eyes widened as she scanned the rocks for danger and felt certain the canyon was closing in upon them. To her, it was now a breathing beast with a heartbeat.

"We've been in here all day, and nothing evil has happened to us." Colton snickered. "I think you're scaring yourself."

She suddenly grabbed his shoulders from behind and shouted, "Look!"

He jumped away from her grasp. "Whoa, why did you do that? Are you trying to scare me to death?"

Her silence made him turn to see her wide-eyed and pointing at a red figure painted on the rock wall about fifteen feet above them. It was an inverted, life-sized handprint with a spiral on the palm.

She trembled, and her expression changed to one of distress. "That is not a good sign," she whispered. "This *is* an evil place."

Colton squinted and shook his head in confusion. He stepped toward the handprint, but she held out her arm to stop him.

"The hand can mean health and the spiral the eternal path, but the hand is upside down. That means death. We should—" She quickly put both hands up to her ears.

"What is it?" Colton asked.

She placed one hand on his mouth to silence him, leaned forward, and tilted her head to listen.

He moved her hand aside and whispered impatiently, "What do you hear?"

She sighed. "Onoon'ooweench . . . thunder."

"It can't be. Look." He pointed at the top of the canyon walls nearly a thousand feet above them. A narrow band of sunny, blue sky assured him of clear weather. Colton shook his head. "Star, I don't think that is—"

"Shhhhh," she interrupted. Her brown eyes widened more. She snapped upright and yelled. "Weech ooweech! Kawkawd' uh!" She grabbed the boy and pushed him toward the canyon entrance.

Colton complied with Star's urging and ran; he knew the Paiute words for "flood" and "run away."

Then he heard it: a distant rumble that sounded like giants playing marbles with boulders. The ribbon of blue sky soon turned an ugly shade of gray brown and poured sheets of rain onto the terrified sprinters. Lightning flashed, igniting a dead ponderosa pine on the summit. The entire slot canyon immediately blazed in brilliant white and resounded with thunder so deafening it nearly knocked them to the ground. The uprooted pine, now aflame, hurtled toward the canyon floor. Smoke mixed with a foreign odor created by the lightning that smelled like burning metal.

Star ran with arms flailing wildly, screaming in Paiute, "Suhpeng' oa! Get out!"

Colton gasped for breath and wondered if the evil ones were indeed right behind them. He ran for his life, but the wet, sandy trail made him feel like he was picking his way through a sticky maze. She continued yelling at him, but he couldn't understand what she said. As he ran, he glanced back toward her and saw a torrent of chocolate-colored water, rocks, and tree limbs roaring only two hundred yards behind. It sounded like a freight train smashing through a forest.

Star grabbed his hand and pulled him toward a rotting tree limb. She picked the tree limb up and braced it against the canyon wall. "Get up there," she insisted.

"I'm not leaving you down here."

"Do as I say!" she said, putting her hand on Colton's cheek for an instant. "I am not strong enough to pull you up there. You go and pull me up." She pushed him up the limb toward an overhanging ledge. "Climb! Hurry, Colton. Faster!"

The limb bent and cracked under his weight. A small branch splintered into his thigh. He yelled in pain but kept climbing. He pushed with his other leg and stretched for the ledge with his fingertips. Using the strength of fear, he pulled himself onto the narrow outcropping just as the decayed limb shattered in two, the upper branches pinning him against the rock wall. He wedged himself next to a small boulder and reached down for Star.

"Quick, take my hand!"

She stood on her toes and stretched upward, but the gap between their hands was at least three feet. The smell of wet, churning soil filled the air. She turned her head and saw a huge wave of brown water crashing around the bend, roaring the last thirty yards toward her. Star looked up at Colton, then lowered her arms.

"Mother!" he yelled. Straining to reach her, he groaned, "No, no, NO!" But his voice could no longer be heard above the liquid thunder.

"I love you, Colton Grey," she said. He could barely make out the words, but he knew them by heart.

Then she was gone.

His first thought was to leap after her into the roiling mix of water, mud, logs, and boulders. But the thick web of branches prevented him from going down. It was hopeless. He couldn't save her now and most certainly would die in the attempt. All he could see and hear was the rampaging river below.

"It should've been me." He sobbed. "It should've been me."

The maze of branches soon started to lift as the rumbling floodwaters rose. He looked skyward and blinked against the pelting rain. The thought of leaving the canyon, of moving on in a life without Star, felt unbearable, but there was no time to mourn. The only way out was up. He stood and reached, tightened his grip on another small ledge, and inched his way toward the summit. He strained to grasp another thin ledge, then another, and another—

2

The Inside Passage

Alaska, 1900

R ED . . . guess I *miss* red." It was the simple answer to her question. He leaned a little farther over the passenger ship's rail, staring down at the white foam of the bow wave as it hissed northward over the cold, green-black waters of Alaska's Inside Passage.

"Red?" She smirked.

"You asked me why I'm leaving Alaska. Red is a good answer."

She cocked an eyebrow and pursued a better answer. "Is *Red* the name of your horse, your dog . . . or the color of your woman's hair?"

He sighed and removed his hat, allowing the breeze to stir his sandy-colored hair, but continued gazing into the deep waters. He was six feet tall, wore a forest-green shirt, a tan wool jacket, and tan pants.

She stared at his face—the square jaw, and steel-gray eyes—then leaned back against the railing as her eyes scanned the ship. When she saw the large letters CG enclosed in the diamond-shaped logo on the smokestack, her eyes darted down to the fine leather bag at the man's feet. The same CG logo was engraved in silver on the bag's clasp. It was also on the silver ring on his right hand. Realizing who he was, she moved closer and tried a more seductive tone. "So, Mr. Grey, red *is* a woman, after all?"

His head remained fixed, but his eyes glanced toward her only for a moment. "Utah," he said as he returned his gaze to the sea.

"Well, Mr. Grey, what do you think of *this* red?" She unpinned her hat and shook her head. The sheen on the auburn hair cascading down her shoulders accented her look-me-over stance as she placed her hands on her hips and turned sideways to show off the feminine curves in her blue-satin pinstriped dress. Her boldness made other men passing on the deck stop and stare.

Sensing something had happened, he turned toward her, still leaning casually with one elbow on the rail. Looking at her face, he felt the most dangerous weapons in the world were the lustful eyes of a beautiful woman. They had the power to make men do insane things, but he had learned that they always promised far more than they could ever deliver. Her eyes reminded him of the blue ice that fed the Tanana River during the spring melt. He noted how her eye shadow and dress were of the same stunning blue. Bright-red lipstick framed a flashing smile. He grinned but decided to remain silent.

The redhead moved closer, cocked an eyebrow, and whispered, "Can *this* red do anything for you, Mr. Grey?"

Pushing away from the rail, he locked his gray eyes onto those of blue ice. She moistened her red lips with anticipation and moved so that their faces were only inches apart. Still staring at her, he stooped and picked up his bag, touched the brim of his hat as he walked past her, and replied, "Brunette . . . she was brunette."

Leaving the stunned auburn beauty with her hands on her hips and her mouth agape, he strolled toward the ship's stern to resume his position at the rail.

The sun was approaching its sizzling immersion into the sea. Banners of copper-colored clouds accented the darkening sky as the ship steamed past countless forest-covered islands garnished with lacey waterfalls. Colton's gaze wandered from sunset, to cloud, to island, trying to capture a journal's worth of visions before nightfall. Pulling his collar up and putting his hands into his pockets provided a little cover from the cool evening breeze.

His fingers felt a folded telegram. It had lain crumpled at the bottom of his pocket since the day a messenger boy had delivered it a month ago. He was used to receiving telegrams, he'd completed a number of business deals through them, but this one spoke of things he didn't want to think about. It called him back to memories of canyons, an unforgiving father, a merciless brute . . . and the brunette. He opened it again.

WESTERN UNION

```
COLTON GREY
CG SHIPPING LINES
SKAGWAY, ALASKA


CHARLES HURT LOSING ALL -STOP-
FINALLY BROKEN -STOP-
DON'T LET ETHAN WIN AGAIN -STOP-


AMBER DUNCAN
SPRINGDALE, UTAH
```

No, it wasn't just the color red calling him back to the desert.

Utah had been an easy enough answer when it came to throwing that woman off his scent. It was already on his mind, but the truth of that answer was as unclear to him as the morning mist and as elusive a figure as Amber had always been.

Why in the world would I go back to fight all those battles again? he angrily thought to himself.

There was a reason why he'd left. It felt like personal weakness to return at Amber's mere request. She had made her choice, and he wasn't about to let her take it back now. Endless work had provided him with power, respect, and money. He'd made a good living for himself, and he'd done it on his own. Amber could do the same.

Crumpling the cable into a tight ball, he threw it over the railing and into the sea. He was headed to Portland, and that was

it. Frustration pricked his heart as he squinted at the sun setting on the horizon. He slammed his hand down on the railing and squeezed it.

3

Ethan's Rifle

Southern Utah, 1900

SLAPPING HIS HAND around the wooden stock of his rifle, Ethan Morley pulled the Winchester from its scabbard and pointed it at the nervous farmer. His piercing dark eyes squinted at the setting sun for a second, and then he sneered, "You're trespassin', Harold. You know I can't allow that. Why, if I let you do it, every cotton farmer down in that valley will be up here cuttin' down my trees." His expression sobered as he growled through thin lips and a mustache. "And I like my trees."

"Look here, Ethan, you've cut down more trees than all of us in the valley put together."

"Gotta feed my sawmill, Harold. Towns are growing down there." His grin returned. "Just take a look over the edge of this cliff, and you can see the smoke from their chimneys: Saint George, Santa Clara, Silver Reef—Why, do you know they discovered silver in that town?"

"Of course I know that. Everybody knows that." His belly shook as he continued with a nervous chuckle. "They also know you're the one who bought the mine claims just before the price of silver dropped. We all understand how that could get you upset."

The grin disappeared from Ethan's face as he pulled the hammer back on the rifle, spit on the ground, and stepped forward. The scowl on his face was accented by thick, dark eyebrows that matched his mustache. "You think I'm stupid!" he yelled. "All you farmers think you've got everything figured out, don't you? Well, ya don't!" Holding the rifle at hip level, he pointed it at Harold's belly. "Selling my lumber to the townsfolk down there gets me enough money to open new mines. Silver prices will come back."

Harold's smile faded as he retreated a step and stammered, "I-I'm sure th-they will, Ethan."

"But you've got five problems now, farmer. One, you can't grow enough cotton down in that desert to keep food on your table. Two, you folks cut down all the trees in the canyon. Guess you farmers ain't as smart as you think."

"We . . . we needed houses, corrals, fences, and barns. We've got families to raise." Harold grew a little bolder. "There are plenty of trees up here on the mesa. And I paid to come up here to cut timber from Amber Duncan's forest, not yours."

"Problem three, farmer Harold, is that no woman is going to tell me what I own and what I don't. You come up here *anywhere,* and you're trespassin'. Cuttin' my trees makes you a thief. That's problem four." He took another step forward and poked the end of the rifle into Harold's stomach.

Harold's eyes widened as he continued stepping backward. "Look, Ethan, be reasonable. We'll pay you double what we're giving Amber. We can be friends about this."

"Pay? You mean owe! You cotton farmers don't have enough money to pay anybody for anything. And what do you mean, friends?" His face grew red with anger. "I'm not forgettin' the way all you treated me years ago at your stupid cotton festival." Ethan continued forward and poked Harold in the stomach with each step.

Beads of perspiration now appeared on Harold's face as he was forced closer to the cliff's edge. "Th-that was a long time ago, and you put yourself in a mess when you started manhandling Amber in front of everybody." He stared down at the rifle and swallowed hard. "Please put the gun down. Let's talk."

"Don't bring the Royal Miss Duncan into this." Gritting his teeth and narrowing his eyes, Ethan spit on Harold's boots, then poked him much harder, backing him to the very edge of the cliff. "Problem five, farmer, is that people forget how slippery sandstone can be. Sometimes it's like walking on little marbles. Once you start to roll, it's kind of hard to stop. Looks to me like you're walking on a real dangerous ledge." Lunging forward, he rammed the rifle into Harold's stomach.

Harold gasped for breath, grabbed the barrel with both hands for balance, and swayed as one foot slipped over the edge. "Ethan, wait! Don't shoot! I'll—"

There was no shot. Ethan just let go of his rifle.

Stepping to the edge of the cliff, he placed his snakeskin boots exactly where Harold's had been one second before. Putting his hand to his ear, he listened to the scream descending two thousand feet to the canyon floor.

"Stole my trees, stole my rifle. Careless hiker. That's my story." He stepped back, took off his hat, wiped the sweat from his forehead and short red hair, and squinted at the sun sinking below the horizon.

4
Sailing South

THE FAMILIAR THUMPING of Zeb's limp across the deck caused Colton to turn around and blink himself back to the present.

"Gettin' dark, but it's still good ta see Vancouver Island again," Zeb croaked through teeth clenched around an unlit pipe as he joined Colton at the rail. "You'd miss this country, wouldn't ya, Cole?"

Colton nodded as he returned his gaze to the verdant slopes of the island.

"This here's a lot different than where you're goin', you know... where you're from."

"Sure is," Colton responded without thinking, but he quickly corrected himself. "Wait, what do you mean where I'm going?"

"One of the cabin boys was passin' your way when you was tellin' that redhead about Utah."

"Just trying to get rid of her. She's not my type." Colton responded in what was meant to be a breezy tone, but it fell flat.

"What girl *is* your type?"

Colton glared at him but remained silent. They shared the view at the rail as Zeb waited for him to speak. But Colton's mind was playing tennis with the message in the cable and his upcoming business in Portland. It was at least five minutes before he broke the silence.

"Alaska will be famous someday, Zeb. So many fish they can't be counted; trees that march on forever."

"What about the gold?" Zeb asked, shivering a bit with excitement while stroking his short gray beard.

Colton glanced at Zeb. "Sure, Zeb, the gold. But I think someday the water up here might be worth more than all the gold found
by a few lucky prospectors. Why, if they had this much water in
Utah . . ." He paused as he remembered Star and the flood. "Never
mind."

"Huh, what you talkin' 'bout?"

"Nothing."

"You never did look for gold, did ya, Cole?"

He sneered, "Like those hundred thousand fools who went into
the Klondike? Only a handful made any money."

"Well, you done all right," Zeb reminded him. "You done *real*
good."

"And I did good by not hauling fifteen hundred pounds of food
over the Chilkoot Pass and watching twenty-five thousand horses
die along that trail," he barked.

"Easy, Cole. Didn't mean ta get you all riled up."

"Look, Zeb, it was tough up there. Real tough. I remember
there was a young guy named London. He thought he was going
to get rich finding gold, just like everybody else. He seemed smart,
full of energy, but, like most folks, he never made a strike. He
wound up spending his time working for other men until his mouth
turned black and his teeth started falling out."

"Scurvy?"

"Yeah. Looking at him made me decide the way to make a
fortune in Alaska wasn't killing myself looking for gold. It was
buying and selling claims and the tools prospectors needed for mining, cabins, sluices, gold pans, and—"

Zeb raised his hands in surrender. "Whoa, partner, I get ya."

"It's just that most people can't see the . . . ah, forget it."

"What ya gettin' at, Cole?"

"What I'm getting at is there's a lot of ways to make money,
if it's important."

"Ways more important than findin' gold?" Zeb wondered aloud.

"Look at those waterfalls and think big. People live where there is water. Where do people need a lot of water? Can it be piped? Or what about fuel? Did you know that oil was drilled on the shore of the Cook Inlet in '96? And Henry Ford's got folks believing everybody can own an automobile." Colton paused and stroked his chin as his mind pondered another venture.

"Water? Oil?" Zeb began scratching his head. "Them two don't mix."

Colton sighed, then smiled. "Let's try another idea. Population's going up fast all along the Pacific Coast. People have to eat. Can you see why I pulled out of the gold-mining game and bought all those salmon fishing boats?"

"And built them canneries?"

"And the canneries. The trick is to stay *ahead*, figure out what people need before they even ask for it."

"But people don't fish from off these here ships. They're too big." Zeb smiled as though he had finally won a point.

"People movers. People will be coming this way for a lot of reasons, if nothing more than to see mighty Alaska. And you can help them enjoy the journey."

"You know, maybe you don't belong up here. I ain't never seen *no* man turn down that redhead before, and all ya ever done is worked and looked for ways to start a new business. Never did see ya spend your money crazy like the other men around here. Looked like the only reason they ever worked a day was ta spend their money on drinks, cards, and women like her. But you—"

"All right, Zeb."

"No, I mean it. Ya don't fit in here. Who else would've jumped in that icy water to save an old fool like me? That boat was bustin' up good. If you hadn't—"

"If I hadn't wanted to get that last run on those salmon, that boat would still be here, your leg would be good, and—"

"Stop it! You've heard from every man on those boats a hunnerd times. We all knew the risk. It was worth tryin' ta get that extra catch. Best year we ever had on the runs! But I don't want ta think you got me this job cuz yer feelin' guilty. With my leg all busted up, I couldn't find any place that would take me, and I've been meanin' ta thank ya again—"

Colton interrupted him by slapping him on the back. "It's not guilt or charity. It's the least I could do for an old fishing pal. I think you do a grand job running the galley and welcoming people into the dining hall. Folks always tell me how much they enjoy your adventure stories."

Zeb smiled, turned, and headed for the galley but yelled back, "I better be headin' inside now and get back to work. You might want to get inside too. I can't figure this weather lately. For some crazy reason, that sky ta the north has been blushin' red every mornin' for a week, but not a drop falls. Could be tonight it'll be dumpin' some rain on us, and big floods inland. See ya in the mornin'."

Colton nodded, but Zeb had just triggered a memory buried fifteen years ago. He shook his head and blinked hard to erase it, but as he looked up at the clear sky, another memory came to the surface. On the ship's aft smokestack was a painting of the Orion constellation.

Years ago, he and Amber had enjoyed an evening walk along the Virgin River. On their walk, they had paused to look above the horizon and had been captivated by that group of stars hurtling over the crest of Eagle Crags Mountain. Holding her close, he had told her that the three stars in Orion's belt meant *I love you*, and if there was ever a time they couldn't be together, she was to look at those three stars and remember that night. She had told him he was a romantic.

"Mushy," he mumbled to himself as he shook his head, attempting to remove the memory.

What was I thinking? he wondered. *Young kid. First romance stuff. First romance . . . and last romance. I haven't looked up at those stars in years. Not since I left her after she . . .* He tried to convince himself, but there was a reason why he'd chosen that name and insignia for this ship. Sighing, he finally conceded, *And tonight* Orion *will be nearing the end of his winter run.*

5

The Warning

THE ENTIRE DECK had now emptied as darkness became his only companion. The ship's running lights came on as it slowed in preparation to dock. He fixed his stare just past midship, out where the water was still glassy-smooth. On the reflective surface, something caught his eye. He leaned forward over the railing to get a better view. It appeared to be a woman struggling in the water and reaching her hands toward him. He could just barely make out her long black braid; it felt like someone had poured glacier water down his back.

"Hold on!" he yelled as he grabbed a ring buoy and line.

"Colton, climb!" she shouted from the dark water. Her voice was so familiar.

He flung the ring with all his might and shouted, "Grab it!" But the instant the ring struck the water, the woman vanished and silence returned. She hadn't sunk, just disappeared. His eyes scanned the surface in vain. There was no one there, not even a ripple, and he suspected there never had been.

Feeling a little foolish, he began pulling the line in and winding it around his arm. She sounded just like . . . no. It couldn't be. This is not the time to lose my mind. He spun around to see if anyone had observed his futile attempt to rescue what must have been an apparition.

"You saw her too, didn't you, Colton?" A gruff voice spoke.

Startled, Colton saw a tall, lean figure slip out of the darkness. The man wore a conical hat of woven reeds and a knee-length black shirt adorned with a red eagle—signature clothes of the native Tlingit people. His stride, though silent in tall leather moccasins, indicated a sense of urgency.

Colton recognized him as a member of a local tribe he had partnered with in Alaska; a man named Chitina.

"Have you watched the morning sky?" Chitina questioned. "Seven days now it is red, but still no rains come. Fire in the morning sky, but no rain falls, is a bad sign. The rain waits for us to give you warning."

"Us? Who do you mean us? And a warning about what?"

"A woman has come to my dreams for seven nights. She tells me to warn you about the water." An expression of stress masked his face. He looked seaward trying to interpret the meaning of his next statement. "Then she says you must fear the fire too." His eyes focused a solemn stare at Colton as he continued. "This is why she comes to my dreams."

"She who?"

"You saw her in the water just now."

"I didn't see anybody," Colton denied.

Chitina looked at the wet lifeline around Colton's arm. His voice was now a whisper. "I do not know the woman's voice. I cannot see her face. But she is one of us. She cries to me to warn you of the water and the fire."

"Doesn't make much sense, does it? Why doesn't she come to me?"

"She did. In the water. This woman is . . . is . . . she knows things only our people know."

Colton glared. "Am I not one of your people?"

The Indian winced as he replied. "In every way except by blood. Maybe she does not speak to you because there is no room for her in your heart and mind. They are too full of hate."

"It isn't hate that supplied your village with salmon these past winters."

Chitina's pride seemed bruised by the barb. He cast his eyes toward the deck. "This woman tries to warn you because of deep love. I have come to do the same. We do not forget those who treat us as family. Wherever you go, I will be with you in spirit. But the water and the fire . . . there I see you stand alone." A puzzled expression creased his face. "Yet there are others there. The dream is like a waterfall to me—easy to see when it starts, but when it hits the rocks, it goes everywhere." His eyes moistened as he grinned. "I think maybe I am becoming an old man."

He grabbed Colton's right hand with both of his and advised, "Drive out the hate. People you know need help."

"I don't hate anybody."

Chitina stared so intently into Colton's eyes that he became uncomfortable and looked away.

"There are a few people I don't like," Colton admitted, "but that doesn't mean—"

"Drive out the hate. Help those in trouble. Maybe she will come to your dreams too. Listen to her. But watch out for the water and the fire. I don't think I will see you again." He did not wait for a response. He patted Colton's hand, turned, and vanished into the same shadows from which he'd appeared.

As Colton leaned against the deck railing, pondering all that had been said and what it could mean, he wondered whether he'd seen one apparition or two.

6

The Second Cable

S HORE LIGHTS TO the west indicated the Orion ship had docked at Port Victoria to pick up a few passengers and unload a cargo of C-G canned salmon. Even at this late hour, business pushed on; Colton admired how reliable it was.

A young lad sprinting up the gangplank drew Colton's attention away from the crowd along the dock. He wore a Western Union uniform and was holding an envelope. Once cleared for boarding, he ran directly to Colton.

"Cable for you, Mr. Grey," the boy puffed.

Still staring at the crowd, Colton automatically extended his hand behind his back to accept the cable.

The boy placed the telegram in Colton's hand, then waited patiently with his own hand extended. But Colton seemed hypnotized by the sights, sounds, and smells on the dock.

"Umm, Mr. Grey."

Colton turned, shocked to see the boy still standing behind him. "How do you even know who I am?"

"I think most everybody along the Inside Passage knows who you are, Mr. Grey."

Colton smiled, then handed him a silver dollar. He chuckled when the boy's eyes grew wide and his mouth fell open. "A whole dollar? Thanks, Mr. Grey." He put the coin in his pocket, turned, and sprinted toward the gangplank.

Colton removed his hat, ran his fingers through his hair, and mused over the pros and cons of telegrams as he opened the envelope.

WESTERN UNION

```
COLTON GREY
SHIP ORION

10,000 ACRES GOOD SOIL IN OREGON -STOP-
AWAIT YOUR APPROVAL TO PURCHASE -STOP-

MERRILL INC
EUGENE OREGON
```

"Hey, boy!" he yelled at the courier now running along the dock. "Come back up here. I've got a message to send back with you." He pulled a pencil from his coat pocket and wrote on the back of the telegram as the boy spun around to return. The youngster soon arrived and put his hands on his knees to catch his breath.

"Yes, sir," he wheezed, "what would you like me to do?"

"Take this back to the Western Union office to send off right away."

> *Merrill Inc*
>
> *Eugene Oregon*
>
> *Buy it STOP*
>
> *Will sell to farmers for good price STOP*
>
> *Forests and vineyards good too STOP*
>
> *CGrey*

As the boy reached for the paper, Colton noticed the patches in his coat and pants.

"Did you have a fall off your bike, son? What's your name?"

"It's David, sir. People want their messages delivered fast, and I don't have a bike, so I run. My mom buys big shoes for me so I can use them for a few years and grow into them. Sometimes I run too fast and . . ." He was embarrassed and turned away.

"I understand. Here's twenty dollars to send that cable."

"But, Mr. Grey, that message might only cost two dollars at most!"

"Well, prices keep going up, and I'm not sure what telegrams cost nowadays. Take that and keep the change." Colton winked, then put the money in the boy's hand.

"But you just got a cable from me a minute ago, and that only cost—"

"Better hurry, son. You don't want that office to close while you're here, do you?" He put his hand on the boy's shoulder and turned him toward the gangplank. "Use the extra to buy yourself a bike. Tell your mom it's a thank-you for patching up those torn pants."

"Yes, sir," the boy said, eyes moist. He put his head down to hide the tears. "Thank you, sir."

"No, David, thank you. You better go. It looks like rain's coming any minute."

The boy sprinted down to the dock just as the wind started to pick up. Colton looked over the railing to watch him and saw a woman with a long black braid come out of the nearby bakery and motion the boy over. She must be preparing tomorrow morning's inventory, Colton marveled as he watched her and the boy exchange a warm embrace. She slipped a piece of bread into his pocket just as the owner of the bakery waved her back to work inside.

The black braid of the mother stirred Colton's memory back to Star. It seemed he couldn't escape her these past few days.

Colton stretched and yawned as he again shook the memory of Star from his mind. He hadn't slept in two days. He bent down, grabbed his bag, and started up the stairwell toward the cabins. He leaned into the door to keep it open as he swung his bag into the hallway. As the door slammed behind him, startled passengers jumped and stared at his blustering entrance. They were dressed in their finest clothes and were being directed to the dining room by Zeb, who, in formal attire, now resembled a waddling penguin.

Colton turned in the opposite direction of the moving crowd and nearly collided with the auburn beauty, who was now clinging to the arm of a white-haired, aristocratic-looking gentleman who wore a black-satin vest and leaned on a golden-tipped cane. She stuck her nose in the air when she recognized Colton.

He smiled broadly as he approached the couple. "I see you're out for a nice evening with your grandfather," he said with a tip of his hat.

The woman stiffened at his comment and opened her mouth to respond, but he brushed past her before she could say a word.

She had asked him about "his woman" earlier that evening. He chuckled at his snide answer, "She was brunette." But, as with his responses about red and Utah, the truth was a mystery.

Was Amber his woman? She had been . . . once.

He brushed against the wall as he squeezed past more passengers on their way to the dining room. A few of them called him by name and asked him to join them for dinner. He declined. He was tired, and his mind struggled with thoughts of Amber, Portland, and the woman in the water. He entered his cabin, closed the door, and collapsed on the bed. His arm crossed over his eyes to make the room as dark as possible.

The thought of Amber always had a pull on him. He had already decided not to go—he'd thrown her cable into the ocean—but the idea of seeing her again kept bringing him back. The very thought of being able to stare into her eyes again sent him in endless circles.

Seeing Amber again would be a bitter-sweet experience. Was it worth the cost? No matter the circumstances, her appearance would garnish the surroundings more than anything else on earth. He remembered her as the most breathtaking woman he had ever seen. The most breathtaking woman he had ever dreamed of. The first time he saw, her he had stood openmouthed and deaf to everything around him. It was her eyes that riveted his stare that first time, and every time thereafter. Long dark lashes framed an amber-copper luster that seemed to melt into ever-changing shades. Even the sunlight would seek her out just to reflect off that color. He was certain God had not, maybe could not, create that color again anywhere on earth. He used to wind her long dark hair around the fingers of one hand while he stroked the satin-like skin of her face with the other. They would spend hours walking and talking, planning a future together. A young Colton had thought she was the source of rainbows and everything else that had color. There was turmoil in his heart just thinking about her. She should have been his.

His last coherent thoughts convinced him that a return to Utah would be aggravating at best. "Amber . . . Ethan . . . water . . . fire. I'm not going," he moaned as the unconscious hum of sleep conquered him.

7

Astoria, Oregon

THE PATTER OF rain against the cabin window, and the drone of the ship's engines, helped Colton sleep through the night. However, the sound of distant chamber music caused him to stir in the morning. It floated from the dining room and wafted under his door much like the pleasant scent of fresh-baked bread. He stretched himself awake as his mind hurtled over yesterday's events.

Way too much work to do to worry about Utah or mystical warnings, he thought as he staggered toward the washbasin, cupped cold water onto his face, and stared into the mirror. *Didn't break,* he mused, *that's a good start.* He resigned himself to the day's tasks, shaved, dressed, and headed out the door for breakfast.

A thousand aromas greeted him as he entered the dining area. He selected the most secluded table and sat with his back to the rest of the diners. The room was nearly filled with early risers, most of whom displayed pompous attitudes toward the galley help. He ignored them, ordered breakfast, looked out toward the sea, and recalled the woman in the water and Chitina's warning. He rested his arms on the table and hoped that a plate full of hotcakes, sausage, and eggs would eradicate any thoughts other than his pressing business in Portland. There would be one more stop at Astoria, then up the Columbia River to Portland.

"Trust you slept well, lad," croaked Zeb as he placed a gnarled hand on Colton's shoulder.

"Don't come up behind me like that!" Colton shouted as he jumped in his seat.

Zeb squinted at him as though he had just accosted a stranger. "Sorry, son," he apologized. "What's got into ya?"

"Nothing," Colton said, lowering his voice. "Just a little tired, that's all."

"Worried about Portland or Utah?"

"Neither. Portland's fine, and I'm not going to Utah."

"But I thought . . ."

"Well, you thought wrong."

"So you'll be staying in Portland, then?"

Colton glared at him for a moment. "Yes."

"Okay, okay. I'll let you finish your breakfast, then maybe you and me can visit on the aft deck."

The invitation helped Colton soften a bit, and he nodded in agreement.

In that brief pause, he recognized a familiar voice. The redhead, with her rather rotund escort, was seated only eight feet away.

"This is a lot of food for only two people," she remarked as waiters brought plate after plate to their table.

"Nonsense," the old man shot in her direction. "Don't let this good smoked salmon go to waste."

The accent on the word waste prompted both Colton and Zeb to glance at the man's ample girth.

"Looks like he let it go to his waist," Zeb said.

Colton chuckled, causing the dining couple to turn and face them.

"Are you laughing at us, sir?" the man demanded as he thumped his gold-handled cane on the floor. The noise brought the attention of a few other guests in the dining room.

Colton pointed at himself and raised his eyebrows. "Me?" he asked with feigned innocence.

"How dare an ignorant fishy person like you act so uppity?" the redhead sneered.

Colton smiled and replied, "Which fish ma'am? Are you referring to anadromous species like salmonids?" She blinked, but before she could respond, he continued. "Pink, chum, chinook/king, coho/silver, or sockeye/kokonee?"

"Salmon, whales, goldfish . . . whatever!" she snapped. "Can't make any difference to big Mr. Grey."

"So you are Colton Grey," her escort continued in a raspy voice, pointing an accusing finger toward Colton. "There's a fair amount of talk that your honor is in question regarding how you made your money off poor prospectors. You're a weasel, from what I hear."

Colton dropped his fork and pushed his chair back to stand, but Zeb put his hand on his shoulder to keep him seated. There was already enough attention focused on them.

Colton apologized. "Excuse me, I'll let you two finish your salmon breakfast and . . ."

But the redhead wasn't finished with him. "Don't act like you know anything about fish. You just hire other men to tie worms on hooks, catch little fish, and kill them."

"Hear! Hear!" the old man cheered as he thumped his cane.

"You really don't know anything about fish, do you?"

Colton stood up from his table and walked toward the couple. The old man slunk back in his chair as he approached.

Her mouth fell open.

"Eggs are laid October to January. They hatch as alevin January to April. Fry emerge April to June. When they're older, they're known as smolt."

She tried to interrupt, but he wasn't finished.

"The smolt ride whitewater rapids hundreds of miles in June and July down to the sea, where they spend up to three years racing away from seals, whales, dolphins, sharks, and dozens of other critters." Then he pointed at her escort's plate. "And those critters are determined to savor that same delicacy hiding the plate of your grandfather here. They're the mainstay of thousands of Indians and feed the people of eight nations."

"Grandfather?" the redhead exclaimed with an outraged gasp.

Colton leaned forward and lowered his voice. "Then the amazing part happens. After surviving all those years and thousands of miles in the ocean, they fight their way up the rapids in the same stream where they hatched. Seems like they need to return to the place of their origin to die and—" His expression sobered. He stared at the floor as he contemplated what he had just said. He stood upright but remained in deep thought.

Zeb decided to terminate the discussion with one more shot. "And another thing, missy, Mr. Grey here is the one who invented the best way to net them salmon. He found that . . ."

But Colton shook his head. "Enough. I think we've made our point. Excuse me." He grabbed Zeb by the arm and led him to the door and out onto the deck.

"Ain't you gonna finish your breakfast, Cole? You never let loud-mouthed fancies push you around before. Why don't you just kick 'em right off this ship?"

Colton remained silent as they walked toward the rail.

Zeb thoughtfully stroked the stubble of his gray beard. "You're figurin' you're just like them salmon, ain't ya? Ya gotta go back to them canyons to end where ya began, ain't ya?"

"That's crazy," Colton snapped a little too harshly. "That's just plain crazy talk. You, Chitina, that ghost in the water—you're all talking crazy. I'm going up to the top deck. I've got some thinking to do before we stop in Astoria. Goodbye, Zeb. I'll see you on my next trip north."

"Sure you will, Cole." Zen sighed as he turned back to the galley. "Sure you will."

Colton bolted up the stairs to the top deck, where he could

see the mouth of the Columbia River flowing to the sea. Along the shoreline was one of his favorite cities, Astoria. The sight of it was a bright light in his dark mind. He grinned as he remembered a reporter from the Oregonian newspaper who called it "The most wicked place on earth," while another hailed its boomtown reputation as the "New York City" of the Pacific. There were bars and brothels but also dozens of shops and restaurants, new locomotive steam engines, hotels, and dozens of canneries accenting its northern shoreline.

Send a cable to Stuart and Emma, he reminded himself. They'll be glad to know I'm getting close to Portland.

He turned toward the bridge but was alerted to the sound of large boots thumping behind him. Colton turned to see a huge man who eclipsed the morning sun coming up the stairs, followed by the gray-haired man with the golden-tipped cane, holding the hand of the redhead.

"This the guy, Mr. Fitch?" growled a six-foot, eight-inch, 275-pound brute in a red flannel shirt and coveralls.

"Yes, Leonard," the grey-haired man, Fitch, answered. "He is the one, indeed."

Puzzled, Colton asked, "Something I can do for you? You certainly finished that salmon quickly."

The redhead slinked forward and sneered, "If you say brunette again, I'll—"

Fitch pulled her back and shouted, "Come on, Leonard, earn that fifty dollars."

As the hired thug stepped forward, Colton backed into the railing.

"He's trapped! Crush him, Leonard," Fitch bellowed, but Colton had made a reputation for not letting anyone push him around, and he intended to stand by it.

Leonard made a massive fist and cocked his right arm. He

swung hard, but Colton ducked at the last moment, and the fist went whistling over his head. Colton lunged forward and punched Leonard hard in the ribs. The big man's face turned purple, and he hunched over to catch his breath, but Colton stayed low and came up under the giant's belly. He grabbed Leonard by the hip pockets of his coveralls and, in one motion, drove his shoulders upward, twisted, and launched his would-be assailant airborne over the rail. The sound of a painful splat on the water caused Fitch, the redhead, and Colton to peer over the rail.

"Seventy-two feet," Colton remarked. "That's a fair dive . . . but he forgot to point his toes." There was no smile from the redhead this time. Colton glared at Fitch, who grabbed the girl and hid behind her. Colton shook his head in disgust and turned to leave but heard the girl groan as she was pushed into the railing. He turned toward the scuffle just as Fitch swung the cane at his head.

He ducked and wrenched the cane free from Fitch's hand. Wedging the cane between the rail and support post, he snapped it like a pencil and flung the broken pieces over the rail with his right hand. His left shot out like a rattlesnake and grabbed Fitch by the collar.

"Astoria's a nice city, Fitch," he growled. "Too nice for you. But some people would think you fit in there perfectly. I think you and your girlfriend better leave this ship as soon as it docks, unless you'd prefer to swim there right now."

"How dare you, Grey," Fitch sputtered. "What is this young lady to do about being stranded in Astoria?"

"Somehow I think she can earn free travel anywhere she wants to go." Colton let go of Fitch's collar.

The ruckus had drawn the attention of two members of the crew, who peered over the railing one deck above them.

"Hey, you two, come down here," Colton ordered when he saw them. Startled, the men sprinted down the stairs.

"Yes, sir," the taller one said. "What can we do for you?"

"We're stopping to dock. Escort these two off the ship immediately. I'll have another man bring their luggage."

"Yes, sir." The crewmen looked stunned but herded the whining couple away.

Colton grabbed a ring buoy and, without a backward glance, tossed it over the rail toward the flailing Leonard.

"Man overboard," he whispered as he walked back to his cabin.

8

Stuart and Emma

Y OU KNOW, STUART, you *could* walk a little faster," complained Emma as they hurried out of the marketplace and onto the busy sidewalks of Portland, their arms loaded with groceries. "How can I get dinner ready for Colton if he arrives home before *we* do?"

"Walk faster? If I go any faster, this stuff will turn into goulash before we get home."

She glanced back at him and grinned. His light-blue eyes and dimpled cheeks flashed a perpetual smile. "You know, good brother, I think you're putting on a few pounds and it's slowing you down a bit. It appears you're having trouble even keeping up with young Todd here."

"Putting on a few—hey, wait just a minute," Stuart complained. He glanced ahead along the busy sidewalk and noticed a wooden barrel that stood about five feet tall. He placed his grocery bags at the feet of his ten-year-old nephew. "Here, Todd, watch these for a minute and prepare to be amazed." He launched himself forward, placed both hands on the barrel top, and leapfrogged over it in a mock, death-defying act. Hands on his hips, he grinned and turned back toward Emma and shouted, "Ta-da! So, missy, how many fat men do you know who can do that?"

"One."

"Momma," quizzed Todd, "how come Uncle Stuart does silly things like that? He's not fat."

"I know he's not, son, but sometimes, I mean many times, men do things like that to prove they're still young and strong."

"That doesn't make any sense. He is strong. He works hard at the lumberyard all day."

"I know, but you'll see, or at least all the women around you will see."

They soon caught up with Stuart, who grunted as Todd pushed the bags of groceries back into his stomach as they passed by. He glanced down toward his belly and sucked it in a bit as he hurried to catch up to them. As they passed the bakery, the pies in the window caught his eye. "You know, Emma, you won't have time to bake one of those, and Oregon blackberry is Colton's favorite dessert."

Emma halted with a puzzled expression, "Colton's favorite?"

"Number one for him . . . I'm pretty sure. And Todd and I don't mind it much either, do we, Todd?" Stuart raised his eyebrows and gave Todd a gentle bump with his knee.

Todd caught the hint and gave Emma his wide-eyed, begging-puppy look.

"See? There's only one left. I'll run in and buy it, then catch you and Todd in just a minute."

"All right, I can't fight you both. Colton's favorite." She laughed.

He placed the bags back at Todd's feet, glanced at his stomach again, and rushed toward the bakery to beat other the customers to the prized dessert. Focused on the prize, he collided with a very stern-looking, matronly woman who wore a full hoopskirt. He tipped his hat and stammered, "I'm just after one thing."

She squinted over her wire-rimmed glasses and harrumphed. "All men are after just one thing." She rapped him once on his head with her parasol, squeezed past him, and stormed away.

Mouth agape, he shrugged his shoulders and looked back at the giggling Emma, then lamented, "Everybody's a comic today."

She smiled, shook her head, and hurried toward home.

Though he appeared confused, Todd yelled, "Don't forget the pie," then dashed after his mother.

Ten minutes later, Emma reached for the front door handle and heard her name called from across the street. It was Elizabeth, a beautiful woman with long brown hair who had recently moved into the neighborhood.

"Emma, dear, you certainly have a lot of groceries. Are you expecting guests today?"

"Hello, Elizabeth," she replied as she opened the door. "Actually, we received a cable from our dear friend Colton saying he will be in Portland tonight. The three of us are anxious to see him. I would love to visit with you, but I have a big welcome-home dinner to prepare for him."

"Well, that's what friends are for, dear," Elizabeth remarked as she crossed the street to help. "Here, give one of those bags to me, Todd." Todd handed off the heaviest sack and acted like kitchen-duty shackles had just been removed from his ankles. "Friends are here to help in emergencies like this, and—"

"Stuart isn't home, Elizabeth." Emma chuckled softly as she motioned for Todd to open the door. He rushed forward and held the door for the two women.

"Oh. Well, I just—" Elizabeth floundered, her face turning a bright red.

"But I would love your help."

"Yes, well, I, um—"

"And you would be welcome to join us for dinner. I'm sure Colton wouldn't mind, and neither would Stuart."

Todd held the door for the two women as they entered, then followed them up the stairs to their apartment above the Landon-Grey Hardware & Lumber Store.

"Emma," Elizabeth said, desperately trying to change the subject. "Why don't you buy a house and move away from all the noise down below?"

"For one thing, work is right downstairs." Emma unlocked

the door to the apartment and stepped inside. "After school, Todd knows that he can find me or Stuart up here or down in the store. And the place reminds me of my Jonathon." Her gaze softened. "He liked the convenience of this arrangement too."

"I'm sorry I brought it up," Elizabeth apologized as she and Emma set the grocery sacks down on the kitchen table. "I had no idea. You must still miss him a great deal."

"It helps to keep busy," Emma said lightly as she pulled a bag of potatoes out of one of the grocery sacks. "We can keep talking if you'll peel those potatoes for me." She handed the potatoes to Elizabeth.

Elizabeth nodded and started washing and peeling the potatoes in the sink as Emma and Todd emptied the rest of the grocery sacks.

"So by Colton, do you mean Colton Grey?" Elizabeth asked as she peeled. Emma nodded. "Would you mind telling me more about him? I don't know much about him other than what you hear in the papers, and I'd like to have something to talk about at dinner."

"You know, even we don't know everything about Colton, especially his past. He just won't talk about it. The most we know is that he came from the desert and has no plans of going back."

"Maybe if we asked Jennifer to join us, she could get Colton to open up a little," Elizabeth suggested. "She's a beautiful girl."

Emma shook her head and started preparing the roast. "I don't think that's a good idea. He doesn't really like talking about personal issues—especially with women. I mean, he's polite, but never really opens up about his feelings or thoughts."

"Has he had any serious relationships since he's been here? The papers have shown him with attractive women at social functions in town." Elizabeth wiped her hands and started dicing the peeled potatoes on a cutting board.

"None," Emma said as she handed Elizabeth a pot for the diced potatoes. "It's as though he doesn't trust women. He even makes certain to review the financial records I keep for the store, and I haven't made a single mistake in those books. I know he trusts me, but he's just so . . . so thorough."

"All right," Elizabeth said, considering. "If he doesn't like to talk about his past, then what does he like to talk about? How did the three of you meet?"

"I'm not sure that's a great conversation topic either," Emma said as she resumed her work on the roast. "We met him the same night Jonathon was killed."

"Oh, I'm sorry, dear. If this is too heartbreaking—"

"No, it's just that it was an event Sheriff Whitacre could never solve, and I'm not sure he really tried. Jonathon was at the edge of the docks with a horse and wagon to receive a load of tools off a ship, like he had done dozens of times before. Stuart was a little late getting there because he was flirting with . . . well . . . he was coming around the corner just as the crane with a pallet full of picks and shovels swung out of control and knocked Jonathon off the wagon and into the water. The cable came loose, and the pallet fell on top of him. Stuart raced toward the river, but out of nowhere, young Colton Grey was already running along the dock-side and immediately dove into the water to rescue Jonathon."

"You know, I heard a rumor that he was the one who caused—"

"You heard wrong." Emma cut her off sharply. "Colton dove deep to save Jon, but he couldn't reach him. He came up gasping for air and barely had the strength to grab the rope Stuart threw to him. As he pulled him up onto the dock, a man came running toward Colton, intent on beating him for stealing some of his tomatoes, but Stuart intercepted the man and told him to leave. Then Sheriff Whitacre appeared, called the situation an unfortunate accident, and turned and left the scene without asking questions of bystanders or the ship's crew."

"Well, that's strange," Elizabeth said as she took the pot of diced potatoes, filled it with water, and put it on the hot stovetop.

Emma nodded. "Then Stuart noticed how thin Colton was, how shabby his clothes were, and learned that he had been living on the streets for a week. He insisted he come to live with us until he could get out on his own."

"I didn't know he lived with you, Emma. I guess I always assumed he was born rich."

"No, he's worked for his money every step of the way. He read everything he could get his hands on, worked incredibly hard for us in the store, and managed to triple our business in less than a year. He acted as though he had something to prove to himself or to everybody else."

"So why go to Alaska?"

"That's another thing I'm not sure about," Emma said as she put the roast in the oven. "All I know is that one day the four of us were strolling down Columbia Street and Colton saw a gorgeous brunette. He spun around, passed Todd over to Stuart, and sprinted across the street toward her. He grabbed the woman by her arm and turned her around to face him, but I guess she wasn't who he was looking for. His embarrassment was obvious. He walked away from us after that and didn't return home until very late that night. Then, the next day, he told us he was going to Alaska to look for gold."

"Well, whatever his reasons, he seems to have done well for himself," Elizabeth said as she started wiping down the sink and counter. "Did he strike it rich?"

Emma shook her head and gave the potatoes a stir. "He was there for a month, then sent a cable asking us to ship every tool we had up to him in Skagway. The next month, he doubled the order. Two months later, he became our partner, and business went crazy."

"So no gold?"

"No gold. But he made a fortune buying and selling claims and equipment to prospectors. Then he got into salmon fishing, which led to cargo and passenger ships. Who knows what else he'll do. Guess we'll find out when he arrives tonight." Emma paused and put her hands on her hips while she considered whether she had done all that was needed. "The roast is in the oven, the potatoes on the stove, and soon we'll have—"

"Blackberry pie," Stuart sang as he climbed the stairs. But the singing stopped when he saw Elizabeth in her cream-colored dress backlit by the windows. He nearly dropped the pie as he stumbled on the last step. "Oh. Elizabeth. You look . . . really . . . good."

She smiled and took the pie from his hands, making sure her fingers caressed his during the exchange. "Thank you, Stuart."

9

Springdale, Utah

THE CLOMPING SOUND of horse hooves pulling Ethan Morley's timber-laden wagons muffled the commotion stirring ahead at Springdale's town hall. A crowd of people jostled about, waving their arms and shouting. What's this all about? he wondered. His curiosity turned to concern when they all stopped talking, stared at him, and pointed in his direction.

"There's Ethan now," one of them yelled. "Get a rope," another barked.

As the crowd stormed toward him, Ethan looked back at the five other wagons driven by his men. "Looks like a farmer-style lynch mob." He grinned. He motioned Stitch to pull up next to him. Stitch did as told, his expression hard as stone, and put his hand on his pistol.

The sheriff stood in the middle of the road, waving his arms for the wagons to stop.

"What's all the uproar about, Sheriff Tom?" Ethan asked.

"Harold Smith has been missing for a week. Today somebody found his body at the base of Deer Trap Mountain, and a busted Winchester rifle with your name engraved on the stock was only twenty feet away." He grabbed the reins and demanded, "You've got some explaining to do, Morley."

Stitch moved his pistol onto his lap, covering it with his hat. He pointed it at the sheriff.

Ethan pulled his hat back and scratched his head in pretended wonder. "So Harold's the one who stole my good rifle. I told Stitch here that my rifle had been missing for about a week." He looked over at Stitch and the rest of his crew and shook his head as though he was amazed. "Harold always seemed like such an upstanding citizen. And he had a family too, didn't he?

I can't believe he was a thief."

"Some folks think you killed him, Ethan," the sheriff growled. "Harold told his family he was headed up to cut timber on Amber Duncan's land but was nervous about going through your place first. Now he's dead. Folks think you're kind of crazy about your land. Maybe you went a little too crazy and shot him."

The word crazy set Ethan off. He stood up and placed his hand on his pistol. Stitch silently pulled the hammer of his pistol back. "They think I'm crazy, do they? Did you find a bullet in him anywhere?"

The sheriff shook his head.

"Then all you found was my rifle, then. I'll bet he stole it, ran scared he might get caught, and slipped off the edge of Deer Trap. That's a long fall. I'll bet his body was all messed up. Now, who in this group is going to accuse me of shooting poor Harold when it's obvious he fell?"

Another farmer yelled out, "How come you didn't report your rifle being stolen to the sheriff? You've had plenty of time."

"I think all you folks know that it takes a long time to bring timber down to the valley floor, whether we go north to Cedar Mountain or south around Kanab. We started this load two weeks ago, and I was heading to Sheriff Tom right now to report my rifle being stolen. And my men will back me up on this, won't you, boys?" The drivers of the other wagons nodded their heads in unison like chickens picking grain off the ground. "Any other stupid questions?"

People shuffled nervously and looked down at their feet.

"We ought to get a collection up to help out his family, don't you think so, Tom? Here's a dollar." Ethan grabbed a dollar bill from his pocket and tossed it at the sheriff. "Why don't you pass your hat around to see what else you can get? Me and the boys got to get this timber to the Saint George sawmill. That town's really startin' to grow."

The sheriff let go of the reins and backed away. He appeared confused as to whether he should apologize or remain suspicious. Ethan scanned the crowd and noticed their expressions mirrored the sheriff's.

"If there's nothing else, Sheriff, remember private property is a man's right, and a person is innocent until proven—"

"Move along, Morley," the sheriff grumbled.

Ethan grinned and tipped his hat to the crowd. The snap of the whip jerked his horse's heads up as they strained to get the heavy wagons moving again. As they neared the west end of town, a woman with long dark hair walked across the road toward the telegraph office. She was clutching a piece of paper and paid no attention to the rumbling wagons approaching her.

"Well," bellowed Ethan as he pulled back on the reins, "if it ain't the lovely Miss Amber Duncan. Boys, tip your hats to the Queen of the Forest. She has more curves than a coiled snake, but she's twice as mean."

The men all laughed as if on cue but were leering at her from top to bottom.

"Yes, indeed. This here lady is the only person, besides me, still holding on to forest land up on the mesas."

"Oh, does that make you a queen too?" She glared through bright-green eyes.

He leaned forward and glared at her. "As a woman, she knows she's got no legal right to own any land in this country. But I made her a good offer on that land anyway, just to show what a gentleman I am. She won't sell . . . yet. But she will. I'll make her an offer she can't refuse," he snarled.

"Congress made it legal for a woman to own land or a business. And is your offer like the one you gave poor Harold? He had a family."

Ethan wrapped his hand around his whip and pulled it out from under the bench seat.

"I don't have to explain myself to any woman, especially one who thinks she's too good for everyone else."

"Not everyone, Ethan." She looked from one driver to another, then nodded. "Just present company."

He shifted uncomfortably in his seat, then tried to change the subject. "So, you're headed into the telegraph office. You sendin' out invitations to a big party? Me and the boys would love to come." The men laughed but continued to stare at her.

Amber was somber. "I'm sending a cable about the Scofield mine. Two hundred men killed. It's the worst disaster in U.S. mining history. Don't you pay attention to what's going on in this state?"

"Guess my schoolteacher forgot to tell me about that," he sneered. "So who needs the cable if everyone is supposed to know about this?"

"Someone who doesn't live in Utah but would want to know the people he cared about were in that mine."

"And who would that someone be?" Ethan barked as he jumped off the wagon and tore the note from Amber's hand.

"Ethan! Give me that!" She reached for the paper, but Ethan simply pushed her aside, causing his men to laugh at her feeble attempt.

"Hey, boss, maybe she wants to wrestle."

"Yeah, let's see how tough she really is, Ethan."

"But watch out for the curves on that rattler."

Amber threw wild punches at Ethan, but he smiled and pushed her away again before opening the note. "To Colton Grey," he read. "Hey, ain't that the kid who was sweet on you back in the day? Me and a few of the boys used to have a lot of fun poundin' on him before he ran out of town. Charlie, remember when we roped him and pulled him through the Virgin River? Yeah, that's the kid, ain't it?"

She snatched the paper and shouted back over her shoulder as she walked into the telegraph office, "He's not a kid anymore, Ethan."

10

Portland, Oregon

PORTLAND'S SKYLINE HAD changed dramatically since his last visit. Hotels, marketplaces, restaurants, and rail-systems surrounded the bustling shipyards and docks of the Willamette and Columbia rivers. The city had come of age as a major center of international commerce.

Colton shook his head, amazed at the clamor of activity. He started down the gangplank, then turned to see Zeb staring down at him from the top deck. He gave a solemn salute to his old friend. Zeb mirrored the motion and nodded. Colton smiled and continued down the walkway toward the luggage-claim area.

"Mr. Grey! Mr. Grey!" yelled a boy who ran toward him waving a white handkerchief.

Colton squinted. "Do I know you?"

"Mr. Grey," the boy gasped, "Uncle Stuart said I should get you into a good hotel before you came over to the store."

"*Uncle* Stuart?"

"Yes, sir. Stuart Landon."

"I know Stu, but . . . are you Emma's boy?" he asked.

The boy nodded, "Todd Edwards."

"Why you were just learning colors and numbers when I was here last. Now look how grown up you are."

"I'm ten, sir," beamed the boy. "Uncle Stuart gave me a silver dollar to make sure I got you into a good hotel."

Colton smiled, reached over, and shook the boy's hand. "And which hotel is a *good* hotel, Todd Edwards?"

"Well, sir, we had quite a few built just this year. There's the Clyde on Stark Street, the Benson on Broadway, the Mallory on Fifteenth Avenue, the . . ."

"Which do *you* recommend?"

"Well, Mr. Grey, they're all really nice. But Uncle Stuart and I think you would like the Benson so he already reserved a room for you. It's fourteen stories tall and has almost three hundred rooms!"

"The Benson it is, Master Edwards." Colton winked, then went over to a dockside porter waiting by the baggage area. He slipped the man a tip, pointed at his two trunks, and instructed him to take them to the Benson.

A bell clanged around the corner. "You know, Todd, it's been a long time since I've ridden a trolley. Can you find one that will take us to the hotel?"

"Yes, sir. We can catch one on the next street over."

"Lead the way."

The boy sprinted down the street, leaving Colton behind, and then spun around and returned to grab the leather bag marked with the silver-diamond CG logo. "This bag is how I knew it was you, Mr. Grey. This, and mother has a picture of you at the store. We better hurry before all these passengers fill up the trolley!"

Colton grinned, quickened his pace, and marveled at the many changes of Portland's inner city as he jumped onto the trolley. Buildings stretched toward the clouds. Every street was laced to another with utility wires and poles. Yet, amid the noisy crowds, Portland had retained a simple elegance. Trees garnished the streets, gardens and parkways bordered the river, and the people radiated an enthusiasm spawned by success.

The varied scenes of commerce kept the two of them entertained until the trolley made a stop near a small mom-and-pop hardware store. Colton pointed out the signs in the windows, "Ah, the Wilson Hardware Store. They're on my list to buy out or drive out of business. We can do that in less than a week. It's all about business, young man," he boasted, "only the strong survive."

Todd squinted at him and said, "But their son is my best friend."

There was an awkward silence between the two of them for the next ten minutes. Colton noticed the boy would no longer look him in the eye. Soon the trolley reached the Benson Hotel. The building's dark-chocolate redbrick, accented with white stone base, made an impressive hundred-and-fifty-foot ascent into the sky. Colton held the door open for Todd and grinned when he saw the boy take his hat off and hold it against his chest. Once he entered the brass doors the boy stared wide-eyed and openmouthed at the hardwood floors, polished banisters, big fireplace, and dazzling chandeliers.

"The Benson was a good choice. You and your uncle Stuart were right, Todd. But remember that *money* built this place, and Simon Benson has a lot of it."

"Sure he does, but he helps a lot of people with his money too. Like paying for all the drinking fountains in Portland. And he doesn't hurt his friends."

Colton was going to respond, but sighed. "You know how to get back to the store, right?"

"Course I do," he replied matter-of-factly. "Mother and Uncle Stuart said for you to come over as soon as you're rested up. There's another trolley across the street that goes right past the store."

"Thanks, I know how to find it from here. I'll come right over." He chuckled as Todd headed toward the door while gaping at the lobby interior as though it were a chapel. The desk clerk interrupted the scene as he cleared his throat and pushed the hotel register in Colton's direction. His posture straightened when he recognized the name being written on the ledger.

"Ah, Mr. Grey. What a pleasure it is to have you reside at the Benson. I assume you know that all the crown molding, the bar, and fine furniture in this hotel were provided by the Landon-Grey Company."

"Thank you. Glad we could help. I have two trunks coming from the Orion ship."

"I'll see that they are brought to you immediately. I trust you will find your stay here very enjoyable. How long will you be with us, sir?"

"Perhaps a week. Then I need to head down to Eugene."

"Our loss," the clerk remarked as he handed Colton the room key, "but we will endeavor to make you wish to remain with us longer, or to reserve a room here at the Benson for your return. Do you know when that will be, sir?"

"Return to Portland? Same time, next year I suppose."

"Very good, sir. I'll make a note of it and have a room ready for you. Enjoy your stay." Colton turned to leave, but the desk clerk stopped him. "Oh, I nearly forgot. Mr. Landon brought this package of business mail over for you this morning. He marked it *urgent*. He wanted me to tell you to 'Get your business done before you come over for dinner.' I believe he also said something like you should just socialize tonight, quit being so stuffy, and prepare for a big surprise."

Colton frowned, grabbed the package, then turned and climbed the stairway to his room on the second floor. He tossed his hat on the bed and shuffled through the envelopes. The one from Western Union caught his eye. He tore open the cable:

WESTERN UNION

```
COLTON GREY
LANDON-GREY COMPANY
PORTLAND, OREGON

SCOFIELD MINE EXPLOSION -STOP-
JENSEN BOYS DEAD -STOP-
TAVACI MISSING -STOP-
```

AMBER DUNCAN
SPRINGDALE UTAH

Stunned, Colton sat on the edge of the bed and stared at the floor. His mind staggered through memories. Tavaci, Star's younger brother, was his best friend. Colton had developed a stronger bond with him than he had with his own father. He was the one who introduced him to Amber and the Jensen brothers.

Colton made a mental note to send some money to the Jensen family; there was nothing else he could do for them. But Tavaci's disappearance didn't have as simple a solution. His heart tugged, but even if returned to Utah, the odds of finding Tavaci alive would be remote.

The thought of dredging up the past and reentering that small world again, only to hold his best friend's corpse in his arms, felt worse than leaving it unresolved.

He crumped up the telegram and threw it in his room's small garbage can. He stared at the telegram for a long moment before a loud knock on the door startled him out of his thoughts.

"Who is it?" he demanded.

"Room steward, sir. I have your luggage."

"Huh? . . . Oh yeah. Come in. Put them by the desk." He gave the steward a tip as he exited, opened his leather bag, and carefully removed a rolled blanket. It was a classic Pendleton, prized by mountain men and Indians. White wool with the signature red, black, and yellow bands. He unrolled it to reveal wooden figurines: a moose, a bear, and a totem, all hand-carved by Tanana Indians. They were gifts for Stuart, Todd, and Emma.

Stuart and Emma had filled the vacuum of friendship within Colton since he had run away from the desert. They had given him shelter and support when he had none. Now, looking at the Tanana Indian carvings, he couldn't help but think of the Paiute

Indian friend he had left. Every tribe he encountered on his travels was so distinct, with their own traditions and ways of life, but he could never escape the memory of Tavaci, or Star.

A wave of melancholy briefly washed over him.

He rolled the carvings back in the Pendleton, placed it in his bag, grabbed his hat, and headed out the door for the trolley.

11

The Dinner

THE DINNER PREPARATION complete, Emma collapsed on a chair to catch her breath.

"Mother, will you please make Uncle Colton tell us about his adventures in Alaska?"

"Todd, I'm not going to *make* him tell us anything. He's a busy man and just traveled a very long way to be here. Let's allow him to relax awhile so he can enjoy himself."

"But Uncle Stuart said—"

"Uncle Stuart needs to let Colton rest too."

"Actually," Elizabeth added, "I would love to hear about his adventures."

Emma's mouth dropped open as she looked at them. "People, let's just go slow and see where the conversation takes him."

Three loud raps on the door halted their conversation.

The knocks were repeated, prompting Todd to sprint toward the door. "It's him, it's him."

Emma stood and made sure her hair was in place, Elizabeth smoothed her skirt, and Stuart straightened his tie. An observer might have expected a drumroll.

Tod swung open and Colton beamed. "Is this where Todd, Emma, and Stuart live?" he asked.

"Uncle Colton, Uncle Colton!" shouted Todd. He grabbed Colton's hand and led him inside, "Please tell us about Alaska, please."

"Todd," Emma cautioned with a glare, "he just arrived, let him have a chance to relax and take a seat."

"He's all right Emma. I don't mind. There are probably a few questions you and Stu would like answered too." He paused and looked intently at them both. "I had no idea how much I missed the two of you."

"And me?" Todd wondered.

"Of course, Todd. All of you." There was a warm and cheerful embrace as Colton grabbed the three of them and squeezed. "It's wonderful to be back home."

"Well then, how about telling us about Alaska?" Todd continued.

"Let's have dinner first," Emma interrupted, leading Colton to the dinner table. "Colton, this is our neighbor Elizabeth." She quickly introduced the two as she pulled out a chair and motioned Colton to sit down. Elizabeth smiled politely and Colton nodded in acknowledgment as he sat. "Now let's eat."

The meal was spiced with talk of shared memories and laughter. As they finished dinner, Colton stood to assist Emma in clearing the table. Todd rushed to help and immediately picked up where he left off.

"Uncle Colton, you promised to tell us about Skagway and the Gold Rush."

"Todd," Emma scolded.

"But he promised, and dinner is finished now."

Emma shook her head as she took an armful of dishes toward the sink. "One thing about the men in *this* group is that when they set their minds to something it doesn't seem to matter what I say."

"Sorry mother."

"Emma, it's all right," Colton chuckled. "What's on your mind, Todd?"

"Tell me about the Gold Rush, and fishing boats, and fighting Indians, and—"

"Fighting *Indians*?" Colton looked incredulously at Todd but quickly turned his openmouthed stare toward Stuart, who had his hand over his eyes. "*Fighting* Indians?" He asked Stuart.

"Well . . . there *are* Indians up there . . . aren't there?" Stuart floundered.

"Of *course* there are Indians up there," Colton said, glaring. "Where did the *fighting* part come from?"

"You know—gold rush, fishing boats . . . fighting Indians. The stories helped him get to sleep."

"Yeah, I'll bet. I wonder how many tall tales I'll have to undo." Colton rubbed his eyes, but finally he sighed. "Look . . . it wasn't the kind of adventure that you've heard about. It was hard out there, and a lot of men were either killed or injured. The avalanche at Chilkoot Pass alone killed dozens of men . . . while I was making a lot of money."

"But, Mr. Gray," Elizabeth interrupted, "you didn't *make* them go looking for gold. It wasn't your fault if they were caught in an avalanche. You should be proud you were so smart."

Colton stared at the floor, then mumbled, "I'm not so proud."

The room became uncomfortably silent, too silent for Stuart.

"Elizabeth is right," Stuart said. "You didn't force anybody up into the snow. And you've helped hundreds of people with your whole operation. You paint yourself and your accomplishments in a far worse light than the papers do, my friend. You need to tell her and Todd what great things you've done."

"I'd rather not."

"Then I will." Stuart proceeded to tell Elizabeth and Todd about how Colton got into salmon fishing, canneries, and shipping. He told them how Colton had kept Indian villages fed with salmon through the winters, and how he had developed one of the most efficient methods of catching salmon ever known. Elizabeth and Todd listened to every word with rapt attention.

"Well, friend," Stuart said when he finished. "Did you forget all of that or do you just like to beat yourself up?"

Looking up at Stuart, he feigned a smile and whispered, "I didn't forget."

"Well then," Stuart shouted while slapping his knee and leaping up to his feet, "we're sure glad you returned to Portland. We should go looking for a house for you while you're here, or at least some land to build one."

"I don't know, Stu. I love you three in ways I can't describe, but . . ." Colton said, trailing off.

"Don't you think we need you here?" Stuart complained.

"Are you in financial trouble? Because I would gladly—"

"Nonsense!" Emma shouted. "We're fine. You need to come downstairs and see what we have done to improve the store. And Stuart started a construction company last year. They have both done so well we've hired managers to run them both. Financial trouble indeed. Come downstairs right now to see, and Stuart will take you to see the warehouse afterward so you can just relax about us."

Colton stood obediently and raised his hands in mock surrender. "Lead the way."

The store had indeed undergone an incredible transformation. Aisles were filled with customers, cash registers were ringing, and the diversity of merchandise was amazing. Emma stood with her hands on her hips in a display of obvious satisfaction.

"You see? And the warehouse is ten times bigger than this. Stuart is dying to show you."

A glance at Stuart revealed a broad grin as he waved Colton down to the exit.

"You've seen how Portland's growing. A guy with your business-savvy could do anything here." He raised his eyebrows in an expression of hope and continued, "Plus, winters here are pretty mild compared to Skagway."

"Stu, I—" Colton protested but Stuart cut him off.

"We can talk about the details later. For now, let me take you to the warehouse. I've got some big surprises for you."

12

Stuart's Secret

STUART QUICKENED HIS pace as he led Colton around the block to the back entrance of the warehouse. He grunted as he pushed against the metal sliding doors. As sunlight entered the dark room, he ran forward and pointed at a huge canvas tarp covering a large, box-shaped object.

"Guess what's under here?" Stuart gasped with excitement.

Colton shrugged his shoulders.

With the enthusiasm of a magician unveiling a beautiful woman who suddenly appears in a glass case, Stuart yanked the tarp aside and shouted, "Ta-Da! What do you think? Huh? Huh?" A wide grin splashed across his face mimicking how a child might show off a new bike.

"What in the world . . . ?"

"It's an automobile, you ignoramus."

"I *know* it's an automobile."

"Well then, it's a Model T, you know, Henry Ford and assembly-line production."

"Yeah, I *know* about Henry Ford. My question is what in the world is it doing *here?*"

Stuart wrung his hands and turned his head in all directions as if trying to avoid being discovered. "Look, it's about Emma. She doesn't even like riding in street-car trolleys, so I decided it would be better—"

"To lie to her and keep it hidden here."

"Yes. I mean *no*." He took a step closer to Colton and lowered his voice. "I am not lying to her. I just haven't *told* her about it yet." His boyish grin returned as he stroked his hand across the shiny green hood, brass lights, and horn.

"I've never seen a green one," Colton admitted.

"Yeah, well old Henry said, 'Any color is fine, as long as it's black,' but I have connections. The point is this machine is fabulous! Women *love* riding in this thing. They don't get their skirts dirty crossing the roads; no hurrying to catch the trolley; and, not that women are vain or anything, but they love the way heads turn when we go down the road. There aren't that many autos here in Portland yet, and this is the only green one." By now he was pushing Colton into the passenger seat and sprinting around to jump behind the wheel. "And in case no beautiful women happen to be in the city of Portland on any given evening, this thing can really get down the road. Do you know it will hit 45 miles per hour? And they're bound to get faster!"

"Going fast is important to you?"

"You bet. Why? Is going *slow* important to you?"

"There's some guy in India, named Gandhi, who said 'There is more to life than increasing its speed.'"

"And how many autos do you think there are in India?" Stuart yelled as he started the engine.

Colton rolled his eyes as he climbed into the car. "Where are we going?" he asked.

"That's my next surprise," Stuart winked, and they bolted out onto the street.

They hadn't gone one block when a shiny, black auto cut in front of them from a side street. Stuart swerved to avoid a collision and pulled alongside the other driver.

"Hey!" Stuart yelled. But the other driver seemed oblivious to the dilemma. "That's Judge Thorndale," he complained as he shifted to full speed, "thinks he owns the road." Colton grabbed his hat as they sped past the Judge, who harrumphed in their direction. Stuart merely tipped his hat and smiled.

"And you think racing judges and hauling beautiful women around town will be kept a secret from Emma, do you?"

"Relax. She has too much to do to gossip with neighbors. Besides, none of the paperwork went through the store accounts; I did a little extra work on the side and paid cash. She'll never know." He reached forward and squeezed the rubber-bulb of the horn. Pedestrians scattered. Colton just shook his head.

As they crested the hills on the east side of the Willamette River, the elegant Palmer House came into view. The car roared up to the sidewalk then came to an abrupt halt, nearly throwing Colton out the door. Stuart shrugged his shoulders and grinned, "It's easier to drive it than it is to stop it."

Colton raised both eyebrows, then stretched his back and groaned as he stepped out of the car. "What are we doing here, Stuart?"

"Well, this is the next surprise, of course!" Stuart said confidently. "I've arranged a meeting with some very important men in this town. I think it might convince you to make Portland your permanent home."

Colton pursed his lips and nodded a silent okay. He began to walk up toward the house, but he stopped when the entire house was exposed. Shaking his head in wonder, he exclaimed, "You know Stu, the more I see of Portland, the more I am impressed with the architects. They've become real artisans."

"Yeah, there are quite a few of these Victorian styles around now," Stuart said. "You know, if you stayed here you could build a place as good as this, or better. Think. The scenery here is spectacular: the hills, forests, and rivers. It's got *boomtown* written all over it. A man could drown in green here. And I mean the forests *or* the cash."

Colton sighed as he proceeded up the walkway. "It's somewhat like Alaska here," he agreed as he thought about the Willamette River slipping around Portland. "And there's nothing wrong with more cash." He paused for a moment, considering, then added in a more sober tone, "By the way, let's leave that Wilson Hardware Store alone. They can't hurt us."

Stuart nodded.

"What is this Mr. John Palmer's occupation?" Colton asked.

"Building contractor. Built this home in 1890. Sixty-four hundred square feet of elegance captured in fine cedar. His wife died a few years after the home was built, so he moved away. The guy who lives here now, Oskar Hoch, is a musician and takes very good care of the place. He's in Europe for a while, but was gracious enough to allow this meeting to take place in his home."

Colton was enchanted by the fine craftsmanship. The exterior was an eye-catching shade that was difficult for a man to describe. "Would I call that yellowish-tan, or . . . I don't know. I'll bet Emma would call it "Seasoned Grain," or "Aztec Gold," or something like that. But the five gables with band-saw and spindle work make this place really unique."

"Did you notice the cast-iron rails running along the ridges of the roof, sentry pillars at the doorways?" Stuart grinned. "Hey, did you know your mouth drops open when you look up?"

Colton closed his mouth and glared at Stuart. "What's this meeting all about that we would come to a place like this?"

"You've been in some pretty big meetings in your day, but I think this one will be the most important one you've ever attended."

"I don't know about that, but I can't wait to see the *inside* of this place."

"Let's get inside then," Stuart said as they approached the door. He paused to admire the stained-glass, double-door entry before he knocked. "It's like a kaleidoscope filled with jewels!" he marveled.

"Why Stuart, you do have an artistic side," Colton joked.

"Of course I do," Stuart retorted with a grin, but then his expression sobered and his voice grew serious. "Look Colt, wait until you hear what these guys have to say. I don't want to cross them. In fact, I'd better not." He looked at Colton. "Please . . . as a favor to me."

Colton nodded slowly, his expression equally serious. "As a favor then."

Stuart took a deep breath and knocked.

A butler soon opened the door and took their hats.

The inside of the Palmer House was as unique as the exterior. The small hallway entrance was bordered on the right by a steep and narrow stairway leading up past exotic stained-glass windows that allowed the sunset to garnish the walls like red rubies and blue sapphires.

Colton grabbed the rail to begin the climb, but the butler cleared his throat and nodded to the left. He opened two sliding doors to reveal a smoke-filled room packed with men in business suits.

13
The Meeting

THE LARGE MEETING room had three bay-windows on the west that coaxed the dwindling sunlight to splash across the peacock-blue wallpaper. A bald man with a black mustache sat in a leather chair in the center of the room, encircled by fifteen men in suits. The room extended to their left into an adjoining parlor of golden hues where several women were sitting near a silver wood-burning stove. As Colton and Stuart entered, one of the men closed the doors to the parlor. This was going to be a man's meeting.

The man in the chair stood and raised his glass toward Stuart. The others mimicked his salute. "Mr. Landon, so good to see you again. And finally, we get to meet the renowned Mr. Grey. I think everyone is present, save for Judge Thorndale."

"It's great to see you as well, Mr. Halstead," Stuart said. I'm sure the judge will be along any minute. But, before we begin our business, let's become personally acquainted; ask questions; tip a glass or two."

That cued the butler to approach the group to refill drinks.

"Brandy," ordered Stuart.

"Thank you, nothing for me," said Colton as he looked around the room and smiled.

Stuart grabbed his arm, grimaced through a fake smile, and whispered, "Look, how are you going to make new friends and tip a glass or two, if you don't *have* a glass?"

Pursing his lips and nodding as though he now understood,

Colton looked at the butler and said, "Ice water please . . . in a glass."
Glancing back at Stuart, he gave an *is that okay with you* look.

Stuart rolled his eyes and shook his head. "How are you going
to succeed in this world without alcohol, Colt?"

"Clear head," Colton said as he took the ice water and continued to smile.

The man from the chair, Mr. Halstead, stood up and approached
Stuart and Colton. "Mr. Grey," he said. "How do you feel about
politics?"

"Which type?" Colton queried as he sipped from his glass. "The
real politics, or the real *politics*?"

"Your choice, sir," came Halstead's less-than-amused reply.

"I think real politics is the responsibility of everyone in this
country."

"Precisely!" Halstead boomed gleefully.

"But it's also deciding where to place the blame for bad
decisions."

"Umm, we are moving way too fast here." Stuart quickly ushered
Colton away from Halstead and toward the fireplace, but another
group of men approached to continue the barrage of questions.

"Mr. Grey, how do you feel about the management of the
state's budget?"

"It appears the government puts our money where their mouths
are," Colton replied.

"Do you have some sound advice you would like to share
with our current leaders?"

"I think I would prefer just making sounds rather than giving
advice," Colton said with a forced smile. He turned to Stuart. "Say,
what's this all about?"

"Patience, patience," said Stuart.

"Mr. Grey, you are a very successful businessman. Which is
most important, the economy or the environment?"

"Are you inferring that one must choose between the two?" Colton replied.

"He's perfect," Halstead whispered in Stuart's ear. "He answers questions by asking questions."

"Mr. Grey, what is your most prized possession?"

"Comments I haven't made yet," Colton said, gritting his teeth.

"Do you feel the government should help people solve their problems?"

"I'm not sure that many problems were around until the government created a department to manage them," Colton responded with his last shred of patience. "Look gentlemen, I appreciate the hospitality and fine drink here, but I think we have passed the appropriate time for disclosing the reason for inviting me to this prestigious meeting."

The entire group hushed as Halstead stepped forward and cleared his throat. "Mr. Grey, we already have Portland, Salem, Eugene, and Medford in our pockets. We know you can add the coastal cities from Brookings up to Astoria, and the counties along the Cascades. We can guarantee your victory."

"Victory?"

"We want you to represent our group and run for governor in the upcoming election."

"I'm not interested. Politics seems to be involved with finding problems everywhere, making an erroneous analysis, and using incorrect treatments. And I don't like the idea of having cities in *anybody's* pocket. It doesn't sound, shall we say . . . respectable. In fact, it sounds a little suspicious."

Glasses were slammed onto tables, and postures stiffened at Colton's rejection.

"Look here, Grey—" said another man as he stepped through the group, but Colton cut him off.

"No, you listen here, Mr. Whitacre," Colton snapped. "You

seem surprised that I call you by name, but I know you men. Probably a little better than my friend, Mr. Landon. Mr. Dayton runs timber sales. Mr. Whitacre is the sheriff and owns several mines. Mr. Oakland has big ties with the Union Pacific. Mr. Halstead runs a newspaper syndicate. Shall I go on and identify the rest?"

"Very impressive, Grey," Halstead remarked. "So you've done some reading. The idea here is that we can all work together, help each other out, especially if we have a *friend* as governor. You're not against progress and partnerships, are you? Why, if you're our man, we can make certain that your hardware and cannery interests, as well as shipping connections to ports, will be the only ones doing business in the Northwest."

"No, I'm not against business, progress, or partnerships," Colton said, his tone frigid. "But I am intrigued. Honestly, or should I say *seriously,* how do you propose to arrange my success at ports . . . I mean *our* success?"

"Sometimes ships have trouble at the docks, inspection problems, additional fees . . . even accidents," Halstead said in a low rumble. "The men in this room can determine what information is revealed to the public."

Colton stiffened, even though the words were exactly what he'd expected to hear. "There are three reasons people get involved in politics," he said, folding his arms and turning slowly to scan the entire group. "One is to honestly serve the public by having the notion that you could really have a positive effect for the citizens you serve. Two is for the profit involved: making money with endorsements, public speeches, and inside business deals that the public never knows about. And three is for people like you, the *real* machines that run the government. One would become a puppet while they pull the strings." He placed his glass on a nearby table and concluded, "I don't like wearing strings."

"Perhaps you would prefer wearing a rope instead," someone growled.

Colton snapped erect and glared at the group to determine the source of the threat. It could have been any one of them. "I'm not interested in working with a group where disagreement could result in a permanent problem. I think some of you are worried about George Chamberlain being elected. He runs a clean administration. He'll protect the salmon industry, develop the river freight system, and clean up some of the land deals in this state. I wouldn't be surprised if some of you were called in for an investigation by him as governor. I don't know who you will put up against him, but Chamberlain will get my vote."

"And mine," vowed Stuart.

As Colton headed toward the front exit, someone shouted, "Watch your backside, traitor!"

Colton turned and fired back, "Watch my front side." He stood there for a full thirty seconds awaiting a challenge, but nobody moved. "I see. And this is the method you would use to govern the state?" Manners would have prompted him to offer a cordial *good evening* when he departed, but he sensed an ominous vapor filling the room. He kept his focus on the group, nodded at Stuart, and called for their hats. The two of them backed their way out the door and started down the walk toward the car in the now darkened night sky. They were halfway there when someone yelled, "Grey!"

Colton turned to see a figure in the shadows fifty feet away. In the next instant, he saw a flash and felt leaves and branches shower over him as the sound of a gunshot exploded in his ears. He and Stuart dove to the ground as a second shot ripped into the trunk of a nearby tree.

Wide-eyed, Stuart yelled, "What the—?" But Colton already had a pistol pulled from behind his coat and was aiming at the place where the would-be assassin once stood. Hearing footsteps coming from the car he wheeled and pointed the weapon at the approaching man, who seemed quite at ease amidst all the commotion.

"Gentlemen, you seemed to have gotten your clothes rather soiled," said Judge Thorndale as he cleaned his glasses with a handkerchief.

"Didn't you see or hear what just happened?" Stuart gasped.

"Did something happen?" The judge grinned. "I can only assume that you men refused to cooperate with the alliance. That's unfortunate. As you can see, some of the gentlemen tend to become a little upset when things don't go their way."

Colton glanced back at the house. "Stuart, I think we need to go, *now.*"

"They have the Judge, *too*?"

"Apparently. It's a good thing that guy was a bad shot."

"Not at all," the Judge said, "they're all excellent marksmen. That individual was either taking revenge upon this tree or firing a warning shot."

Colton glared at the Judge. "Start the car," he said to Stuart. "Quick."

Stuart bolted down to the car to fire the engine while Colton stood, keeping the judge between himself and the house.

A pop sounded from under the hood, followed by a growling rumble. "Colton!" Stuart yelled. "Let's go!"

With his eyes continually scanning the grounds, Colton backed toward the car and vaulted over the door to join Stuart.

As they backed into the street, Judge Thorndale yelled, "I suggest you keep your heads low, at least until the election is over."

14

Secret Revealed

W HO WAS HE talking to?" Stuart yelled to Colton as the car lurched forward. "Me? You? Or both of us?"

"I don't know," Colton replied, looking over his shoulder as the Palmer House faded from view. "Just keep driving."

"You'll help me with this, won't you?" Stuart asked as they skidded around a corner.

"You're the one who got us into this mess," Colton growled.

Stuart looked at him, wide-eyed. "Please, Colton. You've got to. Why I don't know what I'll—"

A streetcar's loud clanging bell signaled a near miss of their rear wheels and brought their attention quickly back to the street.

"All right!" Colton yelled over the sound of the bell, "I'll help."

They drove around a corner as Stuart headed past the railroad station and down toward the river. "What are we going to do?"

"I don't know about *we*, but *you* had better keep this thing on the road."

"Hey! I can drive this thing on two wheels if I had to."

"Sure. The front ones or the back ones?"

The bickering continued well after they crossed the river bridge into downtown Portland. Stuart pulled into a grove of trees, shut the car off, and immediately turned around to see if anyone had been following them. His eyes continued to scan the horizon as he nervously sputtered, "There's no use us getting after each other because there are a bunch of guys already doing that."

"What can they do? They can't *make* a person run for governor."

"No, but we both know too much about their group now. We have to figure something out. At least until the election is over."

Colton stared intently at Stuart. It was the first time he had ever seen fear cross his friend's face.

"We'll figure something out, Stu," Colton said, putting a firm hand on his friend's shoulder. "We've gotten out of some rough scrapes before."

Stuart's eyes met Colton's as he nodded.

There was no discussion during their return drive. Stuart drove as fast as he could, while Colton was lost in a maze of thoughts. As they pulled up to the warehouse doors, Emma was carrying a large basket toward a side entrance. When she saw them she unlocked the sliding bolts of the large double doors, swung them open, and stood with her hands on her hips.

"Uh-oh, I don't like it when she stands like that," said Stuart as he pulled his hat down to his eyebrows, drove past her into the warehouse, and parked. They got out of the car quickly.

"Look Emma, I'm sorry for not telling you about the car," Stuart apologized as he began covering the car with the canvas tarp. "I know they're dangerous and—"

Emma put her basket down and hurried over to help him. "Don't be silly," she laughed. "I knew about this car the day after you bought it."

"What?"

"Heavens, yes. Sylvia's husband sold it to you. And within an hour you had given Elizabeth a ride. I'm sure you asked those ladies not to say a word to me, but we all have sort of bond of sisterhood that motivates us to share little things . . . like *secret* cars."

"So you've been deceiving me all this time."

"Deceiving *you*?"

"I hate to interrupt a good sibling rivalry," Colton said, "but what was in the basket you were carrying?

Emma sighed. "I was going to pack the car for our picnic tomorrow."

"Picnic?" Colton asked.

"Yes," Emma said. "Todd and I thought we should celebrate your return to Portland by going to Multnomah Falls. It's silly to have you finally come home and do nothing but work, work, work."

"But, Emma—" Colton protested.

"Taking time for a family picnic will not break you." Emma cut him off, her hands returning to her hips. "The most important journey you may ever take will be in meeting people halfway. And I'm doing this for young Todd too. He's never been on a picnic with you, *or* seen the Falls, *or* had a ride in Stuart's secret car."

Colton's expression softened. "All right Emma, I can't fight you both. The Falls tomorrow. Now, if you'll excuse me, I'm heading back to the Benson. It's been a long day, and Stuart's given me a lot to think about."

Stuart shuffled his feet. "Look, Colton, I didn't know Emma would be here and—"

"Don't worry about it. The walk will give me time to think things over."

Emma glanced back and forth between Colton and Stuart, but she decided to let it pass. "So it's agreed. The *secret car* will pick you up at eight o'clock in the morning. We'll spend a wonderful day together relaxing at a gorgeous place."

Colton smiled and nodded, then he pulled his hat tighter onto his head and walked off toward the Benson.

15

Ethan's Water

Tom ran over to the men at the fence line, ready to argue. Four of them were driving horse-drawn wagons loaded with boulders and logs along the stream toward the edge of the mesa. Ten others stood near the brink of Cougar Creek's small waterfall, manning a wooden-beam crane and pulley system to lower the loads into position in the water.

"Ethan, what's going on here?" Tom asked, outraged, as he stormed over to the man in the cobra-skin boots. He tore off his hat. "I don't think we should—"

"I don't pay you to think, Tom. Just do what you're told."

"I understand that." Tom shuffled his feet a bit as he dusted his jeans with his hat. "But the folks down in the valley will need this water too. They depend on it. It's life to them."

"Sure, just like it is to us," Ethan said. He peered over the edge of the canyon and yelled, "Hey, you men down at the bottom, get moving or you'll all get fired!"

"There's only me down in the very bottom, Boss," a ranchhand yelled back.

"Then spread out!" Ethan yelled, then turned back to Tom, "Sorry for the interruption, but are you workin' for me or them cotton farmers down below?"

"I've worked for you for a long time, Ethan. Helped you do some things I wondered about later, but I did 'em cause you're the boss. But I don't hold with you on this one. Folks ain't gonna like you dammin' up that stream."

"It's just one stream, and a small dam. We need the water for our horses. And they ain't gonna know, are they?"

"But Cougar Creek and the Virgin River are the only waters in the mountains that run all year," Tom protested. "There's only twenty of us up here. We can take whatever we need right from the stream just like we've been doin'. But buildin' a dam here will wipe out half the folks in the valley, and you know it."

"Too many farmers down there anyway." Ethan shrugged. "I'd just as soon get rid of all of them."

Tom's mouth dropped open as he shook his head in disbelief.

"Look, Tom, we'll just tell them it was a mild winter up here and there's no runoff to be had. They'll never see this dam from down in the valley, and the only reason folks come up this high is to steal my trees. That's why we build fences and guard the road. Nobody needs to know about this dam."

"Oh, they'll know, they'll know." Tom put his hat on and pulled it down near his eyes, "Guess I'm finished up here. I'll get my gear."

"Have it your way, Tom. Been nice workin' with you," Ethan said nonchalantly, but he glared at Tom's back as he watched him go toward the bunkhouse to gather his stuff.

When Tom was out of earshot, Ethan turned to "You been doing any *thinkin',* Stitch?"

"No, sir."

"Got any questions?"

"No, sir."

"Make sure he's far enough away that nobody will hear the shot. And that means nobody up here, or down in the valley. I don't want to know what you do with him after. Just make sure he's never seen again."

"I know a place." Stitch nodded. He swung up onto his saddle and patted his rifle.

"Don't miss," Ethan warned.

"Never do."

16

Amber's Dilemma

SHE SAT ON the river bank soaking her bare feet in the cool water. Her shirt was soiled, her long hair wind-tossed, but her green-eyes remained bright and alert. Though she had the heart to maintain a valiant fight, her body was ready to raise the white flag of surrender. Fatigue and stress had pummeled her until she sought comfort in the gentle currents of the Virgin River.

"Amber, is that you?" A young woman's voice called behind her.

Amber turned, surprised, "Oh, hello, Danielle. I didn't expect anyone to be in this area."

"I'm sorry if I'm disturbing you. I was just taking a stroll by the river. I'll walk back to Springdale."

"No, don't go. I'm fine. I'm just . . . I don't know . . . just sitting here, thinking."

"You don't look fine. What's happened to you?"

Amber turned away as tears trickled down her face. "I don't know."

"Oh, Amber." Danielle walked down to the bank to sit beside her. "What's the point in being friends if I can't help you when you need it? You work harder than most men, taking care of Charles Grey, plus owning a sawmill. Why don't you stop? Stay home and—"

"And what? Knit a sweater? Only a few people around here like Charles. And now he's sick. Real sick. And if I stop running the sawmill, Ethan Morley will . . ." She shook her head and sighed.

"Maybe I can help you take care of Charles. And the sawmill can—"

"Three men quit today, Danielle. Old Hank and I had to load, drive, and unload the lumber by ourselves this last week. I'm tired. Maybe I should just sell out to Ethan."

"Don't do it, Amber. If you do, he'll raise the price of lumber sky-high, plus cut down every tree on the mesa. He doesn't care about leaving any seed-trees standing or replanting what he's cut."

"Nobody wants me to sell, but nobody wants to help either. My life wasn't supposed to turn out this way. When I was a girl I would dream of being with . . . well, I did a lot of dreaming."

"I know. You hoped you would be with Colton Grey and live happily ever after."

"Hah! You've read too many fairy tales. I have nothing to do with Colton Grey *or* happily ever after. He doesn't care about anything, or anyone, down here."

"What do you mean, down here?"

"Down *here!* What everybody calls Dixie. There are times I think the pioneer idea of settling this area was crazy, and having prosperity is just a dream. This place has worn me out. The cotton crops have never done well. My parents died years ago. All the men around here are after me. The trees in the canyons have all been cut. It's either drought or flash floods. No wonder Colton left. Anybody with half a brain would."

"Amber! Listen to yourself. You're tired. You don't know what you're saying. It's beautiful here. And you're gorgeous and single. How can you complain about the reactions that causes? I feel sorry for you, but you ought to be thankful you're—"

"Ughhh, stop, Danielle. I know I shouldn't complain . . . about anything. I suppose I'm just having a bad day."

"I know you're carrying more than your share. But weigh this out. We've been here for years, and we'll be here for many more.

Nobody said it would be easy, but things that are worthwhile never are. You've always been such a fighter. And your parents wouldn't want you to give up and abandon their land. You're the source of strength of so many people here, including me. You're *my* strength. I need you to keep *me* strong."

Amber looked down at her feet in the river. She wound her wavy hair around her fingers for a full minute before she stood up, fists clenched, and eyes glaring at Danielle. "I'll stay here until Charles Grey dies. Then I'm out. I'm sorry I can't be the source of your strength, but that's *your* job, not mine."

"I know it's been tough on you, losing Colton, and then your parents. But I'm still here, and I'm sure there are others who will be glad to help you. What about Lewis?"

Amber shook her head. "You have your own family to worry about. And Lewis is almost as eager for me to sell as Ethan. It's just me and the trees up on the mesa. I've got one more season in me, Danielle, then I'm done."

"Well, I read about Colton in the paper not too long ago. Maybe you could contact him somehow."

Amber picked up a rock and threw it into the middle of the river. "I've already sent him two cables, one in Alaska and one in Portland. I told him about his father and the Scofield mine explosion, but it had as much effect on him as the ripples from that rock had on the river. They're gone."

"And how do you know for certain that he ever received them?"

Amber's mouth dropped open. She looked puzzled, as though she had never considered that possibility.

"You need to try again, Amber. For Charles's sake, *and* yours."

"Maybe. Maybe someday, Danielle."

17

Multnomah Falls

THE MORNING STREETS of Portland mimicked a busy ant-hive working on a beautiful sunny day. Colton whistled as he descended the stairway of the Benson Hotel, but it was only to disguise the storm inside of his mind; the night had been filled with terrible dreams of Tavaci, Amber, and the Jensen brothers being consumed by flames and drowned in the ocean. He knew they had just been dreams, but that didn't make them any easier to shake.

He arrived in the lobby just as Todd burst through the revolving doors. "Uncle Colton, we're parked right outside. Are you excited to go to the Falls?"

"I am now, young man. Lead the way." Colton smiled and followed Todd.

They stepped onto the sidewalk just as Stuart coaxed a loud *aooooogah* from the car's horn.

Colton covered his ears, "What? You couldn't see us coming through a *glass* door?"

"Oh, I saw you. It's just Jenny's way of saying hello and let's go!"

Colton raised the brim of his hat and leaned over to search for this new female passenger.

"Jenny? She must be pretty small. I only see Emma and Elizabeth in the back seat."

"Jenny is the car, stupid. Ever hear a girl go *aooooogah*?"

Todd laughed, but Colton just sighed, glared at Stuart, and climbed into the front seat while Todd scrambled into the back.

"You better hang on to that hat, partner. Jenny is ready to dance." With that, Stuart opened the throttle, popped the clutch, and promptly killed the engine.

"Sounds like you stepped on Jenny's toes," Colton said with a smirk.

Todd, Emma, and Elizabeth laughed until their laughter was finally drowned out by the engine sputtering to a start. A quick belch of smoke and off they went toward the bridge spanning the Willamette River.

The friendly conversation was soon replaced with silence as views of the mighty Columbia River dominated the scene on their left, while verdant blends of ferns and trees graced the mountains on their right. There had been a gentle rain the night before. Droplets adorned every leaf and frond. The air was rich with the smell of green. The day couldn't have been more perfect if an artist had painted it.

"Do you notice how we women both sit with our hands properly clasped upon our laps, while the men each have one hand outside the open windows to feel the rush of the passing wind?" Elizabeth remarked to Emma as they drove.

Colton became suddenly conscious of his open hand stroking the wind and smiled.

"Colton and Stuart have a child hidden inside them not much different than Todd," Emma replied, laughing. "I don't think the desire to play ever leaves most men. It just gets smothered by work, and problems—"

"And women," Stuart added with a chuckle.

Elizabeth looked down and bit her bottom lip.

Emma grabbed Elizabeth's hand and squeezed. "Don't worry, Elizabeth. You're wonderful. Stuart just hasn't realized it yet."

The drive was truly magical. They passed a series of small, lacey waterfalls: Latourell, Shepperd's Dell, Bridal Veil, and

Wahkeena. Each of those sites fueled their emotion to see the towering Multnomah. And, somehow, their passion increased speed but slowed time. Soon the car was parked in a place where they could see the top of Multnomah Falls to the right, as well as the Columbia River on their left.

"It's like being in between a diamond necklace and a silver bracelet," Colton mused as they got out of the car.

"My partner is waxing eloquent these days," Stuart teased.

Colton looked at the ground, his ears reddening slightly.

"Leave him alone," said Emma, pushing Stuart away. "I think that's a beautiful comparison. Go on Colton, what else do you see?"

Colton eyed Stuart but continued cautiously. "It's beautiful here. It isn't anything like where I grew up. I wish that she could have—" He caught himself. "Never mind."

"Who? Do what?" Emma pleaded.

"Nobody. Nothing. I'm just tired."

"Of what, Colton?"

"Of wishing she would have . . . ah, forget it." He put his hands in his pockets and strolled toward the falls.

"Stuart!" Emma demanded, "What's going on with him? I've never seen him like this before. And who is *she*?"

"I don't know," Stuart shrugged. "It's the first I've heard of it."

Emma grabbed her brother by the collar. "Stuart, that is the most I've heard Colton talk about his home in all the time we've known him. That's not something you just shrug off. Tell me everything you know. You two were gone an awfully long time last night, he must have told you something."

"He didn't tell me anything," Stuart said as he scrambled out of Emma's grip. He sighed. "But maybe it has something to do with this letter from Utah." He pulled a slightly crumpled envelope from his pocket. "It's signed by an A. Duncan."

"How long have you had that letter, brother?" Emma snatched the letter from Stuart's hand and turned it over to look at the postdate.

"Only a week. I was—"

"A week? Look at him!" She gestured to Colton. "Have *you* ever seen him like this? He's always been a pillar of strength. Stronger than any of us. And seeing these falls nearly brought him to his knees. And you've had a letter for him for a *week*?"

"Emma, we don't do any business in Utah. This has to be a letter from Colton's hometown. What if they want him to go back? He has important business here. He's everything to our business. Why, there were some men in this town who wanted to make him governor. And—"

"And *what,* Stuart? You don't know what could be in that letter. I am so ashamed of you right now."

"Stop it! It's a *woman's* handwriting, it's from Utah, and I didn't—"

"Didn't *what,* Stuart? Huh? What?"

"I didn't want him to leave us again," Stuart said, his voice breaking. He cleared his voice before speaking again. "There. You happy now? It's not about the business or anything like that. He's closer to me than anyone on this planet. And he's finally home. Want me to shed a tear to two? Because I won't."

"Oh, Stuart, I'm so sorry," Emma said softly as she cupped her hands over her mouth. "I knew you were close, but—"

"Yeah, well sometimes what you know, and ten cents, will get you a newspaper and that's all." Stuart grabbed the letter back from Emma and walked off to follow Colton. "I'll take the letter to him right now."

Elizabeth ran beside Stuart and placed her hand on his shoulder. "Stuart, if there's anything I can do . . ."

"There isn't," Stuart replied shortly, shrugging her hand off.

"Maybe we can sit and talk," Elizabeth persisted.

Stuart paused to look at her. His expression softened. "Look Elizabeth, I love you just the way I am." He kissed her softly on the cheek, then hurried after Colton.

A small tear rolled down Elizabeth's cheek as she watched Stuart walk away. "I'll wait," she whispered. "He'll see. Someday."

18

The Letter

"COLTON. WAIT UP a minute. Stop walking away, will you?" Stuart panted as he ran to catch up.

Colton stopped and turned. "What do you want, Stuart? You want to see me make a bigger fool of myself?"

"Not at all, partner. I just want to walk and talk for a while. Maybe share some news along the way. The spray from the falls will help cool you off." He patted Colton's back and walked him toward the base of the falls.

"What news are you talking about?"

"Oh, nothing in particular. Lighten up a bit. Enjoy the view. Have you ever hiked to the top?"

"Never had time."

"You've got time now."

"How tall are those falls anyway?"

"Over six hundred feet. Why? Aren't you up to this?"

He glared at Stuart, "Lead on."

The hike took them along a shaded forest trail as it wound its way upward. An occasional glimpse of the Columbia, and the muffled sound of the plummeting Multnomah, spurred them along the trail, but they frequently paused to enjoy the verdant landscape.

Near the top, they met a couple of attractive women walking back down the trail along the spring-fed stream. Stuart immediately stopped and removed his hat to strike up a conversation. Colton smiled at them but continued to follow the stream toward the falls.

Colton stopped fifty yards from the brink and closed his eyes to listen to the swirling water as it rushed by. It reminded him of the serenity he often found along the Virgin River in Southern Utah. He took a deep breath and tried to savor the moment, but he was alerted to the sound of splashing.

He opened his eyes to see a woman struggling in the current as she was being swept toward the last pool overlooking the edge. Her long, black, braided hair bobbed along on the surface as she thrashed about, looking for a handhold to safety.

"Hold on!" he yelled as he sprinted toward her. "Hold on! I'm coming! Grab a rock or branch!"

"Run Colton! Run! Hurry!" she yelled just before she sank into the pool and went over the edge.

"Wait!" he yelled.

He was running to plunge into the pool when Stuart tackled him from behind.

"Are you *crazy*?" Stuart yelled through the cloud of dust. "You go in there and you will *die*!"

"I had to," Colton gasped. "Didn't you see her in the water?"

"See who? I was right behind you. Nobody was in the water. Colton, look at me."

Colton's chest was heaving as he shook his head.

"Colton, *look* at me . . . nobody was there."

Colton turned, stared openmouthed at Stuart, then back at the waterfall.

"If you had gone in the water you would have been swept away."

The words *swept away* put Colton's memory in a tailspin as they echoed in his mind. It had been her again. It had been Star.

He lay on the ground and covered his head with both arms as the memory of the canyon flood returned. It was as vivid as though he were living it that moment. He could see it. He could hear it. He could smell it. He closed his eyes tight to remove the nightmare.

Stuart began shaking him. "Colton, are you all right, partner? Colton!"

"Huh? Yeah. Sure," he mumbled as he uncovered his head and rose to his feet. "You sure you didn't see, or hear, *anything*?"

"No. I heard you yelling, so I left the ladies and sprinted to tackle you before you did something stupid."

Colton glanced back to see the two ladies covering their mouths with their hands and staring wide-eyed at him as though afraid he might be contemplating jumping over the edge. That same concern crossed Stuart's mind.

"Look, Colton," Stuart said gently. "Let's head back down."

"Yeah. I'm all right. I just wanted to help—"

"I know. I know. Look, you mean a lot to me—"

"I wasn't going to jump," Colton barked.

"All right. I don't know what you saw, but I'll believe you. Because I always have. And your happiness means a lot to me."

"If you try to kiss me, I'll—" Colton tried to sound serious but he couldn't stop himself from smiling.

"Don't be stupid." Stuart smiled, then turned serious again. "I just wish you would stick around here. Emma and I . . . well, we consider you family. That's why I thought the governor thing might at least keep you in Oregon for a while. And Todd thinks you're terrific."

"Where you going with this, Stuart?"

Stuart looked down at the ground, reached in his pocket, and pulled out the letter.

"I hope this doesn't change your plans."

Colton took the letter and turned it over. His face went sober as he saw the name "A. Duncan" on the return address. He tapped the envelope on his empty hand as he contemplated opening it or throwing it over the falls.

"Maybe it's good news, Colt."

Colton glared at him, looked up at the sky, took a deep breath, and tore the envelope open. He was careful not tear the return address.

He unfolded the letter and read it with deliberation.

"Damn it!" he yelled.

"What is it? What's it say?" Stuart asked, startled.

"It's all coming together now. The woman in the ocean by ship, the telegrams, the woman I just now saw go over the falls, and now this letter."

"What woman? What are you talking about?"

"Nothing."

"Who is A. Duncan?"

"Nobody?"

"And *nobody* wrote to you about *nothing*? That makes no sense!"

"Look Stuart, this is complicated. It starts way before you and I even met."

"*Complicated* sounds like it could use some help. Come on, at least give me a hint about what's in that letter. What's got you so tight-lipped?"

Colton wadded the letter into a tight ball and threw it at the falls.

"I need to go back to Utah," he said finally, then he turned and started back down the rail.

Stuart stood with his mouth open in confusion as he watched Colton walk away, but he noticed the letter had landed on top of some rocks on the water's edge. Three quick steps and the letter was in his hand. He looked to see if Colton was no longer in sight, then he uncrumpled the letter and read:

Colton,

I've sent several cables to you but never received a reply. I've almost given up hope in you ever responding, but Danielle tells me I should try again.

It costs too much to send a telegram with too few words, so I hope this letter reaches you.

Words cannot express the gratitude I felt when I learned that you were alive and well. All these years I have wondered and worried about where you were, what you were doing, and if you were thinking about me as frequently as my thoughts lingered on you.

You left too soon. You didn't even say goodbye. You never asked me what happened that night you saw me with Ethan. You just left. Why? Did you really think I would choose to kiss Ethan after all we had together? He grabbed me and I couldn't get away from him. At a time I needed to be rescued, you got on your horse and disappeared. For years.

But it's difficult for a famous person to hide forever. And I'm not even sure that's what you're trying to do. I just don't know. Please tell me, will you? I don't know what course your life has taken, but I do know you have been successful. I would have expected no less. I always saw greatness within you. Without your fame, I never would have known how to reach you.

There is much that has transpired in your absence. Your father may be dying. I have been looking after him since you left, but I cannot replace his need to reconcile with you. Tavaci has been missing since the Scofield mine explosion. My parents have been killed and I've taken over their timberland and sawmill. Ethan is pushing me to sell. He is relentless, and I'm so tired. I can't do this anymore.

Yours always,

Amber

Stuart folded the letter carefully and put it in his pocket. *This changes everything,* he thought as he headed back down the trail.

19

Emma Insists

EMMA AND ELIZABETH had finished laying out lunch on a blanket and were watching Todd skipping stones across the stream when they saw Stuart and Colton strolling toward them. Elizabeth stood but fought the urge to run to Stuart when she heard Emma clear her throat.

"Elizabeth, stay calm. He'll come to you, and you can sit by him." She turned toward the men and noticed how quiet and serious they were as they approached. "Well, boys, how was the hike to the top of the falls?"

"Fine," they said in unison.

"See anything special up there?"

"No," they said in unison.

The two women looked at each other quizzically, but they decided not to press the issue. "Stuart, why don't you go and sit down by Elizabeth over there, and Colton can get Todd from the stream and sit next to me so we can enjoy this delicious lunch together."

The men quietly did as they were instructed, which created more wonder for Emma. Lunch was enjoyed, but the conversation was sterile and brief.

"So how was the view up there?" Emma asked.

"Beautiful," Stuart replied.

"Spectacular," said Colton.

"Was anyone else up there?" Elizabeth asked.

"Stuart met some girls," Colton said.

Elizabeth almost choked on her sandwich. Emma patted her knee and raised her eyebrows at Stuart.

"Only spoke with them for a minute," Stuart defended, then he cleared his throat to change the subject. "Well, this has been fun. Why don't we clean this up and head back to Portland?"

"But Stuart," Emma complained, "it's such a lovely day, and we could enjoy a walk down to the river or—"

"We really should go," Stuart emphasized with a glare. "There's work to do at the store, and Colton's got business to attend to. We need to go. We'll do this again real soon." He stood up, motioned for Colton to do the same, then helped Elizabeth to her feet.

Emma sighed and began returning items to the picnic basket. "That sounds fine, brother. We'll clean up these things and enjoy the ride back home."

Stuart winked at her, picked up the blanket, and headed toward the car.

The return ride was scenic but silent.

As the car pulled to a stop at the Benson Hotel, Stuart left the driver's seat and rushed around to open Colton's door.

"What are you doing, Stuart?" Colton asked as he got out of the car.

"Just helping a buddy and—"

"I'm fine. Really. Take the ladies and Todd home, and I'll see you later tonight."

Stuart patted him on the back, returned to the driver's seat, and pulled away.

Emma reached forward and tapped him on the back. "Stuart, what's going on?"

"Going on? Is something going on? I just want to get my beautiful Elizabeth home safe and sound. We'll see Colton after dinner tonight, and Elizabeth can join us then too. Right, Elizabeth?"

"That would be wonderful."

Ten minutes later Stuart walked Elizabeth to her door and gave her a quick kiss goodbye.

He turned quickly and ran back to the car to find Emma had moved to the front passenger seat. Todd slept peacefully in the back seat, as he had the entire drive.

"Stuart, do you want to explain to me why we left the Falls so early? How did Colton react when you gave him the letter?"

"Emma, something's wrong with him," Stuart said as he got back into the driver's seat and drove to their apartment. "He said he saw a woman going over the Falls and he was going in to save her . . . but nobody was in the water. I had to tackle him or we might be driving his body to the morgue right now."

"What brought that on?"

"I don't know for sure, but he said it happened before on the ship, and he mentioned cables he's been receiving."

Stuart pulled up to the warehouse. Emma got out of the car and opened the doors to let him park.

"So did you show him the letter?" Emma asked once the car was still. She lifted Todd from the back seat into her arms.

"Yeah, but he threw it at the falls after he read it," Stuart replied as he pulled the tarp over the car.

"My goodness. I wonder what was written that would cause that reaction?"

Stuart smiled and pulled the crumpled letter from his pocket as they approached the door to their apartment.

"You devil, you," Emma said as she unlocked the door and they walked inside. She quickly laid Todd in his bed and returned to Stuart. "That's a private letter."

Stuart nodded and started to return the letter to his pocket.

"Still," Emma said, "it might be real important and give us an idea how to help him."

Stuart grinned and unfolded the letter. Emma grabbed it from him and sat down on the couch. She started to read aloud, but soon mouthed the words silently.

"Stuart, do you know what this letter means?" she asked when she had finished.

"Well, I, uh—"

"It means Colton's made a mistake. I don't know who this Amber is, but there was a real connection between those two."

"Then why's he never mentioned her?"

"Why would he? He thought she had abandoned him for another man. He's been living a lie but didn't know it. And now his father is dying!" Emma shook her head in disbelief. "This woman must be hating her life right now."

"I don't know. She sounds pretty tough to hang on this long and go through all that." Stuart looked over to see tears streaming down his sister's face. "Emma, are you crying?"

"Brother, sometimes you are so smart, and other times . . ." Emma said through her tears.

"What? You don't know this woman."

"I may not know her, but I know some of what she's going through. It's been so many years since Colton left his home, and she didn't know where he was all that time or if he was alive." Stuart gave her a handkerchief and she blew her nose on it. "I would give anything to have Jonathon alive and back with me. Sometimes I miss him so much I would—"

"Stop it, Emma. I know. I know." He started wringing his hands.

"It's clear from this letter how this Amber feels about Colton, and I think I know how Colton feels about her too." Emma used the handkerchief to wipe away her tears.

"How do you know that?" Stuart asked.

"Do you remember years ago when we were walking downtown and Colton ran across the street to speak to a woman he saw? He was nearly hit by a trolley."

"Umm, not really."

"Think. He grabbed her by the arm and spun her around. His face literally shined with excitement. And then, when he realized she wasn't who he thought she was—I'm guessing this Amber—he was so embarrassed. That was the same day Colton told us he was going to Alaska."

"I remember now. That girl was gorgeous. Long, dark, beautiful hair; small white hat; white gloves; a sky-blue dress—"

"Stuart!" Emma smacked him on the arm. "You are unbelievable. A classic womanizer."

"Well, what do you suggest we do?"

"We have to tell Colton we know about Amber and the issues she's facing, and that he needs to return to Utah . . . now." She folded her arms and looked at Stuart with tear-filled eyes.

"All right, all right! You realize he will know I read his letter, right? And that's after he threw it away. How do I explain that?"

"You'll find a way, brother. You're better at deception than I am."

"Thanks—hey, what do you mean *deception*?"

"Secret car. Leading women on. Shall I continue?"

Stuart stared at his feet, then winced as a wave of guilt prevented a reply.

"Stuart, you are a good man," Emma said in a softer tone. "I know that. You just deal with things in your own way." She put her hand on his shoulder. "I don't mean to chastise you, but this Amber, *and* Colton, need our help."

Stuart nodded in agreement. "I'll talk to him tonight after dinner."

"Forget dinner. Go to his hotel and talk to him now. I'll explain things to Elizabeth." She smiled. "Who also has long, dark, beautiful hair."

"Emma, don't start," Stuart said as he headed out the door.

20

Tickets to the Past

COLTON WAS WORKING through his stack of business mail when he heard a knock at his door. He opened it and there stood Stuart.

"What are you doing here?" he asked. "Come in. I thought we were having dinner at your place later tonight."

"Yeah, no big dinner tonight." Stuart took off his hat and walked into the room. "We need to talk."

Colton sobered. He closed the door and gestured Stuart to take a seat. "Trouble with the hardware store, or lumber yard?"

"Neither." Stuart shook his head. "Everything's fine. Well, maybe . . ."

"Maybe? I mean, I trust you and Emma completely, but why *maybe*?"

Stuart walked past him to the window where he tapped on the glass and considered what to say next. "Look Colton, I think of you more as a brother than a business partner."

"Likewise."

"And well . . . I . . . umm . . . I—"

"It will save us both some time if you just say what's on your mind."

"Remember the Utah letter and how I worried it might tarnish our friendship?"

"Yes. No harm was done. Things are fine between us."

"I read it."

"What? Why would you do that?"

"Not because I'm nosey. Okay, maybe a little. But the way you acted up at Multnomah Falls made me concerned for your welfare. That's why. I'd never seen you like that before."

Colton sat on the edge of the bed and wrung his hands. "I don't know what to do. I've never been in a situation like this." He turned and shook his head. "I've always just decided on a course of action, worked hard, and trusted things would be fine. So far, I can't complain. But this . . . I hate the conflict it boils up in me."

"You've done amazing things in just a few years, my friend."

"That's not the way I see it." Colton sighed. "Life before I came to the Northwest was . . . well, I needed to leave Utah."

"So the letter says. But Emma and I think you should go back. At least for a little while."

"Emma knows about this too?"

"She's got that woman's feel for knowing the right thing to do. And I believe in her. You know that we consider you as part of our family. We love you."

Colton gave a small smile. "I know."

Stuart leaned against the window. "Think about this, Colt. Your father is dying and wants to make amends for the past. Are you too proud to let a man apologize before he dies? And this Amber woman. I know you miss her."

"I do not."

"You do. I'm being honest with you, so don't lie to me. And it's obvious that you've misread her actions. Sounds to me like she's actually in trouble. And I've never seen you turn down *anyone* in trouble, from the poor in the streets to the native people of Alaska."

"It's not as simple as you and Emma make it sound. Do you think my father is really going to apologize, or accost me again for all his troubles? He'll probably blame me because he is dying. And it's not just Ethan that causes problems down there. He has a gang that works for him. And maybe he forced himself on Amber, and

maybe not. That's her story, but I know what I saw. The one thing
that really does both my is Tavaci. He and I were inseparable; I
consider him my brother. If he was killed in that mine . . ."

"She didn't say he was killed."

Colton pulled a paper from his pocket and held it up. "Stuart,
when I have tough decisions to make, I write two lists. One with
pros, and one with cons. These are the Utah lists, and when I put
all this on a balance scale, they tip heavily for reasons *not* to go.
It's a bad risk. And I weigh my risks *very* carefully."

Stuart nodded. "But what if she's telling the truth? Is that on
your list, Colton? You will hate yourself forever if you don't try
to help her. Did you ever consider that she could have left that
place the day after you did? But she stayed there all these years
helping others and trying to do what's right. Why? What kind of
a person does that? She sounds like an amazing woman to me."

Colton joined Stuart at the window, bit his lower lip, and looked
into the sky. The Orion Constellation had emerged from the East
and seemed to fill the entire sky. He shook his head and sighed.
"Emma was right. Look, Stuart, I'll go, but you need to understand
that I might not be able to return."

"Don't be ridiculous—"

"I'll go, provided you'll let me sign over my share of the business to you and Emma."

"No need to—"

"That's the deal. Take it or leave it. I won't go any other way.
And I'm not having the two of you struggle with attorneys if I
never return, if you know what I mean. Are you in or not?"

Stuart considered for a long time. "Make the contract out to
Emma's name." Colton stared at him. "I'm going with you."

"Stu, I—"

"Listen, we can kill two birds with one stone: get out of town for
the election and solve this problem of yours. If we can figure out

a way to convince Emma she should take Todd to Seattle to visit our sister for a while, that would keep them safe too. Joe is a good manager who will take care of the business here until we all return."

Colton nodded. "I'll get the train tickets tomorrow morning."

21

A Done Deal

THE APARTMENT WAS dark when Stuart returned home. Emma and Todd's soft breathing were the only sounds he heard. He tiptoed quickly to his own bed and tried not to think about all that tomorrow would bring as he lay down and let sleep take him.

In the morning, Stuart got up early and ran to the shops. Emma knew about the possibility of Colton going to Utah, but she had no idea about his sudden decision to join him on the journey, and he hadn't even mentioned Seattle yet. He went into a shop, grabbed the first sentimental card he could find, bought it, and ran back to the apartment for breakfast. He hoped that his offering would be enough to convince her.

Emma was setting the table when he entered the apartment. "Good morning, Stuart," she called to him.

"Good morning, Sis," he said as he walked over to help her. "How was your night?"

"Well, Elizabeth was disappointed we didn't have dinner. But I slept well if that's what you mean." She looked up from the table and spied Stuart suspiciously. "What do you have behind your back, Stuart? It better not be another letter."

"No letter this time, but I did get a card for you."

She took the card from him and opened it, then held it to her heart. "Why Stuart, the inscription is so sweet and heartfelt. This is honestly the nicest card I have ever received."

"That's great . . . what does it say?"

"Brother, you're incorrigible. You just bought a card and gave it to me without even reading it."

"Well, there was a gorgeous woman riding by in a new type of car I hadn't seen before and I—"

"Really, what color was the car?"

"Blonde."

She shook her head and rolled her eyes, "Just have a seat and we'll have breakfast."

They shared a simple meal with Todd, who then went back to his room.

As they were clearing the table there was a knock at the door. Stuart went down the stairs to find Colton standing outside with two train tickets.

"Let's keep these tickets in our pockets," Stuart whispered. "I haven't told her about our trip to Utah yet."

"You should be the one to tell her, I'm staying out of this." Colton insisted.

"Why just me?"

"You're better at deception than I am."

"Thanks—hey, what do you mean, deception?"

As they entered the kitchen the expressions on their faces mimicked children who had just broken an expensive vase. Emma instantly detected the anomaly in their behavior. Unfortunately, she went directly to Colton.

"What happened?" she asked.

He snapped to attention. "Happened? Umm, nothing. I . . . uhh . . . we went . . . I mean . . ." he stammered before looking wide-eyed at Stuart in a silent demand for rescue.

Emma turned on her heels and marched directly over to Stuart. "Well?" she demanded.

Fearing he would duplicate Colton's stammering, he opened

his mouth but began gesturing wildly with his hands while looking around the room.

"Stuart," Emma shouted. "What is going on with you two? I have never seen you speechless before." She hesitated for just a moment, then displayed an *I just figured it out* expression.

Colton raised his eyebrows at Stuart's lack of speech but started to slowly edge his way behind him so he wouldn't have to field Emma's queries.

She smiled. "Why don't you boys just tell me what you've been up to."

Stuart turned toward Colton, who was nodding his head urging *him* to speak.

"Colton's going back to Utah," Stuart blurted.

"What?" yelled Colton.

"Oh, Colton, I'm so proud of you," said Emma as she gave him a warm embrace. "But I have to say I'm concerned about you making a 750-mile journey only to find yourself surrounded by troubles. I know you might think you are invincible, but—"

"Emma, I made that trip alone coming up here when I was much younger, and I've been to Alaska and back several times. I'll be fine."

"I hope so, but the other trips didn't have an evil gang attached to them," Emma said.

Colton clenched his jaw and looked away from her.

"But they also didn't have a beautiful woman there who seems completely dedicated to you and doing what's right," she added.

Colton softened a bit and stared deep into Emma's eyes.

"I think you need a partner," she said. "Stuart should go with you."

"What?" said Stuart.

"Yes." She turned to Stuart. "I think you should go with him.

You've been here all your life. Don't you think you should see something of this country before you die?"

"Die?" Stuart's eyes widened. "What have you heard?"

"Don't be silly. The Northwest is incredible, but I've heard Utah is one of the most diverse states in America."

"I thought it was just a big sandbox with a salty puddle in the middle."

"Stuart, if you're not going to travel you should at least read more. It isn't all desert like some people think. There are fantastic mountains, forests, rivers, and all kinds of wildlife to go along with the red sandstone arches we hear about." Looking at Colton, she gushed, "It must be spectacular."

"It is," Colton said. "Or it was, the last time I was there. That salty puddle was once part of the huge freshwater Lake Bonneville. It covered large portions of Utah, Nevada, and even into Idaho."

Pretending sincere interest, Stuart asked, "So how come it's smaller and salty now?"

"Most of the Lake drained away to the North thousands of years ago. Now it doesn't have an outlet for water to flow out of it to keep it fresh. What comes in just evaporates into the air leaving behind salty minerals."

"Is there anything you *don't* know?" Stuart sighed.

"He reads a lot, Stuart," Emma said.

"The more I learn, the more I realize how little I know," Colton replied. "Like why Emma would suggest that you *supervise* me on such a long journey."

"I've been too selfish I suppose," she answered. "I know that Stuart cares about me. So much that it affects his personal life. By now, he should have married and settled down. But he thinks that he needs to care for Todd and me more than himself."

"That's not completely true," Stuart protested.

"Can you name one woman who you've dated more than three times?"

"That's ridiculous. I've been with lots of women."

"That isn't what I asked. Name one who you call a steady girl."

"They're all steady until they start to drink." His smile was not matched by Emma or Colton.

"What about that Jennifer you started to date? She had a wonderful personality, and would have made a fine wife."

"Yeah, well she needed to make her *outer* beauty a lot more jealous of her *inner* beauty."

"What are you talking about? She was pretty and you know it. All you men are fixated on a woman's appearance. There's a lot more to us than just attracting men."

"Look Sis, men have to be *attracted* to their outside *before* we can appreciate their inner-self. And I'm dating Elizabeth now. She's beautiful outside *and* inside."

Emma put her hands on her hips and glared at him. "She is, but she's also the sweetest girl I've ever known. Don't you *dare* hurt her feelings!"

Stuart intercepted her next argument with a quick, "So you think I'll find a girl in Utah? Is that what you're saying?"

"I'm not saying that at all." She sighed. "I'm saying that Todd and I are going to get away for a while whether you go with Colton or not. Once I learned that he was returning from Alaska, I figured we could visit our sister, Marla, in Seattle. That would free the two of you to run the business and work on developing some serious relationships . . . here, there, or anywhere. So my question is why are you two being so evasive about your trip?"

Looking more passive than ever, Colton and Stuart glanced toward each other, then held their train tickets in front of their faces. "They're for tomorrow," they said simultaneously.

Emma's mouth dropped open as she stared at them in disbelief.

They both shifted their feet nervously, grimacing as they considered what to say next.

But her expression soon widened into a broad grin as she pulled two train tickets from her purse. "They're for tomorrow."

The hearty laughter from the three of them soon brought Todd out of his room to investigate. For no apparent reason, other than the contagious effects, he soon added his soprano giggle to complete the quartet.

"Well," admitted Stuart, "we have some packing to do."

Emma blushed, "Todd and I finished while you were at your meeting."

He turned to face Colton, who said, "My stuff is ready to go at the Benson Hotel."

"Then I appear to be the anchor in these anticipated journeys. We head South at 7:10pm."

"And we head North at 7:00pm sharp."

The laughter, and then the smiles, faded away as the group realized that mere hours were all that remained for them to share.

"Stuart, Todd, and I can take a trolley car to Union Station on 6th Avenue."

Colton added "It's only about ten blocks down Broadway from the Benson Hotel. I'll walk it. It will be sort of my farewell tour of Portland."

"Don't say that Colton. You can come back with Stuart . . . and maybe his new wife."

"Yeah . . . maybe. Maybe the three of us." He grinned.

Emma's smile faded, and her expression was a clear indication she didn't believe him. She started to sob thinking this might be the last time she would ever see Colton.

To console her, Colton offered, "Look, I have too much luggage. Can I leave it in your warehouse, next to the secret car? I'll get it when I return."

"Of course." She smiled while drying her tears. "Nobody will be driving it until you return. You can just leave it inside the car and cover it all up with the big tarp so it will be safe." Glancing over at Stuart, she grinned. "Some people think it makes the car invisible."

22
The Parting Contract

THE UNION STATION Depot reminded Colton of an anthill that had just been kicked. Conductors rushing people aboard, passengers scrambling for seats, and luggage-toting porters dodging each other. The moving mass obscured any sight of Todd, Emma, or Stuart. The sounds of the locomotive engine building steam pressure, and the din of hundreds of people talking, reminded Colton why he disliked cities so much.

"Serenity is under-rated," he said aloud.

"Colton!" someone shouted. He turned around to see Emma, Todd, Stuart, and Elizabeth entering the depot. Porters checked their tickets and directed their luggage toward the appropriate north or southbound trains.

The adults paused and looked at each other, as though they didn't know what to say or do. It was Todd who made the first move as he dove toward Stuart and tried to crush him with a loving embrace. The women pulled kerchiefs out and quickly put them to use. Todd then gave the same farewell to Colton and sobbed, "Will I ever see you again?"

Colton opened his mouth but could not reply. The best he could do was shrug his shoulders. Todd looked hurt.

"Of course you will," Stuart consoled Todd as he glared at Colton.

Colton blinked, then echoed Stuart with an "Of course." He then turned to Emma and pulled some papers from his coat pocket. "Emma, I know how important you are to the success of all our business ventures. You manage all the books, you've trusted my judgment on marketing our tools and lumber, and you've helped me get solvent enough where I've been able to invest in shipping and land deals. You know the operations nearly as well as I do. And I know you like to take charge whenever you can."

Emma's mouth dropped open as she furrowed her brow to protest, but Colton put his index finger to his mouth to silence her as he handed her the papers.

"There is no time for arguments or debates," he said. "I'm giving you contracts already signed by Stuart and me. They will give you ownership or management rights to our companies in case . . ."

"What do you mean, *in case*?"

"You know what I mean. There's no reason to discuss this in front of Todd. Take these now. If all goes well, Stuart and I will return to keep things going as they are now. Agreed?"

She took the papers, then pulled Colton and Stuart close. "If anything happens to either of you, I'll . . ."

"You'll be fine," Colton said softly before pulling away. "Time for us to get on board."

The four of them clung together, sharing a group-hug with emotions mixed between adventure and potentially *final* farewells.

Elizabeth stood fighting back tears. As the group finally parted she ran toward Stuart, placed her hands behind his head, and pulled him forward to share a long, passionate kiss. "Your lips are soft," she whispered. "I'll be waiting for you when you return." She turned, clutching a handkerchief, and ran toward the exit without waiting for a response.

Emma watched Stuart stare at Elizabeth as she disappeared through the doors to the north. Then she glanced at Colton who was gazing at the tracks leading to the south. "What will happen to my men?" she whispered to herself.

"Board!" yelled the conductor.

23

Brother's Reunion

"Y OU KNOW, IT'S a lot more scenic here than I expected," Stuart
admitted as they stepped off the train in Utah and grabbed
their bags.

Colton looked at him and responded with a disgusted,
"Really?"

"All right, it's beautiful here. Green everywhere in the Northwest, and red down here. A great color combination I think."

"There's green here too. You'll see. Let's catch a ride to Springdale, it's about 35 miles east of here." He noticed a few cars parked
over by the livery stable. "Maybe we can catch a ride, or get some
horses over there."

"Horses?" asked a wide-eyed Stuart.

"Sure, they won't bite . . . usually," Colton replied, grinning
as he walked toward a man leaning against the hitching posts.

"You gents ain't from around here," barked the man as they
approached.

"Why do you say that?" Colton asked.

"Not too hard to figure. You wouldn't be needin' a ride if you
had your own close by. What's your names?"

"Grey and Landon." Colton said, gesturing to himself and
Stuart. They both reached out and shook his hand.

"I'm Bill Rogers. Don't believe I've heard your names around
here before."

"I used to live near Springdale. Just returning for a short family
visit."

"Grey? Grey . . . hmmm . . . near Springdale? You related to Charlie Grey?"

"Yes."

"They got problems over in that area now."

"What kind of problems?

"Don't want to mention no names. Don't need that trouble over here. Let's just say that people wind up missin' or dead if they get in a certain somebody's way. Yep, if I was you I'd stay away from there and have family come over *here* to visit with you."

"He can't travel much anymore. And I want to see the old place again."

"Got any friends over there? Names I might know?"

Colton glanced at Stuart wondering if a response would be a good idea or not.

"Go ahead, tell him," Stuart said without hesitation. "Maybe he knows something that will help us."

"Well, there's the Duncans—"

"Oh yeah, I know the Duncans. Too bad about them. Nice folks. We'll miss 'em. Don't know if their daughter is even around here anymore. She used to bring timber over here, but that was awhile ago. Tough life for her. Don't know how she hung on so long. Anybody else?"

Stuart just looked at the ground.

"Don't say anything about her Stu," Colton said to Stuart, intercepting what he might say. "Nothing I can do about the past." He turned back to Bill. "I also had a good friend, a Paiute named Tava—"

"Tavaci?" The man said, finishing Colton's sentence. "How about that? He works down the road at the General Store. Helps folks with canned goods, tools, and so on. Funny guy, but he works hard. Folks like him."

Colton could hardly contain his excitement. "Thanks, Bill. We don't mean to run off, but I haven't seen him in years. Maybe we'll see you again."

"No problem," the man chuckled. "Hope your visit goes well, and you don't have no troubles."

Colton grabbed Stuart's arm and nearly tore it off as he bolted through the door and headed down the road. "There it is! The General Store." They ran up the steps, opened the door, and stood in the doorway looking at the back of a man putting cans on the shelves. He was wearing work boots, dark pants, a light-blue shirt, and a buckskin vest. His long black hair was graying on the sides. He held three cans in each hand as he placed them on the shelf.

"I'll take a can of peaches," Colton said.

"Yes, sir," Tavaci replied as he walked forward and placed a can on the counter without looking at Colton's face.

"Actually, make that one hundred cans, please."

Tavaci had turned back toward the shelf before he realized what had been said. He turned back to face the joker and dropped a can on the floor when he realized who had made the order. Stunned, his mouth dropped open as he silently mouthed the name, *Colton.* He leap-frogged over the counter and ran toward the doorway as Colton ran to meet him. The embrace was like a vise. Tears formed in each other's eyes, though they would never admit it later.

"Last I'd heard of you, there'd been some mine explosion and you were missing," Colton said as they separated. "I came down here to find you. What are the chances that I find you when I'm not even looking?"

"It's as impossible to explain as it is good to see you, my friend." Tavaci grinned. "Now who's this fella?" he asked, gesturing to Stuart.

"This is my friend, and business partner, Stuart. He, and his sister, took me into their home in Portland when I had no place else to go. He's also the reason I'm here today."

Tavaci slid into joke mode immediately. "So, should I be happy about this guy, or mad at him?"

"Your choice," Stuart said as he stepped forward, extended his hand, and decided to join in the humor. "Tavaci is an interesting name. Sounds like an Italian dish. All right if I call you Tav?"

"Stuart, huh? Sounds like a beef dish. All right if I call you Stew?" He turned and went back to the counter.

Colton quickly approached Stuart who was standing mouth agape with his empty hand still extended. "Don't even try to keep up with him. You'll lose," Colton laughed. "Tavaci is Paiute for Sun. Pretty impressive name, I think. Tavaci is one of the finest people I know, but don't get on his bad side. I believe you two will become good friends."

"You do, huh? Well, this wasn't a good beginning."

"You started it."

"It was a joke. He should laugh."

"Likewise."

Tavaci finished putting the cans up on the shelf. "You headed back to Springdale?"

Colton nodded.

"Well, I'm done here for the day." He dusted his hands off on his pants. "Let me take you. I've got a buckboard out back."

"Why, that will be just as comfy as Stuart's invisible car," said Colton.

Tavaci stared at Stuart. "Your car is invisible?"

"Only to Colton. Everybody else can see it," Stuart said as he winked at Tavaci.

"You been drinking something funny Colton?" asked Tavaci with his hands on his hips.

"You know I don't drink. Stuart's kidding you."

Tavaci squinted at Stuart for a moment, then displayed a big smile. "Maybe you and me are going to get along real good."

The ride was pleasant as Stuart listened to stories about the area and the boyhood adventures of Colton and Tavaci as they passed Coal Pits Wash, Grafton, and Rockville. Then they turned south toward Eagle's Crag and Tavaci's village. He stopped the horses near the top of a small hill. "I'll be back in a minute. Just goin' down to tell the misses what I'm up to, line up some horses for you for in the morning, and then we can head."

"You're married?" Colton gasped.

"Sure, ain't you? It's been a long time brother. What are you waitin' for?"

"I've . . . been real busy."

"Hey, you still sweet on Amber Duncan? She might still be around here somewhere. Don't know for sure. If she is, she's probably at your father's cabin, or maybe up on the mesa cuttin' trees. Come to think of it, I haven't seen her in a month since she was taking care of your father and . . . anyway, I'll be right back."

They climbed off the buckboard and walked up the small hill as Tavaci ran over the crest and out of sight. Stuart joked a bit as they made the ascent, but Colton made it a point to stare at his face and note his expression as the village first came into view. The joking stopped as soon as Stuart witnessed the collection of very small, simple houses along dusty roads. His lips parted, but he stared silently until he whispered, "This isn't Portland."

"No. No, it isn't, but it's all they have."

"Where would one even begin to help them?"

Silent contemplation ruled until Tavaci came up from his home. He saw their sober faces and turned to join their view of the village. "You know, if I had a million dollars . . ." he said quietly, then he paused and stroked his chin in deep thought. "I'd be rich." He slapped both of them on their backs, climbed up onto the driver's seat, and grabbed the reins, "Where to, Colton?"

Stuart's brow furrowed and his mouth remained open as he stared first at Tavaci, then his village, then at Colton, who advised, "I told you, don't try to keep up with him. Now close your mouth before you swallow a fly, and jump on board." The two of them climbed into the buckboard.

"Okay Captain," Colton said to Tavaci. "Let's go to our Big Rock cabin near Parunuweap if it's still standing."

"It's still there. Maybe a few spiders in it, but nobody's messed with it. Hang on." Tavaci flicked the reins and they pulled away from the village.

24

Big Rock Cabin

IN A FEW hours, they arrived at the cabin, and Stuart shook his head in wonder. "It's not the Palmer House, but it's amazing. I thought we'd be sleeping in a cave somewhere."

The cabin was made of red sandstone blocks, had a wood shingle roof, and a front porch with a floor of Ponderosa pine. Four columns of Lodgepole pine supported the roof over the porch. There was, true to its name, a sandstone boulder the size of the cabin just off the east wall. Colton remembered where a key was hidden in a small crevice of the boulder. "Looks like we have a home while we're here. Let's see what it's like inside."

"How is it that nobody has lived here for over ten years, but the place hasn't been vandalized?" Stuart asked Tavaci. "That would never happen in Portland, much as I love that city."

"The Grey's have always been good to us. My older sister, Star, married Colton's father. So my people watched over this place . . . hoping someday Colton would return. Here he is, and it is his home again."

"Colton was only eighteen or so when I first met him in Portland. How did he rate having his own cabin so young?

"His father, and pretty much everybody else, figured Colton and Amber Duncan were going to hitch up someday, so he had this cabin built as a wedding gift. Then Colton and his father had some rough spats and, let's see . . ." Tavaci turned to Colton as he walked back toward them. "You moved out here around the time of the old Cotton Festival, didn't you?"

"That's enough, Tavaci." Colton frowned.

"Rough spats?" asked Stuart, "seems like a cabin would make up for a lot of issues."

"You don't know what it was like living with him," growled Colton. "Nobody does. The cabin was kind of a guilt-gift. And yes, Amber figured into this cabin for a short time, but that was a *long* time ago. Look, I don't want to talk about this at all. I came here to find Tavaci, see about making amends with my father, and maybe out some good folks around here. Then I'm out, heading back to Portland and my business. Understood?"

Tavaci and Stuart nodded.

Colton inserted the key, put his shoulder into the door, and pushed. The hinges squeaked but held tight. "It's dark in here. Guess my father boarded up the windows on the outside after I left, but we can remove those easily."

"What about those spiders?" Stuart wondered.

"That's why cowboys wear pointed-toe boots," Tavaci said, "so they can kill them in corners." Stuart's eyes widened and Tavaci laughed. "I'll go get a hammer from the wagon."

"To kill spiders?" Stuart asked.

Tavaci grinned. "To uncover those windows right now so you can see what's in here."

A few minutes of twisting, pulling, and grunting removed the boards and revealed that none of the windows had been damaged, although there were a few spider webs here and there.

The door swinging open had stirred some dust from the floor, illuminated by the sunlight entering the windows. The swirling particles highlighted shafts of angelic light coming in from the west.

Colton removed his hat and entered the cabin in an almost reverent manner. Stuart and Tavaci followed his example. "Memories," Colton said softly. "I remember we had a few rules when we stayed here, and I think they should apply now as well."

"Rules?" asked Stuart.

Colton nodded. "Enjoy the clean air, smell the trees, listen to the water, watch the birds, enjoy sunsets, and be dazzled by stars."

"Good rules," said Tavaci

"And the place is in good shape. No mold, no mice—"

"No furniture," added Stuart.

"There's two handsome wooden chairs in the corner," Tavaci said, "and you can use the wool blankets and straw mattresses I've got in the buckboard tonight. Unless that floor looks soft enough for you." He winked at Stuart, who bit his lower lip and stared at the floor. "Come help me bring them in. I'll see about bringing up some beds tomorrow."

Stuart followed Tavaci out to the buckboard.

"Look at the view," Colton remarked to himself as he stood on the porch, looking out into the distance.

To the west, the view opened into a wide shallow valley with buttes and mesas flanking it on the north and south. To the east, the sandstone cliffs, canyons, and rugged hills added a splendid backdrop for landscape artists to relish for eternity. The layers of red, coral, white, and yellow against a sapphire-blue sky were truly dazzling.

"This is home," Colton whispered.

"What?" quizzed Stuart as he passed by with an armful of blankets. "I couldn't hear you."

"He said he likes the view," quipped Tavaci, following behind Stuart with the two straw mattresses. "I think he missed this place." He set the mattresses inside the cabin and then walked back out to stand by Colton's side.

"Hey, Colton," Tavaci said softly. "I don't mean to interrupt you, but you probably should go see your father pretty soon. He's not doing well at all. In fact, he's pretty bad off. Last I heard he couldn't even get out of bed."

"It's on the list," Colton replied gruffly.

"Tav," Stuart said, joining them on the porch. "You should know this guy makes lists all the time."

"I don't want to forget anything," Colton defended. "But I don't think I'll need lists while I'm here. Just a few things to do, and then I'm gone."

"I've had visions that you were coming back here one day," Tavaci said. "But it was to *stay*." He looked at Colton seriously. "What do you *need* to do while you're here, brother?"

"Not a lot," Colton said, avoiding Tavaci's gaze. Since I found you, making amends with my father pretty much covers it."

"You might run into Ethan Morley while you're here."

Colton bristled at the name, but he shook it off. "Won't matter. I've got nothing to do with him, as long as he stays out of my way."

"Brother, you need to know that he's in everybody's way. He's the main reason our village is so—"

"What's he got to do with your village?" Colton asked, looking at him.

Tavaci sighed. "He decides *who* works and *when* and *where*; he drives the price of lumber sky-high because he has no competition; and he doesn't like our people. He is, umm . . . koomunts." He shook his head. "I can't think of the word."

"Enemy?"

"Yes, enemy. He has men that live up high on his ranch. They cut his trees and run his sawmill. But they do not think. They just do what he says."

Colton stared at him for a moment, then shifted his gaze toward the big rock. "I still don't want to deal with Ethan if I can avoid it, but maybe I can change some things for you . . . and him." He glanced back at Tavaci, "So I have *two* things then, my father and your village."

"Three," said Tavaci and Stuart in unison.

"Three?" Colton asked.

"Amber Duncan," they replied. They smiled at each other and shook hands.

Colton pursed his lips and said nothing.

"It's getting late," Tavaci said, grinning as he walked back to his horse. "Time to head home so the misses won't think I've run off with a young lady. See you in the morning."

He hopped into the driver's seat and rode off just as the sun was beginning to set.

25

Make Peace, or Not

Although it was light, the sun had not yet risen over the crest of the mountains when there was pounding on the cabin door.

"Hey, sleepy-heads," shouted Tavaci, "You goin' to waste the whole day in bed?"

The door creaked open, and Stuart stood there stretching and yawning. "What time is it?"

"Time? We aren't going to be worried about time around here. Where's Colton?"

"I dunno," he yawned. "He always gets up early. Umm, last night I think he said he wanted to go somewhere to think about what to say to his father. Yeah, that's it. But he didn't say where."

"I know where he went."

"Well, go have a nice chat, and come back to get me after the sun comes up." Stuart forced a fake grin and closed the door.

Tavaci turned to the horses, "Cranky when he's tired," he mumbled as he tied them to the rail. He turned East, walked past the Big Rock, jumped over Shunes Creek, and continued up the East Fork of the Virgin River. After fifteen minutes of noiseless walking, he saw Colton sitting under a cottonwood tree, staring across the river at some small, ancient Anasazi ruins.

"I thought I would find you here."

A bit startled, Colton turned and smiled. "So I'm too predictable?"

"I just know a few of your favorite places. Places where you like to go to think."

"And be alone?"

"Hey, I'm sorry. I thought you wanted to see your father today, and I think the sooner, the better. I'm telling you he is not doing well, brother."

"That's why I'm sitting here, trying to think of what to say, or what to do when we meet." He picked up a stone and tossed it into the river. "I thought the long train ride would help me figure it out. But he's been out of my life for a long time now and I honestly haven't missed him . . . until today." He picked up another stone, stared at it for a moment, then threw it forcefully into the river. "What do you say to somebody who was on your back every day of your life? Who made you feel like you were never quite good enough? Who blamed you for the deaths of two . . . ahh, forget it."

"Colton, did you ever try to see things from his eyes?"

"*His* eyes?" Colton glared at Tavaci. "Look, whose side are you on? You saw what life was like for me here. Him blaming me for anything that went wrong . . . guess I should have just toughened up. You know, grin and bear it junk."

"I didn't say it was easy. I just asked if you ever tried to see things from his view."

Colton turned back toward the river, bowed his head, and answered quietly, "No."

"Maybe it's time. Because he doesn't have much of it left. I can't believe that the Colton Grey I knew back then has completely disappeared. You used to be willing to help anybody. And I'll bet that attitude went with you to the north. In fact, I'll bet Stuart could tell me stories about how you would do anything for a lot of people in his town. Wouldn't you do it now for a dying man? Your own father?"

Colton looked at Tavaci, then turned away and stared at the river again.

Tavaci pointed at the river. "Watch that branch floating toward us, brother. Yes, watch it go by very quickly. Maybe that's something like our time in life. Maybe we don't know where it came from. We can only see it for a moment as it is passing. Then it's gone . . . and it's not coming back."

Colton watched the branch disappear over distant ripples. He turned back to Tavaci and said, "You know, you've always had a great sense of humor, but you were also the best teacher I ever had." He exhaled deeply, "All right, let's get Stuart and go see my father."

"That's the Colton Grey I was always proud to know. But I'm not sure that Stu is awake yet."

They both smiled, gave each other a brotherly hug, and headed back to the cabin.

26

Charles Grey

"AMBER?" THE WEAK voice faded off as he lifted his hand and turned toward her.

"Yes, Charles. I'm here."

"Is Colton here?" he gasped.

She grabbed his hand and patted it. "Not yet. But his telegram said he was coming. It's just a long way from Portland. He'll be here, you'll see." Her eyes moistened as she placed his hand back on his chest, then went back to preparing a bowl of stew for him.

"Amber!"

"I can hear you, Charles."

"I've got to tell him how sorry I am for the way I treated him when he was a boy."

"I'm sure he knows th—"

"Not from *me* he doesn't." He finished his statement with fifteen seconds of severe coughing. "Not from me," he whispered.

"Charles, just rest. The stew is almost ready."

"But he needs to know that he didn't kill his mother when he was born. She was weak and sick, but wanted to have a healthy baby no matter what."

"He knows that, Charles."

"But he's got to hear that from me. And I know he didn't take Star into that canyon just to have her die in a flood. They loved each other more than any two people I've ever known. Sometimes, I felt a little jealous watching how she would even give up her own food just to make sure he would have enough to eat. I'm so sorry," he wept, "that I ever accused him of killing her." More coughing accented his remark.

"You've heard how successful Colton has become. People can't do the things he has done unless they are smart and dedicated to a goal. He is smart enough to know that you hurt so badly that you felt you needed to strike out at something, or someone. Give him some credit. I know he hasn't been holding this against you. You'll see, I promise."

"But I pushed him, Amber. I wanted him to learn how to work, and never quit." He paused for a breath. "And I prayed that the two of you would end up together and that he could take care of you, and whatever little ones you might have."

She turned her face away from him and wiped her eyes with her apron. "Charles, please, please don't talk about Colton and me being together. When he ran off, I knew it would never happen. We've each taken different paths, and those will *never* cross. They can't."

"But . . ."

"Don't worry. I'll be here to take care of you until you get better."

"Better?" A weak smile turned up one side of his mouth. "Don't you see? It's my fault. I should be rocking one of your babies now." He looked up at the ceiling. "I was going to suggest you name your first boy after President Lincoln."

"A boy named Lincoln? A boy . . . named Lincoln." She turned and went to the window clutching her apron in both hands. "I told you to stop talking that way. You're speaking about impossible things, and I don't want to hear it anymore. Do you understand?"

"I'm sorry, Amber," he wheezed. "I don't mean to have you *and* Colton hate me. And I know Ethan Morley and every other man in town will be after you when I'm gone."

"You're not going anywhere, Charles," she sobbed. "Can't we just—"

"You see, I wanted him to be strong, to take care of himself, and you . . . and the baby.

And, mostly, I wanted him to be happy. I wanted him to be able to own this land and be proud of it. But he left before I could even tell him that. Or tell him that he . . ."

"What, Charles?"

He took another deep breath, "That he's all I have left in the world that matters. I've lost two wives and drove my baby boy away from me. I've got to tell him." He whispered. "I've got to tell him." He rolled on his side and stretched his hand toward Amber.

She ran over to his bed, knelt down by him, and pulled his hand over to kiss it. "You will, Charles. You will."

"Go find him . . . please."

27

Father and Son Reunion

IT'S GOING TO take me awhile getting used to riding horses," complained Stuart as the three of them approached the Grey Ranch. "Tell me a little about your father so I know what to expect, and so I won't keep thinking about this tough saddle."

Colton opened his mouth but Tavaci cut him off. "He's a changed man from when Colton was here. He is driven, no doubt about it. Wants a great ranch. Wants to help folks. He's one of the few men that the Morley gang won't mess with. He doesn't talk much, but I think it's because he is always too busy working. Well, until he got sick. I think everybody will tell you he is a good man. When you go into town you'll see a new schoolhouse and a store where they can send out Western Union telegrams. He built those." He leaned toward Colton, "But you knew about those don't you?"

Colton stared openmouthed at him, then turned straight ahead to look at the trail.

"Guess you didn't."

Stuart jumped in. "He sounds like a great neighbor."

"I said he had *changed* since Colton left town," Tavaci said. "He's a good man now, but I would agree with the way Colton saw things back then. When I was a boy, I only visited Colton and my sister, Star, when Charles wasn't around. He had a temper."

"But isn't what kind of a person you end up to be more important than what you were like in the past?" Stuart asked.

"Good observation, my friend." Tavaci smiled. "What would

the world be like if we always acted like we were still eight, or twelve, or fifteen, or—"

"I was nineteen when I left," Colton added.

"Or nineteen," Tavaci said. Sensing a little tension, he changed the subject. "So, Stuart, how did you and Colton meet?"

"He was trying to save a man's life, and I wound up saving his."

"Then it appears he is like the Charles Grey we know today."

Colton just glared at Tavaci. "Look, I said I'm here to try and make amends. I'll see if we can build some kind of a relationship again. Just give me a little time, will you? It's been fifteen years, and I swore I'd never come back here again. But I *am* here!"

"Better late than never, right?" Stuart offered.

Tavaci nodded.

They became silent when they first saw the ranch house. Colton's memories blurred his vision. He saw himself chopping wood and feeding horses, he saw the old cottonwood he used to climb as his fort, and he saw the grove of apple trees where he and Amber first kissed. His heart softened as he realized he had good times here, as well as what felt like endless work. As they approached the ranch house, they saw a fancy buckboard and a timber wagon there, but nobody was outside. They dismounted. Stuart looked first at Colton, then at Tavaci, but both of them shrugged their shoulders. Then the door opened.

The woman who walked down the path toward them was so stunning Stuart's mouth dropped open and he was speechless. Her long brown hair swayed in the breeze, and as she approached, he saw that her eyes had a hint of gold in them. He took off his hat and was about to introduce himself, but she stormed past him.

"Hello, Amber," Tavaci said politely.

She paused briefly at the sight of Tavaci, her expression one of surprise, but at the sight of Colton, her expression returned to rage. She took off her apron and marched up to Colton, who was removing his hat.

"Well, the mighty Mr. Grey has finally arrived. And just in time." She wadded the apron into a ball and threw it into his face. "Go on in and join the doctor. Your father just died. But I'm sure that doesn't matter to you!" She shoved him off the path, climbed onto the timber-wagon, and snapped the reins.

"Wait a minute, I just got here." Colton protested.

"I'm making changes in my life, Colton. If you don't hear from me, you're one of them."

Colton stood silently as he watched her drive away. The cloud of dust kicked up by her horse and buckboard drifted over him.

Tavaci and Stuart stared at him, then looked toward the house. "What are you going to do now?" Stuart wondered aloud.

Mouth open, Colton blinked, then shook his head. He started toward the house and replied, "I don't know. Plan a burial I guess." His two friends waited by the horses as Colton opened the door and entered his boyhood home.

"The branch just floated by," said Tavaci to a puzzled Stuart. "It can't come back now."

28

Now What?

COLTON WAS SOMBER as he came out of the cabin, accompanied the doctor to his buckboard, and watched him drive off toward Springdale. He didn't have much to say to Tavaci and Stuart when he approached them. "Look, umm, why don't you two ride back to the cabin. I'll join you later."

"Whoa," said Tavaci, "what are you going to do?"

"The doctor will contact the undertaker, and I'm going to the back yard to dig a hole next to Star's grave."

"Isn't there somebody here who will do that for you?" asked Stuart.

"It's something I need to do."

"Then I'll help you do it." He put his hands on Colton's shoulders and forced him to make eye contact. "It's what a friend would do."

"That makes three of us then," added Tavaci. "And I know Amber well enough that she'll tell Charles's close friends so they'll be here when everything is ready."

"I can see the hate in their faces already," muttered Colton.

THE NEXT DAY, the local Mormon bishop said a few words over the grave. Neighbors would nod at Colton, but they would embrace the tearful Amber while they expressed their sympathy to her. Even though Stuart and Tavaci stood by his side, Colton had never felt so alone in his life. He was losing a battle with his mind. Memories of his father, the Morley gang, Star's death, and struggling to escape in the Northwest refused to be restrained any longer. And now Amber despised him. He was rich, but that could not begin to compensate for his pain.

"You've got some nerve coming back here *after* he died." The voice of a woman broke Colton from his thoughts. He recognized her as Mrs. Jones, an older woman who lived a few ranches over. She pointed a wrinkled finger at him, her face red with tears. "What are you here for? The ranch? Why didn't you come to help him when he was sick?" She continued, but her words became a blur as her husband grabbed her arm and pulled her away toward their carriage. Colton watched them drive away, unsure how to feel.

"Colton," whispered Tavaci. "Colton."

"Huh, what is it?" he replied in a daze.

"I brought eagle feathers for you and me to put on his coffin. Come on."

Colton looked toward him, but his expression was one of a stranger lost in a huge city.

"Here, take a feather and come with me."

"A feather," he whispered.

"Yes, come on." Tavaci took one of Colton's arms, while Stuart grabbed the other, and they gently placed the feathers on the coffin. Stuart and Tavaci then stepped back as Colton stared at the grave.

"I can't fix this," Colton said as he turned to Tavaci. "I can manage companies and start new ones. I have more money than I need. Did you know they asked me to run for governor?" He turned back to the coffin. "But now I have nothing," he said, "I just don't care about any of it anymore."

"You have us," said Stuart. "And don't forget Emma and Todd."

"But I loved him in spite of the way he treated me. I tried to work as hard as I could for him, but it was never good enough.

I let hatred move me to make selfish decisions. I needed to come here to fix our problems and apologize for running away. And now there is *nothing* I can do about it. Nothing I can do about anything." He covered his face with his hands and began to sob, which was the last thing he would ever want to do in public.

"Don't judge yourself by your past," Tavaci cautioned. "You don't live there anymore."

As Stuart stepped forward to comfort Colton, Tavaci noticed that Amber was watching them. He could see that she was moved by Colton's comments, but she remained rigid and silent. Tavaci strolled over to her.

"You can see this is eating at him," he said. "Everybody around here knows how hard you work. The struggles you had when your own parents were killed near Grafton, how tough it is to compete in the timber market against somebody as ruthless as this Ethan guy, how you cared for Charles these last few years. They all know. Maybe you should try to see things the way *he* is looking at them now."

"I don't care what he sees."

"You used to."

She glared at him, "That was a long time ago, Tavaci. That's gone, just like Charles."

"What if he had arrived two days ago, before Charles died? How would you have reacted then? Would you still have thrown that apron in his face? Or would you have been glad to see him, maybe just for the help he could have given? What if—"

"What *if*! '*If*' is the largest two-letter word on the planet. Don't ask me what if."

"Maybe just a couple more 'ifs'. *What-if* he and Charles had gotten along well; *if* Ethan's buddies wouldn't have been after him whenever they could; *if* Star hadn't drowned; *if* he hadn't seen you and Ethan kissing—"

Amber's mouth dropped open. "How *dare* you suggest that I was kissing Ethan? He grabbed me and pulled me in. I couldn't get away."

"Relax, everybody here knows that . . . except Colton. What *if* he knew that Ethan was forcing himself on you? Do you really think he would have left here in such a hurry?"

"I . . . umm . . ." She shook her head in confusion.

"Well?"

"No."

"So you are correct then. 'If' is the largest two-letter word on the planet." He pointed at her eyes and added, "Try looking at things through his eyes."

Amber looked at the ground.

"See you later," Tavaci said. He left her standing with her arms folded as he walked over to Colton and Stuart and escorted them back to the house.

As they reached the door Colton stiffened his back and turned to see the two graves. "I'll be fine. I just had a tough minute there. I don't like it when I'm not in control."

"I know, but you're still tougher than anybody I've ever known," said Stuart. "Remember the Gold Rush, the Palmer House meeting, and a dozen other battles you've had to fight."

Tavaci's eyes widened as his mouth dropped open. "*You* were in the Gold Rush?"

"That's where he made his fortune," said Stuart. "but not by digging through the snow. He bought and sold claims and mining equipment."

"So that's how you—"

"No big thing," Colton interrupted. "It seemed like a smarter way to make money.

"Hey, Tavaci, at least we got his mind going in another direction," Stuart chuckled. "We've probably done all we can here for now. Let's ride back to the cabin. Maybe Colton can show me that place along the river where he used to go to think."

"Glad to," said Colton.

They walked toward their horses when Amber came up to Colton and stopped him. "I want to apologize for throwing the apron and for the mean things I said, but I've been mad at you for a long, long time. I don't want to be a person who holds a grudge against anyone, except maybe Ethan. But I'm sorry, and hope you have a safe trip back to Portland." She turned and walked away, leaving the three of them a little surprised.

"I'm not trying to pick a fight here, Colton," said Stuart, "but that woman is beyond gorgeous. How in the world could you leave her back here?"

Tavaci jumped in, "It starts with the word *if* and I'll tell you all about it on the ride back to the Big Rock cabin."

29

Ethan Knows

ETHAN WAS SITTING at the table eating his lunch when Stitch strolled in. "Got some news, Boss."

"Yeah, what is it?"

"Charlie Grey died yesterday. Had his funeral this mornin'."

"Do tell. No surprise. I heard he was real sick." He leaned back on his chair's hind legs and squinted in thought, then said, "That will mean his land is open to buy, probably just for tax money. Then again, maybe I'll just have a few of you boys just move down there." A big smile appeared. "That valley land will be a great place to build homes. It's got the river running through it, and a few trees that Charlie would never cut down. I think we should go to town and look at making a purchase."

"There's a hitch to it."

"What do you mean, hitch?"

"Charlie's son is back here."

The smile vanished. "His boy, huh? Can't recall his name right now. Coburn, Dalton—"

"Colton, boss."

"Oh yeah . . . Colton."

"He interested in keepin' that place?"

"I ain't heard."

Ethan's face sobered as he stood up and dropped his fork. "Wonder if him and that Duncan girl will be hookin' up again."

"Doubt it. Talk around town was that she hates him. Wouldn't even talk to him at old Charlie's funeral. Did you need me to do somethin'?"

"No. No, not yet. If he heads outta here soon we shouldn't have any trouble getting' his land . . . and maybe the girl too. We'll sit tight for a bit."

30

The "Thinking Place"

S TUART AND COLTON dismounted as they reached the cabin, but Tavaci remained on his horse. "Aren't you coming with us to Colton's thinking place?"

"I think I should go home now. Be-Wa will be wondering if I'm chasing younger women around."

"Be-Wa?"

"It's my wife's Paiute name."

"What does it mean?"

"Heart," said Colton.

Stuart looked at Tavaci with a new admiration.

"Hey, don't get all mushy around me. Her parents named her. But, when I think about it, it fits her pretty good. And I'm not saying I don't chase those younger women." He grinned. "I just can't catch them anymore." He turned his horse, waved his hat, and rode away laughing.

"You know, Colton, I really like that guy."

"I knew you would. I think he'll be your brother too before we leave."

"Hope so. I'd like that. Now, what about your thinking place?"

They tied up the horses and enjoyed a slow and easy walk down to the river. Colton took off his hat and went toward the big cottonwood. When Stuart looked around, he wasn't sure if he had taken off his hat to cool off, or out of respect for the beauty of that place. The river emerged gently from a wide canyon that had shades of red, yellow, and cream-colored stone walls that magnetized his eyes. Maidenhair ferns adorned the base of the canyon, and purple Shooting Stars grew in the moist seeps. Yellow and maroon Columbine flowers seemed to be everywhere, and the songs of Kinglets and Warblers accented the scene.

The setting seemed to give Stuart reason to remove his hat too as he came to sit by the big tree. "Why didn't you build your cabin here?"

"Would you really want to see a house right here?"

Stuart looked around again, then shook his head. "No. You made the right choice. What are those two tall posts on each side of the trail for?"

"Nothing. They're from the past. Forget about them. And I mean it."

"All right, they're forgotten. I'll just enjoy the flowers, the birds, the canyon colors, the gentle river—"

"Easy on that river part."

"Huh?"

"If it rains hard up north, it can rip out trees and push boulders taller than you. And if you're in a small canyon . . ."

"I understand. Nice to appreciate it when it's calm."

Colton nodded.

"Guess I'll use this place the right way and think about Portland, Emma, and Todd."

"And Elizabeth?"

"I wasn't going to mention her, but maybe. How about you?"

"Try to figure a way to repay Amber Duncan. See if I can help Tavaci and the village."

"What about that boyhood mission you told me about on the train ride from Portland? Trying to locate the cave that your stepmother wanted to know about? Aren't you curious to know if it really existed? Or what happened to her parents? You're not a boy anymore, and you have Tavaci and me to help you this time. Besides, I'd love to explore one of these canyons."

"Oh, you would, huh?" Colton sneered.

"Of course, I'd need you to guide me."

"We'll see." Colton sighed, unconvinced. "But, if you listened to a word I said, I don't know why you'd want to explore the canyons."

Stuart shrugged. "Adventure."

Colton rolled his eyes. "So Amber, then Tavaci, then—"

"Do you think you'll confront this Ethan guy?" Stuart interrupted.

"Not if I can avoid it." Colton grimaced. "Remember the evil group in the Palmer House in Portland? He's all their bad qualities rolled into one person. I say we just ignore him. Or does that make me a coward?"

"Easy partner, I would never think that." Stuart put his hands up. "We'll ignore him then." He looked out toward the river. "Have you made plans to settle things with Miss Duncan or help Tavaci's village?"

Colton looked at Stuart. "Haven't had time. That's kind of what I came to my *thinking* place to do." He gave Stuart a pointed look, but he didn't catch the hint. Colton sighed. "I think I'll take a ride with Tavaci tomorrow and try to come up with a plan. He knows what's going on around here, and I trust he'll give me good advice."

"Great idea," Stuart said. "You two haven't had much time together. And you know he'll do whatever he can for you." He rubbed his saddle sores. "I'll probably spend the day around here hoping to heal a bit."

"Good. Then it's time to be quiet and think."

"Maybe if we—"

"You know, Stu, sometimes silence alone is worth listening to."

The birds, river, the smell of green, and a gentle breeze took over the rest of their evening.

31

Wasting Time

COLTON PICKED UP his boots and tiptoed outside so he wouldn't disturb Stuart. He looked at the chestnut horse in the corral, who was staring at him, then scanned the crests of the cliffs to see the light coming through a small arch on the top.

Sometimes I forget why I left here, he thought. *I don't think I've ever seen any place more beautiful.*

The horse neighed and nodded his head, which made Colton smile.

"All right, boy, let me get my boots on, then I'll saddle you up and we'll go see Tavaci."

The ride was pleasant and certainly scenic. In thirty minutes he rode over the brow of the small hill overlooking the village and went to Tavaci's door. Be-Wa greeted him.

"You are Mr. Grey," she said.

"I am Colton," he replied as he removed his hat.

"My husband would talk about you and your adventures when you were boys. He missed you very much when you left."

"And I missed him."

Be-Wa nodded. "He is around back with the boys taking care of the horses. I know you should spend some time together. Maybe you can help each other."

"He needs help?"

"He will never say anything to you, but sometimes I think the white man invented money so he would know how much the Indian didn't have."

Colton opened his mouth to reply, but simply nodded in silence.

"Go around back. He will be happy to see you."

"Thank you. I'm glad we met. I hope we become friends," he said as he left her at the front door.

She nodded in silence.

As he came into the backyard, he saw Tavaci and his two young sons feeding their horses.

"Brother," he yelled.

Tavaci quickly spun around as though he expected an attack. "Don't do that, Colton. Are you trying to scare the life out of me?"

"I'm sorry. I just thought that maybe you wouldn't hear me unless I yelled."

"You are not yelling now, and I can hear you fine," he said as he shrugged his shoulders.

"Can we talk for a minute? Maybe take a ride?"

"I cannot leave now. Come sit with me by the tree. Is there a problem?"

"I don't know," Colton said as he walked over to the tree and sat down beside Tavaci. "It appears that you are the only friend I have in Utah. Well, not counting Stuart."

"We are more than friends. We are brothers."

"You know what I mean. I didn't expect a welcome-home parade, but for a desert area this place feels icy-cold to me."

"You are a stranger here. Nobody knows why you left. People expected you to be at the Cotton Festival, but you never came. When a few of us went to look for you at your home a few days after the festival, your father said he had not seen you for two days. To most people, you left your father to care for the ranch by himself."

"I don't have time to chase down every person in the valley to explain what happened. I'm only worried about you and your family."

"There used to be another."

"I think her throwing her apron in my face took care of that issue."

"Learning something that hurts should make us wiser. Living without any pain will not help us know what is real."

"So pain is good?"

"It could be, depending on how you use it."

"Maybe."

"You need to listen. My wife, Be-Wa, says I never listen to her. At least, I think that is what she said." Tavaci chuckled. "So she would not speak to me for seven days. I thought we got along pretty good that week."

"What's the moral of this story?"

"You have been gone for fifteen *years*. That is a long time to never have fights with your woman."

"She isn't my woman," Colton protested before stopping to consider. "But, I admit, she did try to connect with me through cables."

Tavaci shook his head in disbelief. "The trouble is, you think time is something you can buy, that time will do whatever you want it to. Time has never worked that way, and never will."

"My schedule doesn't give me much free time."

"And that is your problem. You hurry too much. Business all the time." Tavaci gestured to a mountain in the distance. "I think if you were left alone up on that mountain with nothing but your feelings, you might learn that you would not be very good company for yourself. And you do not need a cable to tell you that."

Colton stared at the mountain, then looked at Tavaci, and nodded.

"I don't know if she'll ever forgive me, but I need to tell her everything," Colton said quietly. "She needs to know the truth."

Tavaci clapped a hand on his shoulder. "I think that's the right thing to do, brother."

"When does she head up to the mesa?"

"In two days."

Colton nodded, his expression grim.

"Let's change the subject," Tavaci said, sensing Colton's distress. "Tell me what the ocean is like."

"What do you mean, what's it *like*?"

"I always figured it was like this desert country, only wet."

"It depends."

"What do you mean *depends*?"

Colton smiled, back in his comfort zone. "When the sun shines it can be the same color blue as the turquoise ring you made for me when we were young. If there's a gentle breeze, and white caps frost the wave crests, it dazzles the eyes and makes one want to keep sailing on it to see what lies over the horizon." The smile left his face. "When it's cloudy and still, and you can't see anything but water . . ." He drifted off.

"Yes?" Tavaci pressed.

"Well," Colton continued. "There is a light gray sky, and a dark gray sea separated by a very thin line so very far away. It's flat and shapeless. Life, if there is any, is hidden below the surface. If it's just you in a boat, you will feel more alone there than anywhere else on earth. Nothing to see for fifteen miles in every direction. That's thirty miles if you count the entire—"

"Diameter, not radius," Tavaci said, finishing the sentence. Colton looked at him with mild surprise. "What?" he asked. "You think I didn't go to school?"

Colton and Tavaci shared a look and chuckled together.

"So the ocean is like the desert," Tavaci said finally, returning to the subject at hand.

"No. Not even close." Colton shook his head. "The desert has dunes, mountains, and canyons. *Something* to give it features and textures and dimensions. And you can see life out here. Mount

Mahogany, Pricklypear Cactus, and Joshua trees grow everywhere. And there are Bighorn Sheep, cougars, roadrunners, and snakes. You barely see any life when you're on the ocean, even on a good day."

"We may have life, but storms can be mean here. You know that. What are they like on the ocean? I hear the waves can get pretty big."

"Waves can easily get sixty feet tall, and much higher than that. Storms on the ocean can make you think about God, and that can be a good thing . . . or a real bad thing. It depends on *what* you are."

Tavaci stared at the tree, trying to envision sixty feet high.

"Enough about the ocean," Colton said finally, standing up and out of the tree's shade. "I'll let you get back to your boys and the horses. You've given me plenty to think about."

"It is good to see you again, Brother," Tavaci said as he stood up to join Colton. "You should go back to the Big Rock Cabin or your Thinking Place and rest. Think about what you need to do. Get a good sleep. I will see you early in the morning."

"Maybe you can take Stuart on a sunrise horseback ride," Colton joked. They laughed and shared a knowing glance.

The two walked back to Colton's horse. Tavaci shook his head as Colton mounted. "How can you go anywhere on that old Chestnut?" he asked. "You need a better ride than that if you're going to Amber's ranch." Colton made to protest, but he knew better than to try to turn down Tavaci's kindness. "That will be my work for tomorrow," Tavaci decided. "Be safe, Brother," he said as Colton rode away.

32

Mending Fences?

Come on Sleeping Beauty, get up and see how beautiful the sunrise is on Eagles Crag," Colton said as he pulled the blanket off of Stuart the next morning.

"Ohhh, why does a beautiful scene have to take place at such a ridiculous time of day?" Stuart complained.

"Not only that, but there is a fantastic blonde outside who wants to go riding with—"

"Where's my pants and boots?" Stuart yelled as he jumped out of bed and ran to peek out the window. His face fell. "Hey, there's nothing out there but our two horses."

"Well, yours is a palomino. They're blond. And you'll note that they are both saddled and waiting for riders."

Stuart spun around and glared, "Why would you do that to a good friend?"

"You didn't even look at Eagles Crag."

"If you've seen one mountain, you've seen them all. I'm going back to—" He grunted as Colton pushed his boots into his stomach. "All right, so what's the rush?"

"I need to see Amber before she heads back up on top of the mesa."

Stuart became serious. "So what's your plan?"

"I decided to tell her the truth about everything I did, and why."

"Oh, that can't be a good idea."

"What? Why not?"

"You should tell her you were captured by outlaws and had to do whatever they said or they'd kill you. Or, when you were on board a ship, pirates kidnapped you and held you for ransom. Or, you were lost in Alaska for years during the Gold Rush. Or—"

"Or tell her what really happened."

"Sure . . . I mean *no*. Put some adventure and drama into it. She's not going to believe—"

"The truth?"

"And I have to go along and listen to that boring story?"

"Actually, I thought you and Tavaci could get together for a ride. Get to know each other better. He should be here any minute."

"Well, that would beat listening to you trying to explain fifteen years of absence."

Colton went to the window, stared at the mountain, and tapped his finger on the glass. "Maybe so. Maybe so," he said contemplatively. "I imagine anything would beat that."

Stuart's expression softened. "I'm sorry, Colt. I know this will be tough for you and I was just trying to throw a little humor into it."

The door suddenly burst open and Tavaci yelled, "Hey Sleeping Beauty, sun's up on the mountains! We're late!"

"When did you two plan this adventure for me?" Stuart asked.

"Last night before I left Tavaci's home," Colton answered. "Just a couple of words and we were ready."

"*You* were ready?"

"Enjoy your day, men. I'm off to the Duncan ranch," Colton said as he put on his hat and walked out the door.

"Umm, Colton," said Tavaci, catching up with him. "Going to Amber's may no longer be a good idea."

"Why?"

"There's been some changes. I learned some new things after we talked yesterday. I think we should talk first and let Stu entertain himself."

"All right," Colton consented.

"Yes!" shouted Stuart as he fell back onto the bed. "Go have a nice long chat."

33

Tavaci, the Mentor

I SEE YOU brought an Appaloosa for me." Colton smiled as they approached the horses.

"Yeah, I remembered those were your favorite," Tavaci said. "He's yours for as long as you stay here. Watch him though. He sometimes has a mind of his own."

"Don't we all." He stroked the horse's black neck, patted its spotted rump, then pulled the bridle around to look into its face. "Does he have a name?"

"A Lakota Sioux friend of mine sold him to me. He called him, Wichanpi."

"I don't speak Lakota."

"It means Star. I had to have him." The two "brothers" looked at each other and nodded. They both knew who the other was thinking about. "I still miss her."

Colton opened his mouth, but words wouldn't come. He pulled a small, flat stone from his pocket and held it up. "She marked a star on one side and told me that I should put it in my left pocket. Whenever I secretly did something good for someone, I was to move it over to my right pocket. Each night, before dinner, she would ask to see the stone and watch to see which pocket I would put my hand in to retrieve it. She was a great teacher, and I . . ." He shook his head and closed his mouth tight.

Tavaci nodded, then mounted his horse, motioning Colton to do the same.

"I see you still like Pintos," Colton commented.

Tavaci smiled and patted the horse's neck. "Let's go up Parunuweap Canyon a little ways and talk."

The ride was quiet with only the sound of the horse's hooves to be heard. Tavaci would glance over at Colton now and then to notice how he was absorbing every detail he could in each passing scene.

"Memories?" Tavaci asked.

"So many," Colton replied. "I can see us climbing trees over there. Going into that canyon over there—"

"And then came Amber Duncan. And our times grew shorter."

"Yes, they did." Colton looked at the ground. "I'm sorry."

"Don't apologize. I understood." Tavaci shrugged. "I think everyone figured you two were a promised couple. And I'm sorry that didn't work the way you probably had hoped."

"Too many things got in the way. Maybe there's still time."

"That's one of the reasons I wanted to talk to you, instead of Stu, today."

"What do you mean?"

"All in good time, brother. Let's take the horses up over there by those young cottonwoods and talk. You won't need to tie them up. They won't leave." The two dismounted and strolled over to the trees to sit in the shade while the horses nibbled on grass near the stream.

"All right. What's on your mind?" Colton asked. "This sort of reminds me of a meeting I once had in Portland."

"What does that mean?"

"It means I want you to get to the point. Why are you dragging this along?"

"We should talk about your problems."

"Oh, and what problems are those?"

"Your father, his land, Amber, and one more that you don't know about. But your problems are like the wind coming through the canyon. The wind removes the sand that is not firmly attached to the canyon walls. Your problems will do the same to you, and then you will see who you truly are. Much like being alone in a small boat on a stormy sea."

"What's this *other* problem I don't know about?"

"When you saw Amber, what did you think about first? Be honest."

Colton scratched his head. "I don't know. All this time I convinced I was just coming here to find you, maybe see if my father truly wanted to reconcile, but the first time I saw her . . . I guess secretly I hoped that we could pick up where we left off. An apology of course, but I would hope that we could—"

"Colton." Tavaci stopped him. "You were gone a *long* time. Amber is a very beautiful woman. She is smart, she manages a sawmill, and men around here are after her all the time. The worst part to all this is that she never heard from you. I repeat . . . never."

"And I never heard from *her*," Colton began to defend himself, then paused. "Until this year."

"*Nobody* knew where you were," Tavaci said. "Not even me, until you started getting famous, whatever that means."

"All right, I'll admit that—"

"She's pretty serious with another man, Colt." Tavaci stopped him again. "I just learned about it last night, but apparently it has been that way for about three months."

Colton stared up at the top of the cottonwood tree for a full minute. "After this long, I guess I would expect that. In fact, I figured she was with Ethan all this time."

Tavaci stepped back and frowned. "She hates Ethan, as most people do around here. No, it is someone else."

Colton looked at him. "Who is he?"

"He is new. His name is John Lewis. He has only been here about a year. He bought the General Store and improved it. That's probably why he had a chance with her, him being new. She probably heard all the other guys propose at least twice."

"Well, this is turning into quite a day." Colton forced a grin, but it couldn't hide the panic behind his eyes.

"Brother," Tavaci said gently. "What you are breathing is the air of forever. Take three breaths, and think. Problems are not supposed to freeze us with fear, but to help us build strength to overcome them."

"You have suggestions?" Colton asked, looking into Tavaci's eyes.

"Look inside," Tavaci said. "What would the new Colton Grey do? What do you *want* to have happen? Decide, then do what needs to be done."

"Sounds simple enough," Colton admitted, but he sounded unconvinced.

Tavaci came over and placed both hands on Colton's shoulders. "Isn't that what you do with your companies?" he asked.

Colton nodded.

"Is this so different?" Tavaci asked.

Colton shrugged and walked to the cottonwood. He sat down, folded his arms, and finally nodded in agreement.

"Then do what you need to do," Tavaci said. "Whatever that is."

Colton nodded again. "My good friend, and brother, I need to sit here for a while," he said. "Maybe all night. Tell Stuart that I'm fine and I'll see him in the morning. Then I'm going to find Amber Duncan." He paused. "This isn't going to be easy."

"Remind me of the time when your life was *easy,*" Tavaci joked as he left Colton.

34

Hit or Miss?

IT WAS EARLY in the morning when Colton rode up to the Big Rock Cabin. He was surprised to see Stuart sitting on the porch. "What are you doing up so early?"

"I decided a guy can't sleep his life away," Stuart replied. "And I was a little concerned after Tavaci said you might be gone all night. Not worried, just concerned," he clarified. "What's your plan for today?"

"Same as yesterday," Colton said. "I'm going to talk to Amber if she'll let me."

"Yeah, Tavaci told me she has someone now." Stuart looked at the ground, then looked up at Colton with a serious expression. "This trip hasn't been easy for you so far."

"What makes you think it will get easier?" Colton scoffed.

"I'm not saying that." Stuart paused. "Just reminding you that you're strong and you can accomplish most anything you set your mind to do. I've watched you for years."

Surprised as the genuine tone of his friend's voice, Colton looked down and kicked at a rock. "Yeah, well, I don't know any-body who gets one hundred percent of what they want or need. There are always some losses along the way."

"Don't forget to try using some of those stories I told you," Stuart chuckled. "They would impress her."

"I'm sticking with the truth."

"You might be sorry."

"I already am," Colton said, rolling his eyes. "What are you doing today?"

"Tavaci owes me a ride."

"He's a good man . . . And so are you."

"Are you getting sentimental?"

"Goodbye Stuart," Colton replied with a squint in his eyes.

TWO HOURS LATER, Colton saw Amber's ranch in a grove of cotton-woods. *Those trees sure got tall,* he thought to himself. *But where is the barn, and corrals? Something is wrong here.* He shook his head. He was apprehensive about this awkward meeting. *Maybe this is a stupid idea. I thought what we had was real, but we were so young, and that was such a long time ago. Good chance she'll throw me right off her ranch. Nothing ventured . . . ?* He dismounted, tied his horse to the rail, and knocked on the door. No answer. *Maybe I should just get back on the horse,* he considered for a moment, but he stamped his foot to rid the thought. *No. I ran away before. This time I settle with Amber.*

Sounds of horses pulling a buckboard made him turn to see Amber being driven home by a man who he assumed was John Lewis. The man wore a black coat and hat, a white shirt, and a western bow-tie. He looked very respectable, even with his short mustache.

Colton took off his hat to greet them as they pulled up to the house.

Amber had a very somber expression when she recognized him. "Well, hello Mr. Grey. John, this is Mr. Colton Grey. Perhaps you've heard of him."

"Why yes," Lewis said as he climbed down and extended a handshake to Colton. "You're rather well known in the west.

And I knew your father for a brief time. He was a good man. I'm sorry for your loss." He went to Amber's side, took off his hat, and assisted her down.

"Thank you," Colton said. "I'm just here to—"

"Don't run off because of me." Lewis said, cutting him off. "I'm just dropping her off from an early morning ride. I need to get back to the store, and I understand she is heading up to the timber area." He shook his head. "I wish she would get rid of that anchor in her life. Riding a week or two around the mountains to fill up wagons and bring the timber back in another week or two. It just doesn't make sense. And the store is doing well, so money wouldn't be a problem for us."

"For *us*?" Colton looked at Amber, who was staring at the ground.

"Why, yes," Lewis said, beaming. "Miss Amber Duncan and I are engaged."

Colton paled.

"But if only I could convince her to stop this timber nonsense, her life would be so much easier." Lewis continued. He winked at Colton. "Maybe you can help her see the logic in this proposal."

"The logic?" Colton asked. He looked at Amber for a brief moment, then said, "Maybe."

"That's very kind of you," Lewis said with a smile. "And soon we'll have automobiles here, which will certainly reduce travel time for us, don't you agree, dear?"

Amber nodded her head but continued looking at the ground.

"Well, I'd best be off to the store," Lewis said. He reached forward and shook Colton's hand. "It's a pleasure to meet you, sir. I hope your brief stay will be enjoyable."

Colton nodded as Lewis climbed onto his buckboard, snapped the reins, and headed back toward Springdale.

Hat in hand, Colton stepped toward Amber. "He seems like a nice man," he said.

She nodded again.

"Amber, I'm so sorry—"

"Are you Colton?" She snapped up straight. "Are you? It took you fifteen *years* to say three little words. Well, I'm sorry too. But mostly because you're here. I have a lot of priorities right now, and you are *not* one of them."

"Look, I can leave right now," he shot back.

"Oh no, you have a piece to say, and I can't wait to hear it. Please, do the speech."

He glared at her, but then saw that same defiant pose she used against bullies in school. Arms folded, feet shoulder-width apart, right foot pointed to the side, and her left eyebrow in a menacing arch.

"If you had taken that stance against Ethan that night at the Cotton Festival instead of kissing him, we—"

"I *refused* to dance with him, Colton!" Amber spat. "I was walking away, going to look for *you*, when he grabbed me and spun me around so hard I lost my balance. He pulled me in tight and had my arms pinned against his chest. I was just starting to scream your name when he kissed me so hard I couldn't breathe. And where were you, my hero?" Her eyes were moist as she relived the nightmare.

"I'll tell you where I was," he said softly. "My father thought dances and parties were a foolish waste of time, especially if they were run by the cotton farmers. So he had me do extra chores that night. I think he knew I was planning to meet you; I was going to propose to you at the dance. Instead of gaining a daughter, he would be losing a worker. And I wanted to hurry because I knew every guy in town would want to dance with you. I might never get you away from them." He chuckled coldly. "Guess it's a price to pay for loving a beautiful woman."

She unfolded her arms. "Propose? Why didn't you sneak away? We could have left that night and gone somewhere, anywhere!"

"I *did* leave early. I grabbed that old gray horse and spurred her to run as fast as she could."

"And?" Her stance was softening a bit, but she didn't have all the details yet.

"I got to the dance about an hour late," he said. "But guess who was waiting just for me?"

"That Merrill girl?" Amber bristled.

"What? No!" Colton shook his head. "It was five of Ethan's buddies. They blocked me from going in and told me you had switched over to Ethan. They said they didn't want any trouble from me and ordered me to go home. But nothing was going to stop me from seeing you. I pushed my way through three of them, but then I hit the ground hard. They pounded on me for a while, but I broke free and got to the door just in time to see you and Ethan kissing." He kicked at the ground. "That pretty much ended life here for me. I couldn't stand going home, I'd lost you, and I was too beaten to keep fighting. Ethan's buddies laughed, tossed me up on the horse, and hit her with a stick. I have no idea how far I went that night, but I didn't care, as long as it was north. I was finished with everything and everybody down here." His voice cut out. He cleared his throat and looked away. "But there's no use in talking about before. I was a different person then, and I might be again tomorrow."

"Oh, Colton. I didn't know," Amber said, covering her mouth to hide sobs.

"And I didn't know that Ethan and his buddies had this all set up. I'm sorry I was so weak," Colton said, his eyes softening as he looked back at her. "How did you get away from him at the dance?"

"I don't think you're weak." Amber shook her head. "Neither one of us had a chance that night. I got away when he released my arms and I scratched his face hard. Then big farmer Harold, and some other men, pushed him away from me. I left the dance immediately. I hate Ethan now more than ever!"

"I don't care about him." Colton shrugged. "He was just a typical school bully with some weak-minded friends."

Amber shivered. "They're so much worse now . . . so much worse."

Colton took a long look at Amber. The beauty was still stunning, although she would always deny it and say she was average. Her hair was in a thin braid around the crown of her head, but long brown tresses hung down and moved almost rhythmically with the breeze. An expert sculptor must have formed her face with the narrow nose, high cheekbones, and seductive smile. But it was her eyes that were most unique and captivating. Surrounded by long lashes, they would change colors almost like a kaleidoscope when she was in sunlight. She called them "plain old brown," but he could see shades of mahogany, copper, and cinnamon, accented with sparks of gold. He felt foolish even trying to describe them. All he knew was that they could hypnotize any man.

"You've changed a little," he said softly. "But only for the better."

"Colton, don't, I—"

"You complained about me wasting fifteen years, then stop me when I start getting personal?"

"Listen to me. The only reason I hung on here so long was the remote possibility that my dream might come true. It didn't."

"I'm sorry. I know that means little at this point, but I am. More than you know."

Amber took a deep breath. "I recently decided to forget about you. But then I realized that the only way to eliminate grief in a relationship is to completely dissolve that person from your memory, and that would also mean destroying any possibility of sharing any meaningful happiness with you. It was a dilemma I struggled with for years."

"So, you were alone almost all this time." He shook his head in wonder. "Weren't you ever afraid?"

Amber glared at him. "Was I ever afraid? Every . . . rotten . . . day . . . until I put my whole heart into doing what I *needed* to do. After that, I forgot to be afraid because I didn't have time."

"Time," Colton mumbled while gazing at the mountains to the north.

"What about you?" Amber asked. "Adventures in Alaska, beautiful women in Portland, all kinds of money. It must be thrilling to live that kind of successful life."

"You think I just stumbled into money and my ideas were solid gold?" Colton turned back to her. "I got where I am because I made all the mistakes first. It wasn't so much the stress or hardships. The toughest battle was feeling unneeded or unwanted." His gaze softened. "Amber, if you only knew how much I missed you . . ."

She stared at him with *those* eyes, and time stopped. His eyes were locked on hers as he moved to her with strong steps. She held up her left hand showing a diamond engagement ring. It was a feeble effort to stop him.

Colton ignored it, took her hand, and pulled it behind his back forcing her into his arms. The kiss started softly, lips barely touching, but passion soon rushed through them both like a hurricane. Fifteen years of pent up love was finally released in a kiss that put all others to shame.

Amber finally gasped and pushed away. "Colton, stop. I'm basically engaged," she panted, "didn't you see the ring?"

"No, I only saw your eyes. But—"

She sobbed. "I can never be alone with you again."

"That's ridiculous. Kisses aren't like handshakes. If you kiss someone, that shows there are some real feelings there. And don't tell me you couldn't have pulled away. I saw you close your eyes and lean into me."

"I know, I know. I'm so mixed up. This is going too fast." She backed up two steps. "Let's just agree to be friends right now. I have a commitment now, and yet . . . I still want to—"

"Want to *what*? Be *friends*? Tavaci and Stuart are my friends. And I have friends back in Portland." He turned and started back to his horse.

"Colton, wait," Amber called to him. He stopped and turned back to look at her. "You're crushing fifteen years into fifteen seconds. My mind is spinning right now. There's John, the timber, Ethan, your father's death . . . and now you show up and want to start right where we left off years ago." She put her hands along the sides of her head. "I need time to think about all of this."

"As long as you're happy," Colton said. "You'll solve everything and life will get easy for you."

"You think life gets easier?" she huffed. "It doesn't. I remember when we were kids, wishing we could have the freedom of being adults, to do anything we wanted to do. We both know it doesn't work that way. It gets harder, not easier. You just get stronger, or fade away." She glanced at the mountains, then back at him. "A person's view of life depends on where they're standing. Sometimes it's beautiful, and sometimes . . ." She turned backward glancing at the places where the barn and corrals once stood. "Sometimes it looks like things will just fall apart."

He followed her glance. "What happened here?"

"Two years ago, Ethan was pushing my parents to sell our land to him. He wanted our ranch and timberland. My folks said no. A week later, we had just finished a late dinner when we heard a bunch of horses racing up to our place. The three of us ran out the front door to see about a dozen men with torches and their faces painted black. They started throwing the torches at the barn. Pa went back inside for his rifle. I did the same, but he pushed me back hard and ran outside. He fired a warning shot in the air, but they all shot back and killed him and Ma, then raced away." She had a far-away look in her eyes now. "Life changed for me that night."

"Amber, I didn't know—"

"No, I don't suppose you did. I recognized three of the horses, a white and two buckskins, and told the sheriff what I saw. He said there were a lot of horses around that could fit that description. He was no help at all. But I knew they were part of Ethan's crew. I just couldn't prove it."

"And Ethan's still pushing you?"

"Ethan pushes everybody."

"What can I do to help you?"

"Nothing, I've got it covered." She smiled.

Colton returned her smile and nodded. "You just don't want to appear weak." He began walking to his horse. "Maybe I'll have a word with Ethan," he said.

Her smile vanished. "Don't do that! He's crazy. Nobody can reason with him. But there haven't been any problems here for a while, so don't start any."

"As you wish." He mounted the Appaloosa, then asked, "This Lewis fellow, is he a good man?"

"I think so. People like him, and . . . he would be a good provider." Amber looked at the ground.

"Amber," Colton said softly. "You know I would do anything for you."

She whispered, "I know."

He nodded, unconvinced. "We both have some thinking to do, and some decisions to make. I'll see you again, very soon I hope."

As Colton rode away, Amber wrapped her arms around herself and cried.

35

Two Jokers

TAVACI RODE UP to the Big Rock Cabin to see Stuart brushing the palomino. "Come on Stu, let's do some riding. We'll stop by my home so we can tell my wife and kids what we're going to do."

"I still can't believe you have a family," Stuart remarked as they rode.

"Don't you?"

"I've been meaning to get around to it, but—"

"You are wasting time, my friend. Do you want to be eighty when your first child is born?"

"Child? Hmmm, I hadn't thought about it that much."

"Well, you have a girl don't you?"

"Sort of. I mean, I see a *lot* of women . . . now and then."

"But don't you have a favorite?"

"I guess so."

"Who is she? What's she like? Is she pretty? Can she cook—?"

"Whoa. If I answer these questions can we change the subject?"

"Sure."

"Her name's Elizabeth. She's very nice, she's beautiful, and she's a great cook. There. Can we talk about something else now? Like where are we riding to today?"

"So you see a lot of women?" Tavaci brandished a huge grin. "Last year, I was seeing *three,* twenty-year-old girls at the same time."

Stuart was shocked and a little embarrassed. "Why are you telling *me*? Shouldn't you be telling a village elder or someone like that?"

"Telling *you*? I'm telling everyone!" Tavaci said with a laugh as he kicked his horse to a start.

Stuart shook his head, laughed, and mounted up. An hour later they stopped on the crest of the small hill bordering Tavaci's village. Stuart petted his horse while he looked again upon the simple houses and corrals.

Tavaci noticed his expression of concern. "The white man's justice is to take land from Indians and then call them trespassers. We get no respect. If you understand that, explain it to me someday. Let's go down to the house and then we can go for a ride."

As they neared his home, he saw his ten-year-old son shoveling manure out of the corral. "I thought you would be done with this by now," Tavaci scolded. "When Theodore Roosevelt was your age, he would box, lift weights, hike, and climb mountains just to get stronger."

His son replied, "And when he was your age, he was President!"

Tavaci turned to Stuart and shrugged his shoulders. "See what I mean? No respect."

"Like father, like s—" Stuart began to say.

"Don't say it," Tavaci cut him off with a glare.

Stuart pursed his lips and nodded.

"Come in and meet my wife Be-Wa," Tavaci said. They entered the small wooden-frame home where his wife was sitting on the floor weaving a small rug. Tavaci introduced Stuart to her. She nodded politely but kept working. "Like the threads on that loom, we are weak by ourselves. But what a strong and beautiful rug we make when we work together," he mused. On his way to the bedroom he patted her affectionately on the head and said, "If you sit around too long, you'll be putting on a little extra weight."

She kept working, but replied, "And I know that a woman who puts on a few extra pounds will outlive her husband if he ever mentions it."

Tavaci kept walking, but she winked at Stuart.

So the entire family is like this, Stuart thought. *How fun.*

Tavaci yelled from the bedroom, "If you want to help the boy out there for a few minutes, I would appreciate it. He'll find an extra shovel for you."

"Sure, glad to," Stuart shouted back, hiding his displeasure. *Shoveling manure; guess it's not a lot different than listening to some politicians*, he thought as he went outside to the corral. "Young man, let me help you with that," he yelled. He swung the gate open, stepped inside, then looked at his boots. "Swell, or should I say *smell.*" The boy handed Stuart the shovel and climbed the fence to sit and watch. "I thought there were two shovels." The boy just shrugged his shoulders. After a few minutes of shoveling, Stuart wondered why anyone would ever take care of animals, especially so close to their home. He loaded up once more and asked the boy, "Does your Father or Mother ever do this?"

"Naw," he replied. "The horses did that."

"Yes, I know it's—never mind."

Tavaci soon came outside but Stuart noticed his typical smile was missing. "I just learned that old Two Feathers hasn't been home in three days. He's ninety-two and his wife is worried. She wants me to go find him."

"Any idea where he could be?"

"Yeah." He pointed to the top of a tree-covered mountain.

"Can you send out smoke signals and get some help?"

"Smoke signals? People have been sending telegraphs to Europe since 1866! Smoke signals," he grumbled as he shook his head in disgust. "You're going to be one of those people who will still be riding horses when everyone else will be driving automobiles."

"I already own an automobile."

"You do?"

"Ask Colton. He doesn't like the way I drive, but I love what those machines can do. And they're only going to get better and faster."

"Well, I was kidding. Either you like horses or you're wrong. Now let's get Colton to help us find Two Feathers."

"He rode off to see Amber this morning. I imagine he won't be around until tonight."

"I bet we'll find him pretty easily. If he left this morning, he's probably already back at the cabin or his 'thinking' place. You see, Amber is engaged to somebody."

"What?"

"That's probably what Colton said too," Tavaci chuckled.

"From what you said yesterday, I knew she was pretty serious with someone, but engaged?"

"I just learned about it this morning. News travels fast at the store." Tavaci shrugged. "The guy is nice enough from what I hear, but they don't look like a match, if you know what I mean. He doesn't have half the spark she has. And I've heard he can have a temper. I sure wouldn't want to have one of my family married to him." He shook his head. "But, what do I know about matching people? Maybe it would work." Then he whispered, "But, I don't see how. She is too much woman for him."

Tavaci walked a horse from the stable up to his and Stuart's horses. He hitched the horse up to his saddle.

Stuart considered for a minute. "Maybe Amber is the girl Colton keeps seeing in his dreams, or visions, or whatever you call it," he said thoughtfully.

Tavaci quirked a brow at him. "He's been seeing visions?"

"That's for him to tell you." Stuart shrugged. "Let's find him and look for your lost friend."

As they mounted their horses, Tavaci saw his son still sitting on the fence. "Hey boy, get that corral cleaned up." The boy slowly climbed off the fence and drug his feet over to the shovel. "You know," Tavaci said to Stuart, "I tell my kids they should *stay* in school, but they keep coming home every day. What's a man to do?"

"Let's find Colton. He'll know what to do."

Their laughter could be heard throughout the village as they rode over the hill.

36

Is Death Pain, or Comfort?

"THERE'S WICHANPI TIED to the rail at the cabin," Tavaci said when they were still a great distance away.

"I can barely see the cabin. How can you see a horse this far away? It looks like an ant."

"Are you kidding? A black and white Appaloosa? How many of those do you think are around here? Yeah, it's him."

As they approached the cabin, they saw Colton sitting on the porch whittling a stick. Tavaci looked grim as he spoke to Stuart. "That can't be a good sign. When have you ever seen him just sitting around doing nothing?"

"Never. He doesn't know how to do *nothing.*"

"Yo, Colton!" Tavaci called. "We need your help."

"What's wrong?" Colton asked, looking up at them.

"You remember Two Feathers? He's been missing for a few days. His wife said he went up on the East-side of Cougar Mountain. She wanted me to find him and bring him home. I figured you two should join me since I don't know how long you're going to be here. And I brought an extra horse for him to ride home."

"No problem, glad to help," Cold said as he set down his whittling stick and put his knife back in his pocket. He stood up and brushed his hands off on his pants. "I remember Two Feathers. A gentle and wise man."

"Roll up a blanket," Tavaci instructed. "We may be up there for the night."

Colton went inside of the cabin and soon returned with two blanket rolls, one for him and one for Stuart. He walked over to their horses and started tying the blankets onto their saddles.

"You're an excellent tracker," Colton said as he tied. "You'll find him. Especially with Stuart's help."

Stuart smiled, then turned serious. "How did things go with Amber this morning?"

"I've had better days," Colton said gruffly as he got onto his horse. "Let's forget about it."

"Friends can't just forget about another friend having problems," Stuart protested. "That's why I'm here, remember? What's your story?"

"The story is wasted time, my friend." Colton sighed. "Fifteen years is a long time. Too long. She has somebody else." He turned his head to look at Colton. "Makes me think of that Elizabeth back in Portland. How long have you been seeing her?"

Stuart looked away. "A while."

"Look, Stu," Colton said. "People can learn by *doing* things, or *watching* others do things. Either way, the results can be good or bad."

Stuart nodded. "Got it."

"Now we have a more serious problem than Amber and me." Colton turned back to face Tavaci. "What's your plan?"

"There's a trail Two Feathers showed me years ago," Tavaci explained. "He likes to go up high and think; like your 'thinking place' down by Parunuweap Canyon. He probably went up there for visions to help him, so he could help others. Great Puha can be found up in those dark hills."

Stuart squinted at Colton and whispered, "Puha?"

"Power," Colton replied.

IT TOOK SEVERAL hours for the ride along the Chinle Trail and over Coalpits Wash to the base of Cougar Mountain. Tavaci would watch Colton and Stuart as they marveled at the scenes along the way. Black volcanic rocks to the West, Petrified Forest to the South, the majestic Towers of the Virgin to the East . . . and Cougar Mountain straight ahead.

"We'll take the horses up past Terry Wash on the East side of the mountain, then walk from there. My eyes aren't what they used to be, so I'll need to be closer to the ground to pick up his signs."

"Are you getting old, my friend?" asked Colton.

"You know, it's funny. My skin and hair look like they're getting older, but inside I still feel like I'm twenty years old."

"A perfect match for those three girls," chuckled Stuart.

"Huh? What are you talking about?"

"You remember. The three twenty-year-old girls you were seeing."

"I don't know what you're talk—Oh yeah. That was a good story," Tavaci laughed.

Stuart stared openmouthed at him. "You mean it wasn't true?"

"I told you," Colton laughed, "don't try to keep up with him."

"How do you know when he's telling the truth?" Stuart asked.

"He won't be smiling," Colton said.

"All right, white brothers," Tavaci said as they arrived at the base of the trail. "Let's dismount here. No need to tie up the horses. Let them drink at the wash. They can take care of any young peu'dooks that might approach—that's cougars to you, Stu. The only one they will have to watch out for is big Three-Toes. That cat's been a menace for many, many years. But I'll see if I can fix that problem." He put eight boot-size stones in a circle, then picked up some dead pine branches and used his flint and steel to ignite a small fire in the circle. The needles ignited instantly and as they cooled into ashes he picked up the branches and dragged them across a long line in the ground in front of the horses. "Big cats don't like the smell of smoke," he explained. "If Three-Toes is as smart as I think he is he will head north away from us and that smell."

"Will that really work?" asked Stuart.

"I don't know. We'll see. But I thought it was a good idea at the time." Tavaci smiled. "Now we go for a long walk, maybe two or three miles. Two Feathers could be anywhere, but I'll bet he's by the big spillway right in the middle along the cliff's edge to the west. He would have a good view of the setting sun from there. Take your canteens. I'll grab the rifle just in case."

"In case of what?" Stuart queried.

"In case we need it," Tavaci replied, grinning.

Tavaci was thorough in his inspection of branches, bent grasses, and the sand along the gullies. He looked for tracks and anything else that would indicate a man had passed by. He soon found something along the hard sandstone. "He went this way."

"How in the world can you see a sign on sandstone?" asked Stuart.

"See where there are many tiny ledges stacked up along some section of the hills, almost like pages in a book?" Tavaci asked, pointing. "They are made when water flows over a side hill and washes away the softer sand and undercuts little ledges. They are very fragile. They break if a person steps on them. Normally he would never do that, and I've seen other signs, but he is old and perhaps not feeling well. And it is good that there was a little rain up here last night. The sand will be wet making it easy to see tracks. We need to keep walking."

After another hour walking and searching for signs, Tavaci stopped and snapped erect.

"What's wrong?" asked Colton.

"Nungwud'eku . . . tracks. He is walking right up this sandy trail made by deer."

"That's good, it will be easy to follow tracks there."

"That is *not* the problem. Look." Tavaci pointed down at the sand. There, following the man's tracks, were the prints of a large cougar.

"How do you know it's a cougar, and not a dog or coyote?" Stuart asked.

"Dogs can't retract their claws. Cats pull them in unless they are going to grab something. Seeing it's a big cougar is one thing. Seeing this one only has three toes changes everything."

"It's hunting him, isn't it?" Colton asked.

Tavaci nodded and put his finger to his lips, showing he wanted silence.

Stuart whispered, "Whether a cougar jumps out, or a branch brushes against me, I'm ready to yell."

They both nodded. Tavaci handed the rifle to Stuart. "Just in case," he whispered as he again put his finger to his lips.

The cat's tracks were often on top of the man's, indicating the cougar was following him. Tavaci suddenly stopped and swung his hand to the right, indicating the cat had left the trail. "He's going around to cut him off, but he will still attack from behind. Two Feathers will never know what hit him. We need to make noise now. You two follow the trail. You'll be safe together. I'll go after the cat."

They both nodded, but Stuart's eyes were as wide as dinner plates. "What do we do if we see it?" he asked.

Colton patted his pistol and drew it from his holster. They walked slowly, checking in every direction and behind every tree along the trail as they proceeded up the hill.

Tavaci was running. Now he knew where Two Feathers had gone. Two hundred yards ahead, he saw a large Ponderosa Pine near the edge of the cliff. At the bottom of the tree was the bright red color of a man's shirt. Leading directly to that shirt, were the cougar tracks. And then he saw the cougar's tail close to the man's shirt.

Tavaci yelled as he ran, but the cat didn't move. He yelled again but neither the cougar nor the man stirred.

Colton and Stuart now raced up the trail, and in seconds they saw the black-tipped tail of a cougar extending away from the man.

"It's eating him!" Stuart shouted.

Colton raised his pistol and they ran to the front side of the tree, but Tavaci was already there. He stood with his arms hanging down by his side and his mouth open as though he was stunned by the sight.

"Look," Tavaci said, "they are both dead."

"They *killed* each other?" Stuart wondered aloud.

"No, *look!*"

Three-Toes was stretched out, claws retracted, with his head on Two Feather's lap. The man had his hands on the cougar's head as though he had been petting him.

"I don't believe this," Colton said. "Am I wrong? It looks like they had a pact to die together."

"The tracks show the cougar never attacked him," Tavaci said. "It walked up slowly and lay down in his lap. Two old warriors going to the next life together. I've never seen or heard anything like this before. But I'm thankful I was here."

They stared in silence for a full minute.

"Tavaci, do you believe there is another life after we die?" asked Stuart.

"I've heard it said that to those who believe there is always enough proof," Tavaci answered. "To those who do not believe, there is never enough."

"It's too bad he didn't live longer so we could have taken him home," Stuart said.

"Live longer?" Tavaci turned to look at Stuart. "How long should anyone live? What do you want people to say when you die? That you looked great? That you had a great company? Or that you helped a lot of people throughout your life." He turned back to the scene and looked at Two Feathers's peaceful face. "That is what Two Feathers was all about. And this was an amazing way to die."

Stuart nodded, then turned to Colton. "Colton," he said. "You're awfully quiet."

"I was thinking if two natural enemies like this could reconcile at death, maybe nations could stop wars," Colton said thoughtfully. "Maybe Ethan would be cooperative. Maybe Amber would . . . well." He shook his head. "I guess there are limits."

"Maybe the white man and red man could get along better too," added Tavaci.

The three of them turned their attention to Two Feathers. They were silent but found themselves placing their hands on each other's shoulders during a brief moment of respect.

"I'll go get the horses," Tavaci said quietly.

As he walked away, Stuart stared at him. "I don't know what to say right now," he remarked to Colton. "This has been an experience I never expected to have in my entire life. And Tavaci is an amazing man. I've never known anyone like him before."

Stuart and Colton glanced at each other in sober thought.

"Nobody will believe us about this," Colton said, approaching the two bodies. "Help me move this big cat and get Two Feathers ready to bring back to his home."

37

Then There Were Four

Amber was busy helping John Lewis fill the shelves in the General Store with cans of fruits and vegetables when Colton, Stuart, and Tavaci entered. "Amber," shouted Lewis, "put the cans down and help the customers."

There were a half dozen people already shopping, including an attractive young lady who was having difficulty carrying several bolts of cloth to the counter to pay.

Stuart noticed her immediately and ran to help her take the fabrics to the till. When he had set the fabric down, he turned, took off his hat, and shook her hand. "You look exactly like my new wife," he said.

"Really, what's her name?" she asked coyly.

"I don't know yet. I've just started shaking her hand. Would you—"

"Stuart!" Colton interrupted. "We have to get our supplies for the cabin. Maybe you'll meet this young lady again sometime . . . after we're finished."

The girl blushed, paid Amber, shook her head, and left the store.

"Well, Mr. Grey," Lewis said, walking forward. "I'm surprised you're still around. After spending an entire evening with my Miss Duncan I thought you would be heading north."

"John," Amber protested, "we didn't spend an entire evening together we just—"

"Whatever you say dear, but please don't interrupt," he blurted in. "Perhaps it just seemed like such a long time and—" His eyes scanned the group as he spoke until they finally landed on Tavaci. "What's that Indian doing in here?"

Colton started toward Lewis, but Amber shook her head, so he held still.

"Mr. Lewis," Colton said politely. "Tavaci is my brother. He has been helping my friend Stuart and I to complete a few tasks before we return to Portland, and—"

"Yes, yes, very interesting." Lewis waved his hand. "But if he wants something he can wait outside while you buy it for him."

"I—" Colton began to protest, but Tavaci shook his head.

"Don't worry about it, Colton," Tavaci said. "I don't think there is anything here I need . . . or want." He started toward the door, but Stuart stopped him.

"The *Indian* is our friend," said Stuart, "and he will remain here with us if you want *our* business."

Lewis turned to see Colton and Stuart with arms folded, and Amber with her hands on her hips. Even the other customers frowned at him. He snorted at them all, then returned to putting cans on the shelves while he muttered something about what the world was coming to.

The three men finished their shopping. They put various food items into saddlebags, then went to pay Amber.

Lewis quickly intervened and put his hand out to receive the cash from Colton. "Amber, finish putting the cans on the shelves," he commanded. "I'll take care of these customers."

She looked out the window just before she headed to the shelves. "Well, well, talk about being caught in a pen between two bulls," she remarked, looking at Colton. "Here comes Ethan Morley with a few of his men."

"Ethan?" asked Stuart. "Isn't that—"

"A man who has wandered into darkness so deep even God couldn't find him," Amber growled beneath her breath.

"Colton, is this the guy who—"

Colton shook his head. "He doesn't have anything to do with us, Stuart. Ignore him."

"I will if you will," Stuart retorted.

Tavaci tried to lighten the mood. "Just be yourself," he said to Stuart.

Colton scowled, "That's about the worst advice I ever heard."

The door burst open as Ethan and four of his men stormed into the store. "Where's the story-tellers at?"

"Well, Ethan," said Amber, "we were just talking about your favorite subject."

"Yeah," he sneered, "and what might that be?"

"You."

He grinned at her, then glowered at the other people who quickly left the store. His eyes fell on Colton. "So, the important Mr. Grey has returned to the red rock country. You're not smiling. I thought you'd be happy to see me again."

"Some people make others happy just by entering a room," Colton remarked coolly. "Some when they leave."

"And some folks realize that life doesn't really begin until they understand how quickly it could end," Ethan threatened. "I understand that you three found a cougar in the lap of some Injun, and there wasn't a scratch on either of them."

"You heard right," said Colton.

"Ain't no way a cougar is going to lie down next to a human without ripping him to pieces," Ethan shouted. "You three who brought his body down must have been drunk over your heads to come up with such a tale."

"I'm not young enough to know everything, but I know what I saw," Colton said. "And I don't drink."

"Well, maybe you oughta start." Ethan looked at his men and sneered, "You think so boys?" They all nodded like puppets.

Colton grinned at the men. "It appears that boozing might be one thing that doesn't improve with a lot of practice."

The nodding stopped.

Ethan slammed his hand down on the counter. "I say that cougar story is a lie."

"You're entitled to your opinion, but *not* to change the facts."

"Well, maybe we should vote on it then," Ethan sneered. "You agree with me, boys?"

Once again, they nodded.

"See?" Ethan laughed cruelly. "That's five to three."

"When everybody thinks the same, somebody isn't thinking," Tavaci said from the back of the room.

Ethan closed his eyes for a moment, then stared at Colton. "Did I just hear an Injun talkin' to my men?" His attention snapped to Lewis behind the counter. "And what the hell is he doin' in this store in the first place, Lewis? Didn't I tell you no Injuns allowed in here?"

Lewis nodded.

Ethan's attention turned back to Colton. "You see, Grey, a man's got to have a set of standards to live by, a code of ethics no matter what his job is. You understand that don't you? Of course, maybe you ain't got one since your ma was a Injun."

Colton's face was sober. "Ever hear of Mark Twain? I think he got it right when he said, 'Civilizing Indians is lifting them down to our level.' Tavaci is one of the finest people I have ever known. And there's a lady present, so maybe you can tone it down a bit."

"He don't belong in here, and neither do you! And Duncan ain't no lady!" Ethan roared.

"Can you hear what you're saying Morley?" Colton asked. "Or are you just exercising your voice in case you might have something important to say someday? You're into talking, you're just not into listening."

Stuart joined in, "The problem with you is that your brain hasn't caught up to your mouth yet."

"And who the hell are you?" Ethan blasted as he stepped toward Stuart.

Colton stepped between them. "He's just a friend disguised as a responsible adult. Pay no attention to him."

Stuart pushed past Colton and went right up to Ethan, "I can look you straight in your eyes while you're jabbering and not hear a single thing you said."

"Well," Ethan looked between Stuart and Ethan. "So there are two of you."

"Make that three," said Tavaci, holding his rifle.

"Four," said Amber. She looked over at Lewis who averted his eyes and looked at the floor. "Four then," she said.

Ethan nodded at his men who started toward the others when the bell over door the door rang. Sheriff Lyman, a thin man with gray hair, entered.

"Hello Morley, Miss Duncan, Tavaci . . . Mr. Lewis. And you're Charles Grey's son. I remember you from the funeral," he said politely. "Everything all right? I thought I heard some yelling in here as I was passing by."

Amber cocked an eyebrow and stared at Ethan. "Even if Colton whispers, he makes more sense than all your yelling," she said.

"Someday, Duncan," Ethan replied as he looked up and down her body. "Someday." Then he turned to Colton. "You know something Grey, it seems to me that you and I are going to pick up where we left off many years ago."

"I look forward to that," Colton replied. "I figure if you're upset and confused I've been successful."

"You might consider your success to be very short-lived," Ethan spat, then regained his composure. "By the way, I think it's time I made some financial changes to the community," he said to the group. "Starting with Duncan's trees. Come on, boys. Step aside, Lyman." Ethan pushed the sheriff out of the way and he and his men left the store.

"Mr. Grey," the sheriff said. "There's no use in getting Morley upset. He doesn't forgive anyone who crosses him, whether it was real or imaginary. I think you and your friend should make plans to go home as soon as possible." He tipped his hat and walked outside.

Colton looked over at Lewis, who was quietly standing in the back of the store. He turned to the others and asked, "How about the four of us going outside and talking this over?"

"When we leave through that door, we will be entering a passage into somewhere new," Tavaci advised. "Even if the outside looks the same, time has passed and things are different now. We should think."

"Amber Duncan, your work here is not finished," Lewis spluttered as they started to exit. "You should stay here with me and—"

"John," Amber cut him off. "You just stood there while Ethan insulted Tavaci, threatened my friends, and my forest. I don't know what he is going to do, but if I lose those trees the whole community will suffer. And you *know* that, yet you just stood there. It's *your* store. You should decide what happens in here."

"Listen to me, Missy," Lewis insisted, growing angry. "Ethan Morley has more power here than you can possibly imagine."

"That's why we need to stick together, John," Amber retorted. "I don't know what he's going to do, or how four of us can stop him, but we have to try. You said you loved me. I would expect you to help me when I need it. Will you join with us to see how we can battle this beast?"

"This isn't a David versus Goliath story, Amber." Lewis sighed, his anger deflating. "A few stones won't stop Morley. He has twenty men behind him. Twenty *ruthless* men who will do whatever he tells them. And there's the four of you. Do you think the town's people will join you against him? I want nothing to do with this. If I had to pick a team, it would make the most sense to stick with Morley." His expression turned grim. "And if I have to do that alone . . ."

"You told me once that you would help me whenever I needed it," Amber pleaded. "Now things get a little tough and you admit you would leave me?"

"Not alone, you have three companions," Lewis said with a cruel grin, but then his expression softened. "Use your head and stay in the store."

Amber held up her hand toward his face and shook her head. "John, I have a lot of thinking to do now. I'll talk to you later after I weigh through all of this. And don't call me Missy."

She exited in time to hear Colton speaking to Stuart and Tavaci.

"Look, you two," Colton said. "A friendship is not based on having the same enemy."

"You *three*," Amber corrected as she walked toward them.

"Amber." Colton turned toward her. "Ethan is crazy. I wouldn't endanger you for anything."

"I've been on my own for a long time," Amber replied. "If we all work together, we should be able to do whatever needs to be done."

"So John won't join us?" Colton wondered.

She closed her eyes and shook her head. "Maybe he will later."

"It's just a thought, of course," said Stuart, "but it seems like it would make a lot of people happy if he was pushed off one of those cliffs."

"I was thinking of a different approach," offered Colton. "There was a military strategist in China who said, 'The supreme art of war is to subdue the enemy . . . without fighting.'"

"How in the world would you remember that?" Stuart wondered. "Have you read everything that has ever been written?"

"Some things stick in my mind because they're important," Colton said. "The point is that there are only three, I mean four, of us. We can't overpower his gang. We need to out-think him and beat him at whatever game he is going to play next."

"I have forest land that borders his," Amber suggested. "If there was a way to beat him in lumber production he would fall hard."

"Do you have an idea?" asked Colton.

"Not yet," Amber replied. "But I'll work with you . . . until we can figure this out."

Colton looked back at the store. "And John?"

Amber inhaled. "The only way to know for certain that you can trust me . . . is to trust me."

Colton nodded, his mouth a firm line.

"Answers will come, Colton." Tavaci said softly, "Let's meet at the foot of the Watchman mountain tomorrow to talk about this. Ethan is not your strongest enemy. It is your vision of your own destiny. I think you will learn what to do."

38
Ethan's Plan

TAVACI WAS LEANING against a large rock at The Watchman before the sun's rays hit Springdale. Soon, Colton and Stuart rode up and dismounted.

"How is that Appaloosa treating you, Colton?" Tavaci asked as they approached. "Be-Wa wanted to know."

"So far, so good," Colton replied. "But there are times when he thinks he can go wherever he wants."

"Yeah, that's him all right," Tavaci chuckled. Then he pointed at another rider approaching them. "Look, here comes Amber up from town. She doesn't look very happy."

"Hey, *Missy,* how are you this morning?" Stuart called to Amber as she arrived, trying to lighten the mood.

She cocked an eyebrow at him and glared. "I don't know you very well, Stuart. But if you and I are ever to be on good terms you will never use that term again. Do you understand?"

Stuart's face turned red. "Yes ma'am. I apologize." He glanced at Colton and Tavaci who both wore huge grins.

"Sorry, everyone," Amber addressed the group as she dismounted her horse. "Guess I'm a little tense right now. Ethan just put up notices around town that he will be charging tolls to use the roads going up the mesa whether people go from Kanab or Cedar City. He's in the town square now, telling people how things are going to be."

"Tolls? But—" Colton began.

"And he's doubled the price of all the lumber he cuts at his sawmill in Saint George," Amber continued. "He's going to drive me out of business and break the backs of all the farmers too."

"Let me tell you about lumber," Stuart said. "It should already be built as beds, chairs, and tables and be boxed in stores ready to buy." The prolonged silence of the other three, who just looked at each other, finally broke him. "What is wrong with what I said? Wouldn't that make life easier for everyone here?"

"It sure would my friend," said Colton, "but this isn't Portland. It takes a long time to get up to the trees on the mesa, a long time to cut them down and load them in wagons, a long time to get the wagons back down to the valley and over to the sawmill, and a long time to cut it into useable lumber. Then somebody has to build the furniture, or barns, or fences."

"Yeah, I wasn't thinking about all those steps," Stuart admitted, scratching his head. "And now this Ethan guy is going to make it more difficult for everyone."

"Not if we can help it," Colton said. "Somehow we're going to beat him at this no matter what it takes. I won't leave Amber alone to face this. Not after what she's been through."

"Wait a minute, Colt," Stuart said. "You know the history of that guy. Are you one of those men who never learns from history? You mess with him, he'll kill you."

"He's right," added Amber. "I can't ask you, I won't ask you, to do something dangerous like challenging Ethan and his gang of thugs. If anything ever happened to you—" She turned away to hide her trembling lips.

Colton turned her around, placed his hands on her head, ran his fingers through her hair, and pulled her close. "Amber," he said softly. "I would do anything for you. Anything. Don't you understand what that means?"

She stared up into his eyes and gently shook her head.

"I think it means he loves you, girl," Tavaci said.

They both faced him with stunned expressions and stammered some inaudible comments.

"What was that?" Tavaci queried with a smile.

"Nothing," they said in unison.

"Saying *I would do anything for you* means the same as *I love you*?" asked Stuart.

Tavaci nodded.

"Of course. I see it now," Stuart said. "She's the girl on the street in Portland."

Tavaci tilted his head and squinted at Stuart in confusion.

"I'll tell you later," Stuart said, then he turned to Colton. "Colt, what are the four of us going to do about this Ethan guy?"

Colton cleared his throat. "We'll check with the law, although no lawman ever has enough deputies to protect everyone, or promises that he'll arrest all the bad guys—"

"There is no law in town now," Amber interrupted. "Lyman got sick last night and died. The doctor said he acted like he had been poisoned."

Stuart glared at Colton. "History," he repeated.

"So this will be up to us and the rest of the town," Colton said.

Amber and Tavaci shook their heads to disagree.

Colton looked at them. "We have to try. Let's go down to the town square and see what help we can get."

They rode in silence, each of them considering the futility of their upcoming proposals. As they approached the Square, Colton asked, "So do any of you have ideas we can use?" The three of them shook their heads.

"It's up to you, Colton," Stuart said. "You've always been the idea guy."

"My idea now is to talk to that man standing on the platform, speaking to the crowd," Colton said.

"It's Ethan," Stuart moaned. "How is talking to him going to help?"

They rode up and dismounted. Colton started toward the platform; people automatically moved out of his way. He listened to Ethan's loud speech as he walked.

"Yeah, I'm collecting tolls from everybody who goes up on the mesa," Ethan shouted. "I need to protect my forest."

"But that's where we hunt for deer, bighorn sheep, and game-birds to help feed our families if our herds and flocks die off," a voice from the crowd shouted back.

"Doubling the price of your lumber will break us," another voice from the crowd complained. "We need it for homes and furniture. And Cougar Creek is all dried up for the first time. We don't have much water!"

"Hold on!" Ethan yelled. "It was you farmers who cut down all the trees in this valley. *You're* the ones to blame for this predicament. Not me. My costs are going up too. Why should I be the one who suffers because you made stupid mistakes and weren't more resourceful?"

"You're correct, to a certain point," Colton said when he reached the edge of the platform.

Ethan looked at him and sneered. "Well, look who shows up to do some complainin'. You don't even live here, so nobody cares what you think."

"I still own the Grey Ranch," Colton said. "Who knows where I'm going to live next?"

Ethan disregarded the statement. "You said you agreed with me."

"I do," Colton admitted. "The earliest settlers here cut down all the trees and put themselves in a bind when it came to expansion and larger families. I know because I was one of them for years."

"So what's the problem?" Ethan asked.

"You keeping people off the mesa, and doubling the price of the wood they need," Colton answered, folding his arms.

Ethan walked to the edge of the platform and stared down at Colton. "I did a little checkin' up on you. We're not so different. We both run good business deals. And how many men are there like us in the world? Damn few. And why? Because they don't take chances, they only take orders."

"Sometimes those *orders* are to obey the law."

"Laws are made to prevent people from having to make decisions all the time."

"Clever thought, and somewhat true." Colton shrugged. "But laws are made to help people avoid making *bad* decisions, and to protect others."

Ethan scanned the crowd. Many of them were nodding their heads in agreement with Colton. "I'm telling you, people," Ethan yelled. "This will be a good thing."

"A good thing for you," Colton said.

"You're just not listening to me," Ethan grumbled.

"I'm listening. It just takes me awhile to understand so much stupid."

The crowd erupted in cheers and jeers. Ethan jumped off the platform in a rage. "You wait!" he yelled. "All of you! You think things are bad now? I'm tripling the cost of lumber and tolls as of this minute! Now what do you think of Mr. Grey?" He stormed off to his buckboard and yelled at his men to follow him back up to the mesa.

The crowd became silent. They turned to glare at Colton.

Colton jumped up on the platform and shouted, "Look, we can work together and fix this."

"How, Mr. Smart Guy?" a voice in the crowd asked.

"We can . . . build new roads up to the mesa in both directions." Colton offered.

"You're crazy," someone yelled. "Do you know how long that will take us? We'll starve in the meantime. And twenty new families have agreed to buy land here, but what are they going to use to build homes and fences?"

The crowd began to disperse while they swore at Colton.

"Are you going to be remembered for the dilemmas you fix, or the ones you create?" Amber asked Colton as she, Tavaci, and Stuart joined him.

"I thought the town would—" Colton tried to reply but faltered.

Tavaci put his hand on Colton's shoulder. "You are sleeping on the edge of the world, brother. Do not fall off."

"I thought maybe someone would help me, or at least come up with better ideas." Colton sighed. "I've been thinking about something Gandhi said, 'First they ignore you, then they ridicule you, then they fight you, . . . and then you win.' There *has* to be a solution to this. Ethan seems invincible, but he'll fall, somehow. I just need some time to think and see how it will happen."

"He is an evil man," said Amber.

"I don't know him that well," said Stuart. "Is he really evil, or just very selfish? I know he thinks he's right. That's why he's so dangerous. The real problems in the world are rarely fights between right and wrong. They are usually conflicting issues between two people who think they are both right."

Amber replied, "A lot of us think he has killed people who get in his way. That's evil, and he won't change."

"Coming back here, where things haven't changed much, is a good measuring stick to see how much I have changed," Colton said.

"Do you think you are better now?" Tavaci asked.

Colton sighed. "I don't know."

"There is no reason to compare yourself to others," Tavaci said. "The only real value is to see if you are better than your former self."

Colton nodded. "You always say the right things. Now tell me how to fix this problem."

Tavaci shrugged his shoulders. "I see nothing but still-water now. Maybe Stuart and I will take a ride up high tomorrow to see if a solution appears. I think you and Amber should do the same."

39
Searching Canyon Rims

THE DOOR TO Tavaci's cabin swung open in response to Stuart's impatient rapping. Tavaci's wife stood in the doorway with an inquisitive expression on her face.

"Hello Be-Wa," Stuart greeted her, smiling. "Is Tavaci at home?"

She nodded, then tipped her head to the right, indicating he was behind the cabin.

"Thank you. I've enjoyed our conversation," he said as he backed away and started toward the corral.

She mumbled something to him as she closed the door, but he didn't know the word. As he turned the corner, there was Tavaci feeding his horse.

"Hey, Tav," Stuart greeted Tavaci as he approached. "What does Moa-hup' mean?"

"It means *silly*," Tavaci replied. "Where did you hear that word?"

"It's not that important. I just wondered." Stuart shrugged.

"So you talked to my Pengwu', did you?" Tavaci laughed.

Stuart squinted at him in confusion.

"My *wife*," Tavaci said. "She's not overly friendly with men or whites. Ethan Morley and his gang kind of ruined that for her. He's been nothing but trouble for our people."

"That's why I'm here," Stuart said. "I can't let Colton do all the work. I want to go up the bottom of that one canyon we saw."

"I don't go into the canyons."

"I don't mean to insult your beliefs, my friend, but it's the twentieth century. Do you really think there are evil spirits in there?"

He stared at Stuart for a moment, then looked at the ground.

"I'm just saying that we can take a look for maybe half a day. What if there is a series of ledges or something that would simplify making a road to the top instead of moving an entire sawmill to Amber's trees? Chop the trees, load them up, take them to Saint George. I'm for simplifying things. This whole thing seems like too much work. To me, wood should already be shaped into furniture and sold in stores ready to go. Obviously, that isn't going to work here."

Tavaci nodded. "I remember."

"Will you come with me to look at that canyon?"

Tavaci hesitated, then nodded again.

IN THREE HOURS they stopped their horses and tied them to trees at the wide outlet-end of the canyon. "So far, so good," Stuart said.

"Say that when we're finished," Tavaci grumbled.

"Don't worry, I'm here. We'll be fine."

Tavaci shook his head but didn't argue. "A couple of days ago, you told me that Colton had seen some 'visions.'"

"Yes, but that was only in Portland. Nothing like that has happened to him since then."

"You know, I've heard voices too."

Stuart was very attentive as he glanced sideways at him.

"Yeah, I know they aren't real, but they have some good ideas," he grinned.

Stuart chuckled, then sobered. "Speaking of Portland made me think about my sister, Emma . . . and her son, Todd. Hope they're all right."

"That's all? Nobody else?"

"Well, there *is* a girl," he said as he looked up into the canyon.

"Is it this Elizabeth woman you mentioned the other day?"

Stuart nodded, embarrassed. "I call her Mel . . . I wish she was here."

Tavaci looked into the canyon. "Yeah, my wife isn't that far away, and I wish *she* was here."

Stuart looked at Tavaci. "Are you getting sentimental on me?"

Tavaci smiled. "Naw, I just want someone to carry my pack."

Stuart's eyes met his, but he quickly looked away. "Sure you do. Sure you do."

"Come on, Stuart. Taking a couple of days to search these Canyon rims for new road possibilities will be good exercise."

"I get enough exercise pushing my luck, Tavaci."

"You know, you're a pretty funny guy."

"Colton told me not to try to keep up with *you*."

"Aaah, that's silly. People don't really know what they are saying until they realize what they did *not* say."

"Huh?" Stuart asked with a puzzled look.

"Think about it," Tavaci said, then he turned back to the horses. "Before we ride up high, I want to take you to a place filled with mystery, silence, and wonder. Come with me to where people, and ghosts, lived a thousand years ago."

"Ghosts?"

"You afraid?"

"Should I be?"

"We need to ride down to the East Fork. It shouldn't take us very long. Enjoy the scenery."

"Lead on."

They rode side by side, but Tavaci was observing Stuart instead of the scenery. He noticed how he looked down at the plants along the trail and, in the next instant, was transfixed by the rugged terrain of the horizon.

"Look," shouted Stuart, "An arch waaay up there! Looks like a window into the sky!"

Tavaci smiled and nodded, put his finger to his lips, then pointed at four mule deer bucks with huge antlers that had just been spooked by Stuart's shout. The deer ran from a grove of cottonwoods along the river until they vanished over a hill to the north.

"You know," Stuart marveled. "I used to think that nothing lived in the desert. I've seen all kinds of birds, flowers, trees . . . and now deer. I'm surprised at how truly beautiful it is here."

"More beautiful than Oregon?" Tavaci asked.

Stuart thought for a moment before responding, "It's a different kind of beauty."

"What do you mean, different?"

"The red rocks and canyons here, and the forests and ocean there. They're both beautiful. It's like comparing American women to those from Brazil or Germany, or Japan, or Africa, or everywhere else. They're all different, but they can all be beautiful."

Tavaci stared at him. "Man, you *do* need a girlfriend."

"No, no, listen," Stuart insisted. "Let's take horses instead. Pintos, Palominos, Appaloosas, Buckskins . . . Do you see what I mean?"

Tavaci smiled. "I knew what you meant the first time, but it was fun listening to you try to explain yourself. Now, if we're quiet when we leave, we might also see some bighorn sheep, black bears, coyotes, roadrunners, and who knows what else."

"Bears?"

"Sure, if we're quiet." Tavaci smiled even more when he saw Stuart's head turning in every direction as they continued along the river.

It was quiet for another thirty minutes until Tavaci said, "Over there," and pointed to the base of a mountain about one hundred yards from the river's edge.

Stuart squinted at the strange shapes nestled into the rock wall.

He looked at Tavaci with the astonished expression of a toddler opening gifts. "Can we go closer?" he whispered.

Tavaci nodded.

In a minute they dismounted within fifty feet of stone-wall homes built under the overhanging sandstone ledges. Stuart made a reverent approach to this place that he was certain that Tavaci considered sacred. "Doors, windows . . . what are those barrel-shaped structures?"

"Storage bins, like your farm silos."

Stuart peeked through a window. "And look, there is still beautiful pottery in the homes."

"Handmade, of course," Tavaci said, looking around. "We think this area housed a few families, and we want to keep it just as they left it. This is a sacred place."

"I agree," Stuart said. "And I can picture what life might have been like here. Men and women working, children playing in the area. This place touches my heart."

"I thought it would, or I never would have brought you here. Colton knows about this place, but nobody else, except our people. We should leave this place as quietly as we came. Let's ride up on the canyon rims like we planned, to see if new roads can be built up there."

IN THREE HOURS, they picked their way to the top of a forested plateau that was bordered by four canyons created over centuries of uplifting and erosion. "Not a good place for a road," said Tavaci. "We're just lucky the horses made it."

"Lucky?" Stuart asked. "What do you mean, *lucky*?"

"Nothing to worry about," Tavaci replied. "Horses hardly ever fall off stuff like this."

Stuart's eyes widened. "What do you mean, *hardly* ever?"

"Forget it." Tavaci shook his head. "Let's walk for a while and give the horses a break."

"Good idea. In fact, a little run to stretch my legs would be great," Stuart said as he dismounted and rubbed his rear end. "Here, take the reins." He handed the reins to Tavaci and started running through the trees to the east. Memories of jumping over the barrel in Portland flashed through his mind. *I'm not out of shape,* he thought. *And a run will prove it.*

Tavaci was facing the other way when he dismounted, but he was soon alarmed at Stuart's reckless sprint. "Stop!" he yelled after Stuart. "Cliff!"

Stuart looked backward as he ran. "The name's Stu, not Cliff."

"STOP!" Tavaci yelled again.

Stuart grabbed a tree and slid to a stop just a few feet from the edge of a deep canyon, His feet kicking stones out in front of him. Stunned, he murmured, "Oh . . . *cliff.*" The stones he had kicked rattled and echoed as they caromed down the canyon walls for ten seconds.

Tavaci came running fast. He stopped when he saw Stuart hugging the tree trunk. Gasping for air, he leaned forward and put his hands on his knees to catch his breath. "Are . . . you . . . crazy?" he panted. "You were just worried about bears, and now you go running off into a strange place? If you fall down there you *will* die, and I'm not coming after you."

"I was just—"

"Just what?" Tavaci snorted. "Do you think this is downtown Portland?"

"All right, I'm sorry," Stuart apologized. "I'll be more careful."

Tavaci just glared at him and shook his head. "Go ahead. Take a look down there."

Stuart inched his way to the edge of the canyon rim. It was only eight feet across to the other side from where he stood, but it began to widen quickly as it extended to the north. "I probably could have jumped across here with no problem," he said, grinning.

Tavaci stared at him. "I said look *down.*"

Stuart's grin faded instantly as he peered down the chasm. The walls of gray sandstone gradually darkened as they rippled downward and eventually disappeared into blackness. "What in the world—"

"No, it's a *different* world," Tavaci said. "And I would never go down into that black pit, or any of the other narrow canyons around here. So, if you travel down there by falling, or hiking, you do it by yourself! Understand me?"

"Yeah." Stuart nodded solemnly. "And I apologize for this typical Stuart Landon move."

"What do you mean?"

"I'm the class clown, the one who bumbles along, the sidekick, the last guy picked on a team."

"Is this self-pity time because you almost did something stupid?"

"I'm not looking for sympathy. I'm just saying that I'm always . . . ahh, forget it."

"It is *never* too late to become what you might have been."

"See, there is a perfect example." Stuart threw his hands up in the air. "You always know what to say. Colton can make money in his sleep. This Amber girl is gorgeous and as tough as they come. And you always have the right words."

"Most people are tougher than they think they are," Tavaci said. "Look how you stood up to bad-man Ethan. You didn't even think twice. You just said what needed to be said and didn't worry about what might happen."

"Sometimes that's a really stupid idea," Stuart mumbled.

"Sometimes," Tavaci agreed.

Stuart looked at Tavaci. "Are you telling me you've done stupid things?"

"Name one person who hasn't," Tavaci said.

"Colton," Stuart answered instantly, then he paused to consider. "Wait, he left Amber without checking to see what really happened." He thought for another moment. "My sister, Emma." He shook his head. "No, she still tries to get me attached to a lady at home."

"And that's stupid?" Tavaci asked.

Stuart frowned, turned away from him, and glanced along the rim of the canyon.

"Tomorrow is what counts most," Tavaci said. "It has no mistakes when it arrives at midnight. The trick is to see what we learned from yesterday. Midnight brings us an empty bowl. What will you put into yours?"

Stuart continued staring at the canyon depths. "I suppose you're right. I may not be that smart, or rich, or strong, or handsome, or . . . Now, what was the point I was trying to make?"

Tavaci smiled. "Rainbows don't appear until *after* the storm. I think great things will come to you. Maybe that lady in Portland. Getting a good wife might change your entire view about life."

One corner of Stuart's mouth turned upward.

"What? That only gets half a smile?"

"I just don't know that I would be that good for a woman. They are incredible."

"That is true."

"That must be why I've never seen you fight with your wife."

"Oh, we've had our arguments," Tavaci laughed. "But eventually one of us always agrees that I was wrong."

Stuart smiled, then sighed. "Thanks for the kind words. Things will work out for me. I'm actually more worried about Colton and Amber . . . and that crazy Ethan."

"Me too. We've got to beat that guy," Tavaci said. "Let's look along these canyon rims to see if there is a way to build a road up here, or maybe a good place for a sawmill. A level place with a source of water."

"Well, there's a lot of space up here, and plenty of trees. I'll go around to the east side of this narrow canyon since I was headed that way in the first place."

They both laughed, then parted company. They walked their horses along the opposite rims but looked across the expanse of the mesa as the canyon became wider. After two hours, Stuart had enough. "All right, I'm tired. How do I get to the other side?"

Tavaci grinned. "You *are* on the other side." His laughter echoed down into the depths of the chasm.

Stuart stood with his hands on his hips, glaring at Tavaci. "Let me try this again. Is there a quick way to cross over this canyon and meet you so we can check out another place?"

"No bridges up here, but I agree this canyon is only getting wider. Let's go back to where we first split up and go around the eastside of Parunuweap Canyon, then head north toward Amber's forest land."

"How long will that take?"

"The rest of the day. We'll sleep near the White Cliffs, spend the next day exploring all over the mesa, then go back and tell Colton what we discovered . . . if anything."

40

A Second Chance

COLTON WAS DRAWING potential timber routes in the sand at his "thinking place" along the East Fork of the Virgin River when Tavaci and Stuart rode up.

"I hope you two came up with better results than I did over the last two days," Colton called to them.

"What did you find out?" Stuart asked as they dismounted.

"A judge agreed that my father's ranch was legally mine, but I think everyone but Ethan knew that was going to happen. Other than that, I've been talking to all the old-timers here about finding an easier way to make a road trip up to the forest mesa, but they all said the two-week ride was all they knew about. I've been staring at those cliffs all day to see if I can envision a route, but it's impossible. I've got nothing. What about you two? Any ideas?"

"Stuart could tell you about a *cliff*, but I don't think he will." Tavaci grinned.

Colton looked at Stuart, puzzled.

"I'll explain it to you some other time," Stuart said, rubbing a hand over his face. "We had pretty much the same results as you. But, to make sure I understand this, Amber and some men take a two-week ride to the top of the mesa, they mark trees to be cut down, they drop them with axes and saws, cut them into eight-foot sections, load them on a wagon, then bring them down on another two-week ride to a sawmill in Saint George. Have I got that right?"

Colton nodded.

"I've said it before, she's gorgeous and has a lot of fire inside her, but to me that sounds absolutely crazy. What a waste of time."

"You keep thinking about the Cascade Range in Oregon," Colton said. "Lots of trees up there, lots of sawmills, and lots of men to work in the timber. This place is different. The homesteaders need the wood for sure, it just takes forever to get it. But there *must* be a way to make this more efficient and profitable. I just haven't thought of—" He stopped in midsentence, stood up, and looked out past the two men.

Tavaci turned, looked up the trail, leaned forward, and squinted. "Somebody's riding up the path, but I don't know who. He is too far away."

"It's not a *he*," said Colton, "it's Amber."

"How could *you* tell who that is from this far?" Stuart asked. "Even Tavaci can't see that well. You must be expecting her."

"I had no idea she would be coming here today, or why. But it's easy to see her and her Buckskin, Banner."

Stuart leaned forward and strained to see the image, but he still could not identify it.

"Sometimes the heart can see farther than the eyes, my friend," Tavaci admitted to Stuart. "I think he is right." He turned to Colton and warned, "I hope you know what you are doing. She can either be the greatest blessing that ever happened to you, or the most painful defeat you will ever suffer."

Stuart's head remained still, but his eyes shifted over to Colton. He smiled and said, "It's getting late. Maybe Tavaci and I will go into town for the rest of the day . . . or longer." He continued to stare at him, but Colton was transfixed on the rider. "Umm, Colton? Did you hear me?"

"Huh? Yes, you're going to rest . . . for a long day," Colton mumbled.

"What? Look at my face for a minute and watch me speak. It's like you're in a trance."

Colton reluctantly turned away from watching the rider to focus on Stuart.

"Everyone knows that men are visual. They are interested in what they can see, what they are attracted to, and she is certainly attractive. But what kept you going beyond her looks to build a relationship with her in the first place?" Stuart asked.

Colton thought for a moment, reflecting back to years ago. "She has a soft, gentle voice: the kind that puts babies to sleep, quiets squabbling toddlers, and takes the fight out of men. I fell in love with her laughter too. She was unashamed to laugh at humor, yet she never laughed at the expense of others. I wanted to spend my whole life listening to that soft voice and the music of her laugh."

"You fell pretty hard back then, didn't you?" Stuart asked, but it was a question that he already knew the answer to.

Tavaci nodded. "Yes, he did. And it is strange how one misunderstanding can ruin things for such a long time. It makes me wonder if that isn't what happens to the leaders of nations."

As they pondered that remark, Amber drew near and shouted, "I knew you would be here, but I didn't know I'd be so lucky to meet all three of you at once." She smiled as she dismounted, tied Banner to a tree, and strolled toward Colton.

All three men were on their feet holding their hats. "Hello, Miss Duncan," Stuart and Tavaci said in unison. Colton just stared at her.

"Cat got your tongue, brother?" Tavaci asked Colton, grinning. "Or was it that old cougar?"

Colton blinked himself back to reality. "Hello, Amber. You look beautiful today."

"Why . . . thank you, Colton," she replied as she tried to hide a blush. "What have you three men been doing the last couple of days?"

Stuart jumped in, "Colton insisted that we try to find a possible route for a new road up to your forest."

"You men don't have to do that."

"Colton wanted to do it *for* you, and *against* Ethan."

She stared into the faces of each of them. "Nobody else has ever offered to do—"

Colton interrupted, "I told you before, I would do anything for you. I just haven't finished yet."

"So what did you discover?" she asked excitedly.

All three of them looked downward.

"Nothing," said Colton. "We would need all kinds of road building equipment and dynamite to blast up the side of one of those mountains. And it would take forever."

Her shoulders slumped forward in a moment of despair. But she soon stood straight and declared, "I don't how this is going to work, but somehow there will be a quicker way to get timber down from the mesa to all those people who need it . . . and without bowing down to Ethan's rules."

"It's been a couple of days since I've seen my family," said Tavaci. "I'll ride with Stuart to the Big Rock Cabin on my way home. And I think you two should spend the rest of the evening together, you know, to figure a solution."

"I agree," added Stuart. "I'm tired from all that riding and peering over canyon rims. Let's take a break until tomorrow."

Colton smiled and raised his eyebrows at Amber. "Sounds good to me."

She stared openmouthed at him, but couldn't respond.

"It's one way to know for sure, young lady," Tavaci said to Amber.

"About what?" she asked.

"Another fifteen years."

There was no smile on her face, but it was obvious she was thinking.

"Let's try it," Colton suggested. "I know a place—"

"The gun-sight hill?" she asked.

He smiled. "Unless you know a better place."

"Do I know this place?" asked Tavaci.

"No," Colton said. "I only took Amber there, a long time ago. It was kind of *our* place."

The three of them stared at her, waiting for a decision.

"All right, Mr. Grey," she finally agreed. "I haven't been back to that place since you left. I wonder if it has changed at all."

Tavaci chuckled. "Sounds like the perfect place to talk about building roads." He turned to Stuart and winked. "Come on, let's get going so these two can solve the unsolvable problem." They tipped their hats, mounted up, and rode off toward the cabin.

"Do you remember how to get there, Colton?" Amber asked as they mounted their horses.

"I could never forget *our* place, Amber."

"I'm surprised that you never took Tavaci there. It was always amazing to me."

"I always felt it was our private, special place. Have you taken John Lewis there?"

"No."

"Why not?"

"Because I didn't want . . . just because." She closed her eyes for a moment, then looked away. "Let's not talk about him right now. I have a big problem to solve or some land to sell."

They mounted their horses and rode quietly for two hours. As they rode, they periodically sneaked looks at each other along the way. If their eyes accidentally met, they quickly acted as though it was an accident and would stare off at the horizon.

As they rode up a dry streambed, they saw the landmark for their destination: A huge, coral-pink, dish-shaped formation up on a mountainside to the north. It was the future birthplace of what would eventually be an immense, majestic arch. They stopped the horses and gazed at the magnificent scene.

Colton was astonished, as though it was his first visit to this site. "I know I've been here before, but it is breathtaking to see again. I wonder how long it will take before the stone breaks away and forms a beautiful arch. A thousand years?"

"I don't know. How much time do you have?" Amber smiled.

"As much time as you'll give me," Colton said, turning to look at her intently. "I'll take a thousand if it's with you."

She blushed and turned away. "We're almost there."

"You really *do* remember this place."

"Yes," she said softly. "Petroglyphs should be off to our left, and a dozen connected pools and spillways up ahead. I wonder if there would still be canyon tree frogs in those pools."

"I think we should stay around here until dusk, so we can hear them sing."

"Do you think it will take us that long to design some solutions to the road problem?"

"I certainly hope so," Colton said.

He stared into her eyes, and this time she didn't look away.

"Colton," Amber said. "John and I—"

"You said we were not going to talk about him. Agreed?"

". . . All right."

They stopped near the first pool where they dismounted and smiled at each other. Colton unsaddled Banner, then the Appaloosa. He pulled the bridled face close to his, "Listen, Wichanpi, stay around that water and grass." Then he looked at Amber. "I think they'll both be fine. For some reason I trust him. Will you lead them both over to the water? I'd like us to go up to the Gunsight notch, but I have something to do first."

"Why should we go up there, Colton? Why don't we just stay here in this area close to the pools? It's like a big amphitheater."

"Memories," he said. "And the view is unbeatable, you have to admit that."

She squinted at him. "For the view then."

Amber led the horses over to the pools, where they immediately began to drink. After fifteen minutes she left them and went back to where Colton had been, but he was nowhere in sight. She was about to call his name when she noticed that red Indian Paintbrush flowers had been picked and placed in a line leading up the hill to the Gun-sight notch.

Why would he do that for me? she wondered. *Nobody does things like that for me.* She noticed that her heart was beating just a little faster as she put her hand on her chest. *What's happening here? I haven't even started up the hill yet.*

She bent down and picked up the first flower, then proceeded up the wavy, sandstone hill, picking up blooms every twenty feet. As she approached the tall, solitary Hoodoo column near the top, she noticed there was a small pile of yellow Wallflowers and orange Columbine added to more Paintbrush blooms. As she knelt to pick them up and smell their magical scent, Colton walked from behind the Hoodoo and offered his hand to lift her up.

"Here, put all the flowers in my hat," he said, offering his hat with his other hand. "I'll carry them and help you to the Gun-sight."

She put the flowers in his hat and grabbed his hand, but as he lifted her, he dropped the hat and pulled her in close. The embrace was magnetic and long overdue. They pressed against each other from head to toe, and neither of them wanted to separate for the longest time.

She looked up at him and gasped, "Colton, if you don't kiss me, I *will* kiss you."

He pulled his head back to gaze into her eyes. "Those glorious colors are found nowhere else on earth."

She glanced at the ground, not expecting that compliment. Her long lashes simply accented the colors when she looked up at him again. His fingers softly traced her eyebrows, then stroked both cheeks until they met at the back of her neck.

She shook her head and whispered, "Colton, I—"

"Shhhh, don't." He slid his hands down to her back and pulled her close so that their faces were only inches apart. His eyes now locked onto hers in an almost hypnotic gaze. She tried to escape the intensity by closing her eyes, but he leaned forward and kissed her eyelids.

"Colton, please, I—"

"Shhhh, wait."

She took a small breath and was about to speak again, but she was starting to relax in his embrace.

His left arm slid up behind her neck as his right hand pulled her waist closer to him. "Amber, I—"

"Shhhh, don't," she whispered.

The kiss was soft at first, lips barely touching. Then he kissed her gently along her cheek, down her neck, and up to her ear as he whispered her name. He ran his fingers through her hair until his hands met behind her head as he kissed her with more passion. She was breathing hard. He could feel her heart beating fast and strong. Or was it his?

Maybe this was the fire that Chitina warned me about on the ship, he thought.

She whispered a soft, "Ohhh," and closed her eyes again.

The next kiss was like an electric current that rippled through their bodies. It was as if they had melted into one person. After a minute passed, they looked into each other's eyes, and once again embraced.

"Colton, I . . ." She sighed and tried to catch her breath.

"I know, I know. Too fast." He released her and took a step

back. He shook his head and looked at the sky. "I couldn't help it. I just feel like I've been living in a cave for so many years." He looked deep into her eyes again. "Now you brought me back into sunlight . . . and you have the most beautiful eyes I have ever seen."

She smiled, but then glanced back down the hill to where she had picked up all the flowers. "I think we need to slow down a little. Remember I'm enga—"

"You keep reminding me. But you need to know I don't care anymore."

"What?"

"I'm not losing you again."

"Like I'm some kind of prize?" She grinned. "What do you do if you don't get your way? If you don't win?"

"If it's worth the fight, I'll try even harder . . . until I win," Colton said, determination fired in his eyes. "It's not going to be easy, but I won't give up. And I want you every day, young lady, more than anything in the universe. If I stay here, it's with you. If I leave here, it's with you. You and me . . . every day." He paused to look at her. "So I'm asking you to take my hand and go up to the Gun-Sight Notch so we can talk, just the two of us, for as long as it takes. No John Lewis, no Ethan Morley, no road to the forest . . . just about us." He held out his hand and waited.

She looked at his outstretched hand, then up at the notch where two fifteen-foot tall rock formations formed a perfect "V" against the sky. "I thought we were coming on this ride to figure out a way to create new access to my timberland," she said thoughtfully, "But, then again . . ." She placed her hand in his and smiled. "All right, let's go talk."

Climbing the hill was effortless for him now. He could have picked her up and run to the top. But he led her carefully up to the crest where they saw hundreds of tiny, sandstone balls strewn across their path. "Moquis marbles. The amazing work of water, wind and time," he said as he picked up three of them and placed them in her hand. "*Three* was our number."

"Yes . . . it was."

He put his arm around her and guided her south toward the Notch. "Another hundred yards and we'll be there," he said.

"But what about the stone window?" Amber asked.

"You remembered!" Like a child waiting to open an elegantly wrapped gift, Colton ran and pulled her along toward a thin, eight-foot-tall sandstone column that had a bushel-basket size opening in the middle. "All right, put your head through the window and pose for a photo."

"But you didn't bring a camera," she laughed.

He went around to the other side and looked through the window, "Well, then just pretend. Come on, be the beautiful model." He grinned.

Amber pranced playfully to the window and leaned forward. "A model, you say?" She smiled, pursed her lips, and fluttered her eyelashes.

Colton's smile vanished immediately. He was stunned for a second, then placed his hands softly behind her head and kissed her even more passionately than before. She didn't pull away but responded by leaning into him even closer.

After a moment, Colton leaned back just to look at her face again. "Well . . . that went from playful to—"

"I know," she gasped as she pushed away from the column. "I was lost for a minute, and I . . . we should get back to playful, don't you think?" Her face radiated innocence as she strolled into the vertex of the Notch. "Um, what's your favorite color?"

Colton stood there silently with a puzzled expression. "My favorite *color*?" he wondered aloud as he caught up with her.

"Yes, come on, we're supposed to talk."

"It's green. Do I win a prize?"

"Why green?'

"A few reasons, I guess."

"Let me hear them."

He winced as he tried to figure out the reason for the question. "I like the way it accents the red sandstone," he said.

"Come on. What else?"

"There are more shades of green than any other color," he continued. "It's the most welcome color in the Spring. Umm, the mountains in Oregon and Alaska look like they're garnished with emeralds. How's that?"

"Not bad. But I'll bet there's more." She stopped walking and looked deep into his eyes.

He paused a moment, then added, "It's the color in the *center* of the rainbow. It gives a broad range of light to all the plants that need it."

"Ooooh, science time," Amber teased.

"You asked, I answered," Colton shrugged. "Now, what's your favorite color?"

She leaned her head back and laughed as she shook her head and ran her fingers through her long hair. "Ohhh, I think my favorite is . . . *wild.*"

He smiled at her answer but he couldn't stop himself from staring at her dark-brown hair. He put his hand under the long tresses and let them fall back into place as though he had stroked a harp. "Look how the sun brings out the shades of red, and auburn, and gold, and—"

"Why do you see these things? Why do you see the different colors in my hair and in my eyes? Nobody else does."

"Because I am fascinated by you," he said. "I always have been. I don't understand how so many beautiful things can be part of one person. You're like a living art gallery." He leaned down and picked up a small, twisted branch. "You know, this magic wand could change any of your features so that you would be physically *perfect.* Would you like to guess how I would use it?"

Her smile disappeared. "Yes," she said, imagining all the flaws he might see in her as she scanned her body down to her feet. "What would you, and the *magic* wand, change?"

Colton stared deep into her eyes and he tossed the branch over the cliff. "I would throw the wand away because I wouldn't *change* anything about you."

She cocked her left eyebrow into a questioning arch. "Not a single thing?"

"Nothing," he said, but his eyes darted away for just an instant.

"There *is* something," she gasped. "I *knew* it. Are you afraid to tell me? Go ahead. I can take it."

"Amber, you're the most beautiful woman I have ever seen, ever dreamed of. It's just—" He shook his head and looked downward.

"This isn't helping our relationship, Colton!"

"And neither is *this*," he said as he grabbed her left hand and pointed at the ring.

She looked at the ring, pulled her hand back, then gazed toward the horses near the pools five hundred feet below them. "Looks like Wichanpi is taking good care of my Banner."

"He's doing his job, just like I will do mine. I would do anything for you. Even die for you, if needed."

She turned and faced him in surprise. "Let's hope that things never come to that."

"Who knows what the future will bring. I just want you to be safe and know that I'm always near. It won't be like before."

Amber looked down at her hands and sighed. "Strange how we trap ourselves between the clutches of sadness for yesterday and the fears of tomorrow."

"That's not what tonight is about," Colton insisted. "You can't expect problems to vanish. Life is complicated at best. We both have big decisions to make before we run out of time."

"What do you mean, run out of time?" she asked.

"Sooner or later, time wins," he said. "It only guarantees us minutes and will rob us of the ones we never used. Nobody knows how much time they get. We need to enjoy life while we can. And I need to do it with you. It would probably seem like this is moving way too fast to someone who didn't know us and thought this was our first meeting. But it's taken a long time to get back to this hilltop with you."

"But I think of the years we could have been—"

"Don't think about the love we missed in the past. Just think about the love we aren't sharing now, and what we're going to do about it. We've learned a lot since we were kids, but I'll wager our dreams and goals are still the same."

She looked down at her ring again, twisted it on her finger, and glanced at the sun setting on the horizon.

"The day is gone Amber, and left us behind. Perhaps, if we wait quietly, it will return. Sit with me here, and we'll ask Orion to chase it back to us."

"Orion?" she asked. "Every time I saw that constellation I would remember you telling me that the three stars in his belt meant *I love you*." She closed her eyes and turned away. "Do you know what that was like to see those stars while you were gone?"

"Yes, I know. We were looking at the same stars, from hundreds of miles apart. I even had Orion painted on my ship so I—"

"Colton," she sobbed, "do you know how many times I wondered where you were, and what happened to you? I missed you so much . . . until I gave up, and surrendered to whatever fate was going to overtake me. I just didn't care anymore."

"It was the same for me, only I used my time to get money and control people in order to wipe out my visions of you and Ethan."

"There was no me and Ethan."

"I know that now." Colton sighed. "But now there's you and—"

Amber placed her finger across his lips. *"Don't."*

Colton smiled, put his arms around her, and pulled her close as he kissed her again. It wasn't a kiss of seduction. It was the kiss where two hearts are bound together.

As Amber began to relax his embrace, she pulled him in even closer. She sighed and pressed her head against his chest. "Now I have two problems. The road and . . ."

"Don't," he said as he placed his finger across her lips. They shared a brief smile, then returned to a gentle embrace.

"I suppose you're right," he said after a long moment of comfortable silence. We really ought to think about those two problems you have."

She turned to face the setting sun but stayed within his arms. "Solving problems should never be more important than loving others," she said. "I think it would be wonderful to sit here at the Gun-sight and watch Orion chase the daylight back to us."

Colton smiled, took her hand, and they sat huddled close together. He looked up to where the first stars were appearing. "If the heavens made a diamond for every time I have thought of you . . . the whole universe would sparkle forever."

Amber remained silent.

"What are you thinking about?" he asked.

"I was thinking that you never said goodbye when you left years ago," she answered. "I missed hearing that so much. And now, I don't *ever* want to hear your goodbye. Ever. You are my summer rain."

They sat quietly, enjoying the sounds of silence for two hours. Then Orion made his appearance in the Eastern sky, the three stars in his belt glowing at them. As if cued by a stage prompter, they both looked at each other and simultaneously said, "I love you." They kissed again and embraced each other throughout the night.

41

The Spider

THE MORNING SUN was just beginning to shine on the cabin as Colton rode up and tied Wichanpi to the rail. He stroked the horse's head and pulled it close to his. "Well, my big friend, how can I help Amber and her timber problems? I'm afraid this one's got me beat." The horse playfully nodded its head as though it understood. Colton smiled. "Thanks for the vote of confidence." He stroked the Appaloosa's neck, then stepped up on the porch and sat in a wooden chair next to the railing.

From inside the cabin came a yawn that sounded like a bugling elk. The door soon opened and Stuart let out another loud yawn as he came outdoors wearing nothing but his pants.

Colton was dumbfounded. "Good grief man. Are you trying to start a rockslide?"

"Huh?" Stuart stretched. "Did you just get here? Where have you been all night? Oh, I remember. So did she stay with you all this time? Not that it's any of my business, but—"

"Yes she did, and you're right. It's none of your business." Colton slapped his thighs. "So why am I sitting here? This is tearing me apart, and I am tired of it. How does a man convince a lady who belongs to someone else that he would do anything for her, that her happiness means more than his own, and that he loves her? Can she deal with this and live happily knowing that two men love her and that the guy who *isn't* her *official* partner loves her more than she could ever imagine?"

Stuart stared at him. "I can't answer those questions, but I assume that nothing *happened* between you two."

"You know me better than that," Colton said with a glare. "I care for her too much to do anything stupid."

"That's what I expected. It's the kind of person you are. I hate to ask, but did you come up with any solutions to the road or timber problems?"

Colton shook his head slightly. He opened his mouth to speak, but then closed it and looked at the ground.

"Yeah, didn't think so."

"Look, I thought about it when I held her all night, trying to figure how to save her way of life. I thought about it after I took her home, and for the entire ride back here. I just don't see a way to beat Ethan. It looks like he's going to win again."

"What?" Stuart asked, surprised. "I've never heard you give up before. You're going to raise a white flag in front of this beautiful lady? She didn't quit when *you* left. She didn't give up while taking care of *your* father. This is just another problem. *Something* will happen that will open a window for you and this thing will get resolved so that everybody lives happily ever after. You're a Renaissance man. Sometimes you think you've exhausted every possible solution, but rest assured that you haven't. Remember the Gold Rush, salmon canneries, logging in the Cascades, your ships? Any one of those issues was bigger than this Ethan guy will ever be. You're not a quitter. You might be just one thought away from solving this whole thing."

"I know that complaining never fixed anything. I know we have to *do* something." Colton closed his eyes for a moment, then said, "Stuart, we need a Suez Canal."

"A what?"

"A shortcut. You know, like from the Mediterranean Sea to the

Red Sea so ships don't have to sail all the way around Africa. Taking two weeks to bring timber down from the mesa top to this valley is crazy. There has to be a short cut . . . somewhere, somehow." Colton began tapping his fingers impatiently on the arm of the chair.

"If you're tapping your fingers, you can't roll up your sleeves and get to work," Stuart advised. "Trust me, you'll think of something. You always do."

"And what if I don't? There's no place for a Suez Canal in these mountains!" Colton shouted. "I've been working on this for days, but . . ." He opened his mouth to say more, but no words came. He shook his head and looked toward the river.

"You like to quote people all the time. Here's one for you. Henry Ford said, 'Whether you think you can, or think you can't . . . you're right.' Guess I'll finish getting dressed." Stuart patted Colton's shoulder on his way into the cabin.

Colton nodded but continued staring toward the river. Frustration took its toll as he threw his hat on the floor, put his hands behind his head, and tilted his chair back against the wall.

Looking upward he saw a large spider descending on its silk thread from the roof edge down to the porch railing.

"You're safe, spider," Colton said. "Stuart won't stomp on you as long as you're not in the house."

The spider crawled down to the bottom of the railing and repeated its descent to a branch of a nearby Manzanita bush, where it began the process of spinning a web.

"Persistent little guy aren't you?" Colton chuckled, then leaned forward and brought the chair down on all four legs as a thought struck him. His eyes widened as he yelled, "Of course!"

The shout brought Stuart outside as he was tucking in his shirt. "What's all the yelling about?"

"I think I've got it," Colton said as he picked up his hat and untied Wichanpi.

"Wait a second. Got *what*? What are you thinking? Where are you going?"

"I can't tell you until I know it will work," Colton said as he swung up onto the saddle.

"Hold on, I know it takes a lot to figure solutions to problems, but when friends are around you're supposed to share it *aloud!*"

"I have two main rules when it comes to business. The first is *never* share everything you know."

"What's the second rule?"

"To read the first rule."

"You can't be serious! At least wait for me so I can go with you and learn about this new plan."

"You don't even have your boots on . . . and your shirt is inside out."

"When you shouted I got flustered and—"

"I've got to hurry, Stuart. This might take all day. I'll see you before dark." A soft heel to Wichanpi's flanks, and they raced away toward the main canyon.

"Sometimes that guy drives me—" Stuart muttered to himself as he shook his head and looked up the road in the opposite direction to see dust rising. "Well, looks like I have a visitor." He quickly fixed his shirt and sat on the steps to pull on his boots just as Amber rode up.

"Good morning, Stuart," she said with a smile that would melt the sun.

"Good Amber, morning. I mean morning good to you. Ah, you know what I mean."

Her smile now created small dimples in her cheeks, which made her even more alluring. "May I dismount?"

"Yes, of course." Stuart jumped up to help her off her horse.

She climbed up the stairs and knocked on the door.

"Umm, Colton isn't here," Stuart said, holding the reins of her horse.

She paused. "Where is he?"

"Did he know you were coming to the cabin?"

"No."

"Of course he didn't." Stuart sighed. "He certainly would have waited for you had he known."

"I admit it was a sudden urge to come see him. Where did he go?"

"I wish I knew. He had a sudden flash of light hit him with an idea that might solve your problem. I've seen that look on his face before, and amazing things usually follow soon after. But, if you're not in a hurry, maybe we can get better acquainted."

"That would be nice," she said as she leaned against the railing. "I can stay for a little while, but I do have to go help at the store soon.

"Maybe you and I can put together the puzzle pieces of Colton's life to come up with a clearer vision of who he really is."

"You think he is a mystery?" She smiled.

"You know a lot about him before he left for the Northwest, and I know what he did for the last fifteen years."

"Yesterday is interesting Stuart, but today and tomorrow are a lot more valuable," Amber advised. "I'll make it simple. He had a tough life with a father who worked him hard. He misunderstood my connection to Ethan Morley. Ethan's cohorts bullied him. He left. Wouldn't you?"

Stuart nodded.

"He won't say much about what he did with you up north," she continued. "I was lucky to have seen his name in a newspaper about his ships in the Inside Passage or I never would have known where he went. So I contacted him about his father's poor health. I guess I was a little late with that information."

"He stumbled into me by trying to save another man's life," Stuart offered.

Amber smiled. "That sounds like him."

"He wasn't just a hard worker. He had ideas. Lots of ideas. And all of them were golden. He's a genius. He's like a guy walking around with . . . a paintbrush, looking for a canvas to create a masterpiece . . . or a pen, looking for paper to write classics. Do you know what I mean?"

She gazed at the horizon and spoke softly. "I know what you mean."

"It's frustrating when a guy acts like he knows it all, but it's even worse when he actually does. And yet, he was humble about it all. He would always say when he failed, it was his fault, but when he succeeded, it was due to the help of others."

"I don't care how famous he is," Amber said. "I knew him before all of that, and he was always in my mind somewhere. I think Tennyson said it best: 'If I had a flower for every time I thought of him I could walk through my garden forever.'" She blushed. "Sorry . . . I didn't mean to get poetic."

"You quote great writers, just as he often does," Stuart chuckled. "So, now I wonder why you are connecting with him after this long? It couldn't have been strictly about his father's health. You must have had a lot of other men after you. You're too beautiful not to have had that happening all the time."

"Yes, there were others who chased me," Amber admitted with a sigh. "But none of them was a good fit, and I'd rather be alone than have a bad partner. So I waited, hoping that maybe Colton and I would connect again someday. He was the only hope I had left. I told him last night that he was my summer rain. It was the only thing that kept me here, kept me in the fight. Just because he was gone doesn't mean the love vanished. His absence was to my love like sunlight is to plants; it withers the weak but enhances the great. But the years kept adding up until I finally couldn't . . ." She trailed off.

"You don't have to explain."

"Oh, but I do." Amber sighed. "I'm engaged to John Lewis now. And I don't know what to do."

Lewis gave her an appraising look. "I can tell by looking at your face and listening to Colton talk about you. If you marry this Lewis guy, you might have a lot of kids and have the appearance of a good marriage. And you're the kind of person who would try to make it work because of your children. But when the quiet times come, when you're all alone, you would know that you should have been with Colton from the beginning. You will justify your situation because that's just the way it worked out. You'll tell friends and family that you have a good situation when, in fact, it *could* have been perfect." Amber stared at him. "So I'll ask you a theoretical question and reverse things. If Colton had remained here, and John Lewis came alone, and they both asked you to marry them, would you have chosen Colton instead?"

"In a heartbeat."

"There's your answer, Missy. You're formally attached to somebody, but the *perfect* relationship just rode up that canyon. You know *what* to do, you just have to figure out *how* to do it."

She pushed away from the railing, sat on the steps, and grabbed Stuart's hands. "But they're both good men, and John asked first. I wouldn't know *how* to tell either of them that I am choosing the other."

"I have a feeling something will happen to help you with that choice. Look at the bright side of this. You have *two* men who love you. Think of the many women in the world who have nobody."

She stared at the ground, then closed her eyes for a moment. "Maybe you're right. Something will happen to let me know what to do. Maybe Colton will have an idea when he returns, but right now I need to help at the store." She stood up and mounted her horse.

"Like I said, he's a great idea-man."

"What's the point in having great ideas if you can't put them into action?"

"That's what he's doing right now. And I ask you the same question."

She pursed her lips, nodded her head, and started her horse galloping toward town.

42

The Appaloosa Solution

WHOA, BOY. SLOW down, Wichanpi," Colton said as he gently pulled back on the reins. He looked upward over his right shoulder. "I can see the trees growing along the top of the East mesa. Yeah, plenty of trees right up there, and that's also Amber's land. Very convenient. Now we just have to figure the best place to . . ." He stopped when he realized he was talking to a horse.

He concentrated on closely inspecting the sides of the cliffs as he rode along. *Somewhere,* he thought. *Somehow.*

Colton was on a mission, riding slowly like he was in some kind of hypnotic trance, searching every crevice, ledge, and boulder for the access point he needed to accomplish his idea. He slowed Wichanpi down to a walk. It was quiet now. Only three sounds could be heard as he approached the halfway point up the canyon: the gentle current of the Virgin River; the soft, descending song of a Canyon Wren; and his horse's hooves on the sandy trail. As the canyon widened to several hundred yards, Colton became intently focused on a two-thousand-foot tall mesa to the East. The face was basically smooth from the top nearly to the canyon floor. He was so intrigued by this cliff-side that he didn't notice Wichanpi walking directly toward a low branch of a Canyon Maple. The horse ducked his head as he went under the branch, which then struck Colton in the stomach and swept him off the saddle. Colton crash-landed on the ground. He gasped for air as he lay on his back with eyes closed and hoped that he hadn't broken any bones from the fall.

The horse turned, came over to Colton, and nuzzled him over on his side to face the bottom of the cliff. "Wichanpi," he wheezed as he spit some sand out of his mouth. "Why in the world did you—" then he noticed the horse staring at the same cliff that he had been watching. At the base were three small carvings of big-horn sheep chipped into the sandstone wall. A six-ring spiral was carved just above the sheep.

Glancing back at Wichanpi, he squinted. "No. You *couldn't* have known about this. You're a horse. I'll just consider this as a painful, and fortuitous, situation." He grunted a bit as he rolled to his hands and knees, then grabbed a stirrup to pull himself up to his feet. One more gasp for fresh air, and he limped over to the carvings. He arched his back to stretch, then led Wichanpi over to a fresh-water spring garnished with maiden-hair ferns and shooting star flowers. "Stay here, my friend. And I'm using that term cautiously right now."

Leaving the horse to drink, he walked to the sloping base of the cliff where he noticed that there were narrow ledges running diagonally upward and extending halfway up the mesa. "This could be it," he whispered as he climbed along the first ledge until he was five hundred feet above the valley floor. He stared at the top of the mesa, then back at the valley floor, and repeated that up and down scanning three times. "If I could get up to that saddle between the cliffs . . . Yes, indeed," he shouted. "This *will* work!"

He carefully picked his way back down the ledge to the valley floor, where he grabbed Wichanpi's reins and swung up onto the saddle. "No walking this time boy. It's time to put this idea on paper and change the lives of nearly everyone in this area." A kick to the flanks sent the two of them racing back toward the cabin.

43

The Plan

COLTON SHOUTED AS he rode up to the cabin, "Stuart, get your boots on, we're going to town to get some supplies."

Stuart frowned, pointed down at his boots, and shrugged his shoulders. "Way ahead of you. What's this all about?"

"I think I've got it."

"Got what?"

"The way to beat Ethan and get timber down to the valley folks faster than ever. But I want to draw it on paper and build a small model first."

"I haven't seen you this excited since, well, since you laid eyes on Amber when we first arrived," Stuart chuckled. "And, by the way, she was here about two hours ago."

"She was? What for?"

Stuart shook his head. "And people say there's no such thing as a stupid question."

Colton smiled. "Maybe good things are coming my way all of a sudden. Let's go."

Stuart mounted his horse and they raced the five miles to Springdale.

As THEY PULLED up to the store, Stuart's curiosity overcame him. Colton attempted a detailed explanation about the use of pulleys, stanchions, and cables, but he noticed Stuart was distracted.

"Hey, did you even listen to what I said?"

"Well, that's a strange way to start a conversation."

"What? *Start* a conversation? I've been trying to explain my plan for five minutes. Don't you see?"

"Look, my eyes are wide open but *no* . . . I . . . don't . . . see. What in the world are you talking about? And what does the store have that will help you solve this mystery?"

"Spools of thread, paper, some pencils, and personal connections to the owner of a sawmill."

"And *those* supplies will solve the problem?"

"No, but they'll help me visualize what I need to do. I know it will work."

"Is there anything you don't know?"

"My friend, the more I learn, the more I realize I *don't* know, and I didn't even know I didn't know it."

"Huh?"

"Nobody knows everything. I can use all the help I can get." They tied their horses to the rail, walked into the store, and saw Amber working behind the counter. "Shhh," said Colton, "she didn't see us come in." He walked quietly behind her and put his hands over her eyes. "Guess who?"

She smiled and whispered, "Orion."

"Correct," whispered Colton.

"Oh, Colton, I have a wonderful surprise to tell you."

Stuart rolled his eyes. "All right, you two, no surprises right now. Colton needs some supplies to bring his plan to action."

The smile left Amber's face as she turned to Colton. "You have a plan for the timber and the road? But I need to tell you that—"

"Well, it's just a plan now," Colton said. "But I need a piece of paper about one square foot, a dozen pencils, about four feet of thread, and three empty thread spools."

"That's all? How in the world will that—?"

"No, that's not all," Colton continued. "We need a sawmill

up on your land. Either we build one, or we buy one from somebody and move it there."

As Amber gathered the supplies she said, "Just last week there was someone from Mount Carmel who wanted to sell a sawmill over there. I guess it could be moved."

"Get the name of the owner to Stuart, and I'll start designing the system we need to bypass Ethan's toll."

The mention of Ethan's toll caught the attention of John Lewis from the back room. "Did I hear someone say that there was a way to avoid Ethan's toll fees?" he asked.

"Yes," Amber replied with excitement. "Colton thinks he has a plan that can avoid the tolls and supply the farms and ranches with the lumber they need."

"Is that right, Grey?"

"Well, it's an idea," Colton replied. "I need to outline it on paper first, then see if a model will work. We're still a long way from waving a flag of victory."

"Hmm," Lewis said slowly. "Amber, I need to run to the Blacksmith shop for a minute. But I'm expecting a load of canned goods to be delivered anytime now. Will you stay here to make sure we don't miss it?"

"Certainly, John, but—"

"Thank you, dear, I won't be long," he said as he nodded at Colton and Stuart and left through the back door.

"I could be wrong," said Stuart as he watched Lewis leave the room. He glanced at Colton, "but I think he might be—"

"Yeah, you *could* be wrong," Colton said. "And I hope you are."

"What are you two talking about?" asked Amber.

"Nothing," they said in unison.

Amber squinted at them, knowing she was missing something. "Here are the things you wanted, Colton. I'm really curious to see what you're going to do with them."

"So am I," added Stuart.

Colton took the paper and drew what looked like a large number seven in the center of the page. He touched the horizontal top line and said, "That's the mesa top where the forest is. The vertical line is the side of the cliff going down to the bottom of the page which is the valley floor."

Amber and Stuart nodded.

Then he drew a small rectangle on the mesa top near the cliff's edge. He finished by drawing a diagonal line from the top of the rectangle to the bottom right-hand corner of the page. "Yes, I think this will work."

Amber and Stuart looked at the drawing, then at each other, then at Colton.

"Nice," said Stuart. "What is it?"

Colton took a wooden box and placed it on the countertop. Next, he tied the twelve pencils into an open, rectangle shape that looked like the frame of a house, and put it on the edge of the box-top. He laid a spool of thread inside the framework of pencils, took the loose end of the thread and pulled it over the top pencil at the edge of the box, then had it mimic the diagonal line of his drawing where he attached it to an empty thread spool on the counter. "There," he said, "it will work."

"Of course it will," said Amber with a smile, "but I'm still a little confused."

"Sure," Stuart agreed. "But . . . what is it, and how does it work?"

Colton grinned. "The pencils will be heavy, wooden beams built right on the edge of the cliff. The thread will be steel cable, where we'll attach loads of lumber cut in our sawmill and lower them to the bottom of the canyon floor using a pulley system. We'll replace a two-week wagon ride with a short glide down into the valley. More lumber, quicker, cheaper. And we'll avoid Ethan's toll completely."

"I understand what you're saying now." Amber nodded. "But *that* was the surprise I was trying to tell you when you first arrived."

"What surprise?"

"A local man, named David Flanigan, has designed something just like you're describing. He says he can get timber to the canyon floor in about two minutes by somehow using some steel cables. I heard some men talking about just before I came into the store. I was going to tell John, but he was a little grumpy and put me to work right away."

Colton's mouth dropped open as he stared at his model. "I've been worrying about this for a long time and Flanigan has the idea ready to go."

"He's a good man, Colton, and a hard worker," Amber reassured him. "I guess he's had this idea for quite some time. I just didn't know. I think he already has the structure being tested somewhere above the Weeping Rock area."

"That's great," said Colton. "And I was looking at a completely different mesa range. Just don't let Ethan know about this."

"Well, speak of the devil," said Amber, "here he comes now."

As Ethan opened the front door, John Lewis entered in at the back door.

"What a coincidence," Stuart quipped to Colton, who simply glanced at the two men.

Amber watched Stuart and Colton's expressions. "What's going on?" she whispered.

They both shook their heads innocently as Colton gathered the pencils and spools together.

"Well, well," barked Ethan. "You two still around here? I understand you've got some new ideas kicking around in your heads."

Stuart and Colton immediately turned to glare at Lewis, who looked at the floor.

The small pile of pencils and thread spools made no sense to Ethan. He turned his attention to the paper and reached for it, but Colton was quicker. He grabbed the paper and folded it in half.

"Got some plans drawn up there, Grey?" Ethan asked.

"I'm just writing a letter home, Morley," Colton answered. "Oh, wait, this *is* my home. Guess I won't need to do that after all." He folded the paper again and put it in his pocket.

Ethan stepped up to Colton and demanded, "I want to see that paper, Grey."

"And I'd like to fly an airplane, Morley. But neither one of those things will be happening today."

They stood a few inches apart glaring at each other with such intensity that the others in the room could feel heat rising between them.

"There's no sheriff to save you this time, Grey."

The front door swung open with such force that the windows nearly shattered. There stood Tavaci with a rifle in his hand. "I don't know exactly what is going on in here, but something did not feel right to me, so I thought I would come in to see if I could help someone." He pointed the rifle at Ethan. "Mr. Morley, I think I will help you . . . to leave . . . now."

Ethan looked at the rifle, then back at Colton. "You may be the luckiest man I have ever known, Grey."

"Yeah, my *luck* has changed for the better since I left here as a boy," Colton retorted. "And I think your luck is going to change too. But you're not going to like it, Morley. Goodbye."

Tavaci stepped out of the doorway to let Ethan pass, then closed the door.

Amber glared at Lewis. "Do you realize what almost happened here, John? And I'm sure that you're the one responsible for this situation. Why in the world would you—"

"Amber," shouted Lewis, "Morley runs this town. It's important to choose your allies wisely and—"

"You're right, John. You're absolutely right. And I'll finish with a goodbye to you."

"Look here, Amber, you had better—"

"Better what, John?" She pulled her ring out of her pocket and slammed it on the counter. "*Goodbye*, John!" She stormed toward the door.

Tavaci, Colton, and Stuart stood awkwardly for a moment, stunned by what they had witnessed. Then they decided to tip their hats farewell to Lewis and follow Amber's lead.

When they were all outside, she turned and said, "Gentlemen, I suggest we meet at the Rock Cabin first thing in the morning and see if we can help Flanigan keep his plan moving."

"Yes ma'am," the three men said in unison.

44

Sawmill on the Mesa

THE SUN HAD barely peered over the Eastern mountains when Amber rode up to the cabin.

Hearing her boots coming up the stairs prompted Colton and Stuart to jump out of their beds and nearly leap into their pants. Her pounding on the door made them bump into each other as they scurried to locate their boots and shirts.

"Coming," yelled Colton.

She could hear the muffled commotion inside and it made her smile. "Relax, boys. I'm just a little anxious to help David Flanigan get his plan underway."

The door creaked open as Colton appeared still buttoning his shirt. "No problem, we were just in there talking about who was going to do what."

She continued to smile and nodded her head to accept that explanation.

Colton walked out of the cabin and stood beside Amber on the porch.

"So, Stuart and Tavaci will ride over to Mount Carmel today to help Flanigan arrange the purchase of the Rube Jolley sawmill and get a crew to help move it near the spring, fairly close to the edge of the cliff overlooking the canyon floor," Colton explained. "You and I can start figuring out how to help Flanigan get the wire, pulley systems, stanchions, and heavy beams we'll need to build this contraption and help pay for it." He grinned. "I don't think pencils and thread will do the job this time."

Amber laughed. She walked over to her horse and pulled some bread, apples, and beef jerky out of her saddlebag. "Tavaci will be here soon. I figured we would have a little breakfast before we split up. It will probably be a few days before we're all together again."

"Did somebody mention breakfast?" asked Stuart as he came out on the porch while tucking in his shirt. Diverting attention away from himself, he pointed up the road. "Hey, here comes Tavaci. So we'll all be here with a good morning, good people, good weather, and a good plan . . . I hope."

"Maik'w, friends," Tavaci called as he rode up to the cabin. "That's good morning, Stuart," he added with a wink. "Are you ready for an adventure that will change life for everyone along the Virgin River?"

"I guess I hadn't thought about it beyond what it might do for me," said Amber. "Now I feel rather selfish."

"You? Selfish? You're the most generous person I have ever known," said Colton. "Well, you, and Stuart, and Tavaci, now that I think about it. If this works, it could help everyone around here."

"Except Ethan Morley," added Tavaci.

"You know he won't stand for this if he finds out," said Colton. "And he wouldn't have known anything about it if it wasn't for John Lew . . ." He stopped himself.

"It's all right, Colton," said Amber. "I'm through with him. And I don't trust him either. We'll have to be very careful who we talk to about this plan until things are pretty well arranged."

"Agreed." Colton nodded. "Tavaci knows a narrow trail where he and Stuart can take horses up Shunes Creek and over to Mount Carmel to help arrange the sawmill deal and have it moved to Stave Spring. There are men around who will want the work at the sawmill and help Flanigan finish building his cable system. I'll do what I can there as well. Amber will head to the base of the mountain to signal us if we need to drop another test load. It may be a while before we meet again up at the mill site."

"Thanks to you men for risking so much to help me, and the other ranchers and farmers," said Amber as her eyes became a little misty. Embarrassed, she turned away from the men and wiped away a tear.

Colton embraced her and added, "Let's thank Flanigan. That's the right thing to do."

"But I don't want to be around Ethan Morley when he finds out." Tavaci groaned.

45

Ethan Learns the Plan

THREE WEEKS HAD passed . . . the sawmill had been moved successfully to only a few miles from the edge of the cliff. The engine had been repaired, and soon men would begin cutting trees.

David Flanigan, and some men from Springdale, had fashioned the heavy framework for the pulley system on top of the cliff's edge. They experimented with different types of baling wire by attaching various tree loads and dropping them off the top of the mesa. Several attempts were failures as either the trees smashed, or the wire stretched and became dangerously thin. Some changes needed to happen for the system to work.

"Colton," Stuart said, interrupting Colton's train of thought. "Let's take a break. We've been at this for days. Let's just relax for a while."

"Relax? Soon there will be wagons coming this way loaded with cut lumber, and there are people down in the canyon who need it. There's no time to relax."

"But that's *exactly* the time you need to do it."

"Look, there are two groups of people. Those who work hard, and those who let them."

"And there are those who divide people into two groups and those who don't."

"Stuart, we have to stay on top of this. Those trial loads didn't work, so I invested in this project to help Flanigan get over three thousand feet of steel cable. It's coming in through Orderville and Mount Carmel so we don't have to haul it up the mountain. It could be here anytime now, and Ethan won't even know about it coming if it stays off his road."

"Fine, but how about a day off?"

"That's your problem, you're just not consistent."

"Hey, you can't be consistent *all* of the time."

Colton sighed, but then went back on task. "Flanigan's over at the sawmill. Go get Tavaci and come look at the braking system."

Stuart sighed but did as told. Soon, he, Tavaci, and Colton met Flanagan at the framework. They stared wide-eyed at the heavy beams bolted and lashed into place.

"What do you mean by *braking system*?" Stuart asked.

"Once a load goes over the edge of the cliff, gravity will be in charge," Flanagan explained. He walked toward the back of the framework and continued, "This brake will control the speed of the lumber so it doesn't turn into kindling down there, or kill somebody. So the wire wraps around another wheel over here at the back, and then a lever is applied to slow the wheel turning . . ."

The three men stood with their mouths open trying to visualize what Flanigan had built. Stuart read their minds. "It's not just that he knows a lot of stuff. It's his imagination that's amazing. There's a limit to how much knowledge a person can obtain, but imagination can take you right off this planet."

The men shook their heads in agreement but had no suggestions to offer.

Colton turned to comment, but he stopped and put his hands on his hips. "Well, look who is riding up here," he remarked.

They turned to see Ethan Morley, Stitch, and two other men riding up to the framework.

Ethan nodded his head, "Grey."

"Morley. I'm a little surprised to see you and your men over here. You made it real clear that nobody was ever allowed on your land. I figured you would honor that same idea."

"I go wherever I please, Grey," Ethan growled.

"Well, I guess that opens your place to visitors too," Colton mused.

"Don't ever be stupid enough to try that," Ethan seethed. "Stitch and the boys get nervous with unannounced guests."

"I'll make sure to announce it then," Colton said, then his face grew serious. "Now, what are you doing over here, *unannounced?*"

"Word got around that there was a sawmill up here somewhere, and that there was trees bein' cut at a good rate," Ethan said. "Course I hear your group only takes the big ones. I tell my men to clean out an area before they move to the next one."

"We're a little more selective than that," Colton said. "Take the big ones, but leave smaller trees behind to fill in for the future. We see no point in clear-cutting entire hillsides, like you do."

"It don't matter to me how you do it." Ethan shrugged. "Either way you'll be bringin' loads down my road and payin' to use it."

Colton and the others chose to remain silent.

Ethan eyed the group suspiciously. "So what ya got goin' on behind you over there? If that's the frame for a cabin, your carpenters must have been drunk. Stitch, you ever seen anything so slanted in all your life? How come it's taller by the edge of the cliff than it is at the back?"

"Bad planning I guess, but it will make for a great view," said Colton, who had to raise his voice due to the noise of another wagon pulling up behind him. "We'll level it up later."

"Wait a minute, what are those wheels and drums used for?"

Colton was about to answer when the young man who drove the wagon walked up behind him and said, "Cable for you, Mr. Grey."

Keeping his eyes on Ethan, Colton stuck his hand out behind his back to receive the telegram.

"Umm, Mr. Grey, *this* cable is for you."

Colton turned to face the young man. He was pointing at a wagon containing a huge roll of steel cable. Colton smiled. "Ah, the last piece of the puzzle arrives."

"What ya got there Grey?" asked Ethan.

"The end of your toll road Morley, and new opportunities for everyone down below."

Ethan glanced from the cable, to the wheels and drums, to the framework, and finally the edge of the cliff. His face became red with anger. "Grey! I'm warning you—"

"To do what?" Colton asked before Ethan could finish. "Bow down and pay you to use a road that should be free? Is that your warning, Morley?"

Ethan clenched his teeth and made two fists, but he saw more men had come to stand alongside Colton. "Think you're pretty smart don't you Grey?" he spat. "Well, I guarantee you'll pay for this. You, and everyone else up here, especially Miss Duncan."

Colton stepped toward him, but Stuart grabbed his arm when he saw Stitch put his hand on his pistol.

"Now I'm giving you and your men a warning, Morley," Colton threatened. "Stay away from Amber, stay away from me and these men, and stay away from this side of the mountain. You can change your attitude, or you can go broke. I could not care less which one you choose."

"I think your visit here is finished," said Tavaci, who was now pointing his rifle at Stitch.

Ethan took a slow, deliberate look at each of the men facing him. "I'll remember this. I'll remember this. Come on men, let's get back to *our* side of the mountain."

As Ethan and his men rode away, one of Colton's men came up to him. "You should have a drink to celebrate today!" he suggested.

"I don't drink," Colton replied. "And I quit playing cards when Wild Bill Hickock was killed."

Stuart was surprised, "What? He was shot in Deadwood twenty-five years ago. You were six years old!"

"Yeah, I was a fast learner."

"History is being made right now," another worker added.

"History is written by the winners. We haven't won yet." Colton shook his head. "Let's get this cable unloaded and get ready for Flanigan to drop the box over the edge. I'm worried that we might have miscalculated the cable length."

Tavaci cautioned, "Do not let your worries become your ruler."

"That won't happen," Colton assured him. "I know that only dead salmon stop fighting the current." He turned to the workers. "Flanigan will be here soon. You men help him get that cable spliced and wrapped around the pulley-wheels up here, then drop the other end over the edge. I'll climb down the Indian trail along the ledges, hook the cable up to Banner, and have him drag it over to the pulley-towers we built in the center of the valley floor."

"What Indian trail?" asked Stuart.

"I would have shown him," said Tavaci, "but I didn't think he would be looking for a crooked footpath going up this mountain."

"It's all right, I have either a pretty smart, or mean, Appaloosa who helped me find that trail on the canyon floor." Colton chuckled. "Give me a few hours to make it to the bottom, another hour to connect the cable to the pulley-towers, and a few more hours to climb back up and watch this contraption do its genesis run."

"We'll be right here, and this will be ready to go when you return," Tavaci said. "Be safe."

46

The Test

AMBER WAS RESTING on the grass along the Virgin River when she saw Banner suddenly turn both his ears and his head toward the pulley-towers. She stood up to see what had attracted his attention and noticed Colton checking on the towers.

"How do they look?" she yelled.

"They're perfect," Colton yelled back. "Now we'll see if Flanigan correctly figured the distance from the base of the mountain to the towers. There's got to be some slack, but not too much. Bring Banner over and we'll put him to work."

She grabbed the reins and led the horse over to him. He immediately took the reins from her hand and dropped them to the ground. Her puzzled look vanished as he embraced her and kissed her so passionately it took her breath away.

"Colton," she gasped.

"Yes?"

"Nothing," She returned his kiss just as deeply, then placed her head on his chest and held him close. "I know I've only been here in the canyon for a few days to take care of the horses and make sure the men built these pulley-towers the way Flanigan drew them up, but it feels like forever."

"It does," Colton agreed. "But if Banner can drag the cable over to the pulleys for us to hook it up, I'll climb back up the mountain to tell Flanigan it's ready to drop a test load. If it works, one of your problems will be solved."

"It will work, and the *other* problem is already solved," she said as she grabbed the reins and led the horse to the cable.

Colton checked the saddle to make sure it was secure, then put a small loop of cable over the horn and led Banner to the pulley-towers. There was no problem pulling it until the cable began to rise off the ground. The big stallion strained to reach the first tower where Colton and Amber were able to put it around the pulley. Reaching the second tower took more effort so they asked two passing riders to help Colton wrap it around the second pulley.

"Thanks for your help, men," Colton said once they were finished.

"Thank you, sir," one of the riders replied. "If this thing works, we'll owe David Flanigan and the crew big time."

"What are you names?" Colton asked.

"Leon and Brick Young," the other rider answered. "And we're glad to help."

Colton nodded. "If you men wouldn't mind waiting down here to stop our test-load at the first pulley, I will climb up the trail and tell them to send it over the edge."

The two men nodded.

"Colton," said Amber, "let me walk with you to the trailhead."

Colton smiled. "I hoped you would."

They held hands as they walked, Banner trotting along Amber's other side.

"You see," Colton said. "I didn't think this would work because of my issue with hate."

Amber looked at him. "What do you mean, *hate*?"

"I hate being away from you."

She smiled. "I feel the same. I want you to know that there is nothing grander in this lonely world than hearing the voice, and seeing the face, of the person you love."

"Oh, there's something much grander than that," he said. She tilted her head in confusion, but by then he had her in his arms and was kissing her. He stared into her eyes and said, "This will take a few hours for me to climb both ways, but I'll be back soon."

"I'll be here," she promised. "When I look at that long cable stretching all the way to the mountain top it reminds me of how telegrams can be sent all over the country."

"The telegraph won't be around much longer. You'll see," Colton said thoughtfully. "Soon they'll be speaking on telephones from coast to coast and across the seas. And I'll bet even faster ways to communicate will be coming after that. I wouldn't be surprised if people could see each other while they talked from great distances."

"Your vision of the future excites me," Amber said. "And so does the potential for this cable system. So hurry up that trail so you can hurry back down to me. I'm sure they're anxiously waiting for you."

"Don't worry," Colton said with a smile. "On-time is when I get there."

He turned to walk away while looking at her. Their hands, then fingers, touched until the last possible second.

TAVACI SAT WATCHING for Colton at the crest of the mountain trail. About twenty men, from the sawmill, those cutting timbers, and the wagon drivers, now gathered for the opportunity to witness the dropping of the first load along the new cable works.

"Here comes Colton!" Tavaci yelled as Colton came into sight.

Tavaci raised his eyebrows at Colton to indicate his curiosity about the tower-pulleys on the canyon floor. Colton simply nodded at him and continued walking to the cable framework.

"Let's not take a chance with a load of good lumber going over on our first run with this cable," said Flanigan. "I've got faith it will work, but just in case . . . bring some of those large branches over here and we'll wrap them in blankets. Miss Duncan will signal us with a flag if, and when, the load reaches the canyon floor."

Men drug branches over to the framework and wrapped them in the bedding. Then Colton and Stuart put one end of the branches into a basket that was clamped to the cable and wrapped a chain around the other end. Once it was secured, they swung it over to the front edge of the framework. Tavaci climbed on top of the framework and dangled his legs over the front edge so he could watch the load descend and tell Flanigan, the brakeman, to apply his weight on the brake lever to reduce the speed if necessary.

"What if it doesn't work?" asked Stuart.

"I can't lose. Either I win, or I learn. Are we ready?" Flanigan shouted.

Hats were waved and the men shouted, "Go!"

The brake was released and most of the men ran to the edge of the cliff. They lay prone with their eyes peering down to the canyon floor two thousand feet below and they waited to see the flag signaling a successful transport.

Colton had started counting the instant the load was released. ". . . one forty-seven, one forty-eight, one forty-nine, one—. Look! Amber is waving the flag! We did it! Two and a half minutes instead of two weeks!"

The roar from the men sounded like a choir to Colton. He and Stuart helped Tavaci down from the framework and the three of them embraced and jumped around like happy children at a party.

They ran over to Flanigan to congratulate him. "David, do you realize how you just changed everything for everyone in the canyon, and all the towns, all the way over to Saint George?" Colton asked.

"It's not just the additional wood people will have for homes and fences and such, but you've also provided jobs for a lot of men on this mountain, and who knows how many down below," Colton added. "And with the drying up of Cougar Creek, any extra money they can get will help them move water from the river to their homes and livestock. Well done."

"This took all of us, men. It wasn't just me," said Flanigan. Then he glanced at Colton and whispered, "But you had a pretty good idea too."

Colton whispered back, "Actually, it was a spider, but I'll tell it thanks."

Flanigan quirked his brow but nodded.

Colton turned back to Stuart and Tavaci. "I'm going back down to Amber to take her to her ranch," he told them. "Although my father sold all his animals, she still has a few. Can we meet at the Rock Cabin in two days?"

Tavaci nodded his head, but Stuart grinned and said, "Now about that relaxation day . . ."

Colton sighed. "What were you thinking?"

"Well, I'd love to explore one of those canyons . . . from the bottom this time," Stuart was quick to reply. "Why don't we have one last hurrah and try to find that cave you were looking for as a boy? We've got clear skies and the Cougar Creek is dry so we don't have to worry about flooding when we explore. What do you say?"

"I'd like to finish looking for the cave that Star and I tried to find so many years ago," Colton admitted. "And Cougar Creek being try brings me comfort; that may be the one good thing about it."

Tavaci's face was sober. "I don't like going into the slot canyons, partly because of Star, and . . ."

"What else?" asked Stuart.

"Let's just call it tradition."

"Come on, brother," encouraged Colton. "If it will make you feel better, I'll invite Amber to join us. You *know* I wouldn't do anything to put either of you in danger, or even my Portland partner here."

"Yeah, come join us Tav. You and I have also become like brothers now. And our names even start with letters right next to each other in the alphabet, *S* and *T*."

"In the English alphabet," Tavaci sneered, then apologized. "Sorry, I don't mean to be snappy at you. I'll talk to my pengwu', and I'll meet you at the Rock Cabin in two days to let you know." He sighed. "Sounds like the three of us are headed down to the canyon floor now. Are you going down on the footpath, Colton, or riding Wichanpi with and Stu and I down the narrow trail to avoid Ethan's men? I've got some thinking to do about this canyon hike thing."

"I'm going down the footpath," Colton answered. "It will be the quickest way back to Amber. Just take Wichanpi with you and I'll see you at the cabin."

Tavaci nodded and Colton began the long walk down the footpath.

47

Baiting the Trap

Tavaci and Stuart were riding the narrow horse trail back down to the canyon. Halfway down the trail, they saw a man coming toward them on horseback.

Stuart asked Tavaci, "Do you know that man?"

Tavaci shook his head. "No, but he looks familiar."

"Hello Injun, and Mr.," the man greeted them.

Stuart nodded in his direction, but Tavaci put his hand on his rifle stock.

"What are you two doin' ridin' down this trail?" the man asked. "Ain't you supposed to take the main road around toward Kanab?"

Tavaci just stared at him, but Stuart responded, "I thought that was only for wagons and buckboards. Tavaci here is just showing me a quicker way down to the canyon so we can take a break."

"Been workin' hard, ain't ya? So did ya get a load of lumber down that wire?"

"Yes," said Stuart. "It's going to work fine."

"Well, that will take some serious money away from my boss, Mr. Morley. Maybe I oughta ask you two for a job since he'll probably be firin' me. My name's Clem."

Tavaci remained silent, but Stuart replied again, "I don't see why not. Go up to the sawmill and ask for David Flanigan."

"I'll do that. And what kind of a break are you folks gonna take?"

"Just a little hike up—"

Tavaci put his rifle across Stuart's chest to interrupt him. "We are not sure where we are going."

"Well, I'll tell ya, since we might be workin' together, if I had a whole day off, I'd be explorin' that Cougar Creek Canyon. I ain't never had time to go up that particular crack in the rocks, but I heard it's the purtiest one in the State. And it's dry as a bone. The creek's disappeared and it looks like we got nothin' but blue skies comin' for days. But that's just a friendly suggestion. You suit yerself."

Stuart tipped his hat and smiled, astonished. "You must have read my mind. That's exactly where we're planning on hiking in two days."

"Oh, ya got others goin' with ya?"

"Just Col—"

"Maybe some others," Tavaci interrupted again, "Maybe not. We do not know for certain."

Clem suddenly developed a strange grin. "Well, that's right nice of ya ta have compney. Enjoy your ride down the trail, and have a real good time hikin' in that canyon in two days. And thanks for that job offer. I'll be seein' ya soon." He reached over and shook Stuart's hand.

"Thanks," said Stuart as the man rode past them. "Nice guy."

Tavaci was silent again as he turned to watch the man ride out of sight.

"Mr. Morley," Clem yelled as he rode up to Ethan's cabin. "I just seen that Injun and Grey's partner goin' down the horse trail instead of the wagon road. And guess what? Them troublemakers will be walkin' up Cougar Creek Canyon . . . in two days."

"Clem, you've done real good." Ethan grinned wickedly. "*Real* good."

48

A Dream, or Too Much Sun?

Finally on the canyon floor," Stuart said. "Looks like here's where we part company. I am tired, and you must be too, plus missing your family all this time." He looked at Tavaci, considering. "Tavaci, you are one of the finest men I have ever known. I'll have to talk to Colton first, but I'd like to build a cabin for you and your family up on the mountain top and ask you to help manage the sawmill and the cable works when we return to Portland."

Tavaci shook his head. "You are like my brother, Stuart, and I know your heart is good. But white men will not work for me."

"They will if we say so," Stuart argued.

"No. They won't." Tavaci sighed. "Most of them do not even want to work *with* me."

Stuart twisted his hand around the saddle horn so hard it creaked. "Look here, brother, we aren't leaving here until you and your family are—"

Tavaci cut him off. "You don't understand life here. You think America is free for all men. It is not. It never has been, and maybe never will be. I am lucky I can work at the store in Saint George once in a while to make some money. And I shoe horses and help farmers when they harvest. I even tried working in the mine, but that was a bad idea."

"I don't suppose you would come to Portland with Colton and me," Stuart said weakly.

Tavaci gave a kind smile. "This has been the homeland of my

people for generations. I cannot leave here. My blood is with the people who made those rock carvings and cliff homes I showed to you. I was born here, I live here, I will die here."

Stuart nodded. "That's how I feel about Portland. I miss Mult-nomah Falls, the Columbia River, the hotels and restaurants, the green forests everywhere, my car . . . even the rain. And Mel . . ."

"Everyone wants to be happy. Does that mean owning every-thing? No, it means being happy with your life and the things you have now. It is all right to improve, but be happy while you are doing it. You were kind to come this far with Colton, but I under-stand the love you have for this woman."

"I didn't exactly say *love* . . ."

Tavaci stared at his eyes.

Stuart looked away. "Well, maybe."

"Will Colton be taking Amber back to Portland with you?" Tavaci asked.

"We haven't talked about that, but how could he leave a girl like that behind twice? Besides, he basically is the brain that runs several companies up there. Which brings me back to you, and the sawmill and cable. What if we also hired several men from your village to work for you?"

"A red-man company?" Tavaci laughed.

"Yes, at least partly."

Tavaci stopped laughing and looked at Stuart seriously. "I will think about this, and talk to Be-Wa about it." He shook his head. "But you have a crazy idea."

"Bring her along on that canyon hike that guy was talking about. We'll have all day to discuss it."

"There is *no* way she would go into that canyon. I'm still not sure that I will either."

"Tavaci, I don't think we'll be here much longer. This might be our last chance to be together. Let's do that canyon." Stuart tipped his hat and rode his horse off toward the cabin. "See you at the Rock Cabin in two days and we'll plan that adventure."

"Goodbye, brother." Tavaci started his horse toward his village, but as he approached a little hilltop there was a beautiful native woman standing fifty yards ahead of him. She raised both hands high above her head. Tavaci pulled back on the reins and stared. "Who are you?"

The woman slowly brought her hands down, pointed at him, and shook her head from side to side, then she vanished.

Tavaci's mouth dropped open. He kicked his horse to sprint to where the woman was, but she was gone and hadn't left a single track in the sand.

"Am I so tired?" he asked aloud, "Or was that . . . ?"

49

Coaxing Tavaci

STUART CHOSE TO take a day of rest, Amber and Colton took care of their homesteads, Tavaci spent the day with his family, and those activities were all welcome diversions from their past three weeks. But then came the morning they had agreed to meet at the Big Rock Cabin to discuss what Stuart had described as their *final time together.*

Colton arrived first and walked in on Stuart. "Good morning. Wow! You're up, dressed, and ready to go. Now we just need Amber and Tavaci to join us. Are you ready for a relaxing adventure?"

"Adventure sounds good, and relaxing sounds even better." Stuart smiled. "Look, here comes Amber down the road. I still can't figure out how an average guy like you got a gorgeous, intelligent, independent, hard-working—"

"All right, all right," Colton said. "I understand. Let's just say I'm very lucky and let it go."

"She makes me evaluate myself every time I see her. I may not be that good-looking, or smart, or humorous, or talented . . ." Stuart trailed off. "I forgot where this was heading. What was the question?"

Colton laughed, "There was no question. And I certainly understand the mayhem she can create in a man's mind. But I've never seen you have trouble around women before. Well." He looked at Stuart. "Except one in Portland."

Stuart sighed. "Maybe that is my problem. Amber reminds me

of Elizabeth. They both have that long, dark hair and eyes that can hypnotize a man. I'll bet I'm just thinking of home whenever I see your Amber."

"We both need to start thinking about the trip back to the Northwest," Colton said.

"Will Amber go with you?"

"I don't know, we haven't had time to talk about that. Maybe we will when we take our long walk today." Colton stopped talking and went over to help Amber off her horse. "Hello to *my* Be-Wa. Thanks for adding beauty to our group today."

Amber smiled and immediately kissed Colton and embraced him. "I'm excited for a day where the four of us can just enjoy each other's company and some beautiful scenery as well." She looked around. "Where's Tavaci?"

"He said that he wasn't sure about going into one of the canyons, but he was *positive* that his wife would not approve of this activity," Stuart replied. "But I told him that this might be the last time all four of us would have a chance to be together for some fun."

"The *last* time?" asked Amber.

"Well, Colton and I will be headed back to Oregon soon, now that things are settled with his father, and you, and the Cable Works are going. I assumed that you'd be coming too."

"Stuart," Colton interrupted, "if there's one talent you have, it's speaking without thinking. I told you that Amber and I hadn't talked about the future yet. Don't you remember that?"

He shook his head. "I've been told that I don't listen closely enough."

"Who told you that?" Colton asked.

Stuart shrugged. "I don't remember."

Amber stared at Colton with her mouth agape. "No, Stuart," she said quietly, "we haven't spoken about anything beyond what we had to do here. Did he tell you when, where, and why we would be going?"

"Umm, well, he said that since the cable system was working, and there was this land deal in Eugene that he needed to close, and Emma was dealing with new inventory at the store, and Todd had some school math problems that needed some tutoring, and . . ." Stuart glanced over at Colton who looked completely confused. "Look Colton, I don't think I can be any clearer."

"I don't think you can either."

"Were you *planning* on taking me to Portland in the next day or two?" asked Amber.

"No plans. I already told Stuart that maybe we could talk about our future during today's hike. But I'm sure that you would like to do that privately, just as I would." He glared at Stuart.

Amber continued to stare at Colton.

"Here comes Tavaci," Stuart yelled to divert attention from himself. "I hope he can join us."

Tavaci rode up to the cabin but remained on his horse.

Stuart welcomed him, "Well, brother, come down and join us so we can keep our team together for a little fun for a change."

"My wife didn't even want to hear about exploring any of the slot canyons. I told her that you three were all leaving for Portland in the next few days, but she didn't care too much about that."

Amber glared at Colton, who raised his hands shoulder-high. "I never talked to Tavaci, or anyone else, about our plans to go to Portland," he defended. "I *promise*."

"Am I sensing a little tension here?" Tavaci asked. "Because Colton is right. He never said anything to me. It was Stuart."

"Wait a minute," Stuart defended, "I thought that was always our plan from the time we boarded the train in Portland to come down here." He shook his head. "Like Colton said, we can figure out the details on our walk." He turned to Tavaci. "You're joining us aren't you Tav?"

"I don't think so," Tavaci answered. "I saw a woman shaking her head at me, then she just vanished. I think that is a sign that I—"

"Let's not just *think* about this," said Stuart. "What did she say?"

"She did not speak a word."

"Are you feeling all right Tav?" Stuart asked. "We've all been working hard and—"

"I feel fine. I *know* what I saw."

Stuart looked at Amber and raised his eyebrows.

Amber took the hint. "Tavaci, you've been away from your family a lot, we've all been out in the sun for weeks, I know you have issues with other men in the area not respecting you or your people. Do you think that maybe—"

"I'm telling you she was there," Tavaci insisted. "It was like she was telling me *no* about something in my future."

"Describe what she looked like, brother," Stuart asked.

"She looked like . . . I do not know. I forgot." He stared intently at Colton as though *he* should know, but Colton remained silent and simply returned the stare.

"Look, Tav," said Stuart. "I agree with Amber. We've all been working extra hard for weeks. This is a chance for us to have fun and be together. Colton and Amber will be talking about joining me for a trip back to Portland any day now. And it's been the four of us working together through this whole adventure. Come with us . . . please."

"I agree, Tavaci," said Amber. "You and I are the only ones who have been close the last fifteen years. And Colton and I really haven't talked about what we are going to do. What if we really decide to go to Oregon with Stuart? That wouldn't give us time to be together much longer."

Tavaci sighed and looked at Colton. "You have not said a word, brother."

"One good thing about being quiet is that smart people won't misunderstand you," Colton said. "I know how you feel about the canyons, and, considering what happened to Star, I can understand your hesitation. But Amber's right, we haven't talked about our future plans very much. This hike would give us time, and we want to hear what you and Stuart have to say." He paused to look at Tavaci. "I'll send a cable to Cedar City as we go through town to check on the weather up north. How about if it's sunny, warm, and clear skies we go on this adventure together? Who knows, maybe we'll find a treasure cave," he added with a smile.

"There is still some confusion among you three," Tavaci agreed. "Maybe I will take the chance on joining you for this canyon hike so I can talk you into staying here instead of going north in a few days. But I want to know the weather up in Cedar City first, and you must promise to never tell my pengwu'. That means *wife*, Stuart," he added with a huge grin.

"That's fair," said Colton, "but we sure don't have those answers yet."

"You will never know all the answers," Tavaci said, "so learn to ask good questions."

"My first good question is, do you know where the entrance to this dry Cougar Creek Canyon is?" asked Stuart.

Colton and Tavaci both replied, "Yes."

Stuart flashed a huge grin at Amber and asked, "Young lady, shall we follow these path-makers into a place of adventure and scenery?"

She returned his smile and answered, "Absolutely. Thanks for joining us, Tavaci. Let's go, boys. Mount up. Let's find out about the weather in the Cedar City area and have a fun day for a change."

"Come on then," Stuart said. "Remember, the early bird gets the worm."

"Not too good for the worm, is it?" asked Tavaci. "Let's go, birds!"

50

The Abyss

A S THEY RODE through town, an excited crowd had formed. "We must look pretty good to them," Stuart said, "Colt on his Appaloosa, Amber on her Buckskin, Tavaci on his Pinto, and me on this Palomino. A dashing group for sure. Excuse me, sir," he said to a passerby, "is this crowd really that excited to see us?"

"See *you*? Everyone's excited because there are a couple of new automobiles in Saint George and everybody wants to go see *them*."

"Oh . . . of course." Stuart turned to Colton. "That's called 'being put in your proper place.'"

Colton laughed.

"I sure miss my auto," Stuart said with a sigh. "I can't wait to get back home and start driving that metal-majesty . . . and give all of you some great rides."

"While you wade in your memories, I'll go into the Western Union Telegraph Station now and send that cable to Cedar City to check on the weather," Colton said.

Stuart, Tavaci, and Amber sat on their horses patiently and waited until Colton returned waving a piece of paper.

"There's nothing but sunshine as far as the eye can see around Cedar," Colton said. "We are guaranteed sunny weather."

They all looked at Tavaci, who simply smiled and nodded.

✥

IN TWO HOURS they arrived at the mouth of Cougar Creek Canyon.

"I guess the horses will be fine here," said Colton. "We can go in for the entire day and return here before dark."

"This will be fun," said Stuart. "I've never been in one of these narrow canyons."

"Me either," added Tavaci, which caused a brief laugh from everyone.

They each brought a small pack of food, with canteens of water for the day. The group paused at the fifteen-foot wide canyon entrance.

Colton took a deep breath and asked, "Are all of you ready for this?"

Tavaci stared past Colton into the rust-colored ravine and replied, "How does one become ready for the unknown?"

"It doesn't matter now if it's a good day or a bad one. It's the only day we have right now, and there is only one path," Colton said solemnly.

Colton took Amber's hand and led her onto the dry gravel streambed. Stuart followed close behind. But Tavaci stopped at the entrance.

"What's wrong, Tav?" asked Stuart.

"I am thinking that I am not afraid to die," Tavaci replied. "Everybody dies, but not everybody lives, if you know what I mean. But wisdom should come before an event, not just after. I just wonder if I actually ever lived to do everything I wanted to do, or should have done. Dreams I never followed, or risks I never took. I guess that does not matter now." He stared up the canyon again. "Lead the way. Let us see what is in there."

After walking in a mile or so, they took a rest stop to drink and marvel at the smooth, curved sandstone walls. "That Clem was right," said Stuart.

Colton frowned at him. "Clem?"

Stuart nodded. "He was just some guy Tavaci and I met on

our way down from the Cable Works. Tavaci didn't know him, and he didn't trust him either. But he seemed like a nice guy. He said he worked for Ethan, but figured with the success of the new Cable Works that he, and a lot of other men who worked for Ethan, would be out of a job. In fact, he wondered if he might get a job at our sawmill. I told him we were going on a hike, and he said that Cougar Creek is one of the nicest ones."

Colton looked at Tavaci.

Tavaci said nothing, but his mouth was a firm line.

"I'm just saying, he seemed like a real nice guy," Stuart said defensively.

"I'll bet John Wilkes Booth seemed like a nice guy . . . to his friends," Colton said.

"Well, he was right about this hike," Stuart continued unaffected. "This canyon is spectacular. The walls look like they were made by a professional sculptor." He jabbered on and on about the canyon, and adventure, and danger, until he finally looked at Colton. "I can't believe you were yawning the entire time I was talking. Am I that boring?"

"I wasn't yawning, I was opening my mouth to make a comment, but you kept going on and on."

"I'm sorry. What did you want to say?"

"To just be quiet and listen."

After several minutes, Stuart said, "I don't hear anything."

"I know. Isn't it wonderful?"

"But I—"

"Shhh, let's enjoy it for a while."

"It is not just what your eyes look at, or what your ears can hear, but what your mind can learn," added Tavaci. "This place is dry but was probably home to many small ferns and flowers long ago. Sit and think for a while."

After ten minutes of glorious silence, Colton spoke to Tavaci,

"It's good to see that you've relaxed, brother. I see you looking everywhere. Your fear has been changed to contemplation. That's a good change."

"Speaking about change," Amber said to Colton. "Can we have a brief, but private, conversation?"

Colton paled but nodded. "Of course, let's go over to that boulder. Excuse us, gentlemen."

They strolled another fifty feet up the canyon when Amber turned and grabbed his shoulders. "Colton," she said. "I need to know your plans . . . *our* plans for the future. I don't know where Stuart even got the idea that I would join you in Portland—"

"Wait a minute," Colton interrupted. "Are you saying you wouldn't go with me? I thought we shared the same words about loving each other."

"I do love you, Colton." Amber sighed. "But love goes both ways. Do you assume that because I'm a woman I would just do whatever *you* want? I've been on my own for years now. I can take care of myself. I don't need anyone making decisions for me."

"Why are you being so defensive?" Colton asked. "We haven't even spoken about Portland. It's a great place. And you haven't even been there before." He paused, then embraced her. "I won't go up there without you. But you should give that city a chance. It's wonderful."

"I've been to a city, Colton," she said.

He nodded his head but squinted his eyes. "I see. So that's the way it is. Maybe I'll go ahead up this canyon by myself for a while. I could use the cool shade around this bend. Go on back and visit with those two. I'll talk to you soon. Let me think about this for a while." He turned away, put his hands in his pockets, and walked briskly around the bend.

❖

"Stitch, go and get a few of the men and come over here by Cougar Creek," said Ethan.

"Will do, boss."

In a few minutes, six men joined Ethan over by the dam.

"You men help me wedge this stuff between the base logs here," he said as he carried a pack full of red sticks and fuses down to the base of the dam.

"Boss, that's dynamite!"

"That's right, and one five-letter word we don't wanna hear around dynamite is Ooops. Be very careful."

"But what are we doin' with that around the dam?"

Ethan turned and glared at the men. "First, your job is to do as you're told. No questions. Second, you remember how some of you were worried about the farmers down in the valley bein' short on water. Well, I'm gonna give it to them in just a couple of minutes," he said with an evil grin.

The men looked at Stitch and asked, "Are you in on this?"

"I do as the boss says," Stitch replied. "Just like you're supposed to do."

"Do the folks down in the valley know this is gonna happen?" one of the men asked. "Will they be ready? Do they have ditches or canals dug for all this water rushing at them? I mean, you told them, right?"

"What? Course I did," said Ethan. "Didn't I, Stitch?"

"Huh? Yeah, that's right." Stitch agreed. He put his hand on his holstered pistol and said, "Now you boys get down there and pack those sticks in tight around those bottom logs. Make sure the fuses reach all the way up here to me."

Amber strolled back to Tavaci and Stuart with a scowl on her face. "Well, that didn't go very well. He's got a mind of his own, for certain. But, then I guess I do too."

"Maybe I can help explain him a little," offered Stuart. "It's like he hears voices in his head sometimes directing him into amazing business deals. I don't know how he does it. But I know sometimes he has to be alone to figure out exactly what to do next."

Tavaci leaned over to Stuart and whispered, "You know, I have heard voices in my head for years too."

Stuart glanced sideways at him.

"Yeah, I know they aren't real, but they have some good ideas." Tavaci grinned.

"Not a good time for jokes, Tav." Stuart rolled his eyes.

"I don't know," said Amber, "maybe it *is* a good time. What else were you going to say about him?"

Stuart continued. "Everyone is fascinated with the rebellious entrepreneur because they don't conform with everyone else's ideas. Yet most folks want to see him succeed. And you can't measure his worth by what he has in the bank, or what companies he runs. You have to see what he has done with his success, and how he has helped so many others. Naturally, those efforts stretch from Portland up to Alaska, not here . . . until this sawmill-cable works project was completed. And Tavaci, you need to know he has big plans to help your village. He just doesn't rest. I don't know what he is going to do next, but anything is possible if the end results are still unknown."

"It is the mark of a true friend when they remain close to you when the big problems keep you bound," said Tavaci. "He is the kind of man that history will write his success in stone and his failures in sand . . . as we all should do."

The sudden sound of distant thunder made the three of them stop and stare at each other. Instinctively, they looked skyward, but it remained a passive shade of peacock blue. Not even the wisp of a cloud.

"Had me worried for a minute," Stuart gasped.

They all exchanged reassuring smiles and began to feel at ease until they saw the face of fear rushing at them. It was Colton sprinting around the bend, his eyes wide with terror. "Get up high!" he yelled. "Hurry, it's coming!"

There was no thought to ask what *it* was. Stuart grabbed Amber's arm, spun her toward the canyon wall, put his shoulder underneath her legs, and lifted with all his might. She clawed herself up to a narrow ledge. He flashed a glance back at Colton and saw him stumbling over bowling-ball size rocks, but still coming on.

Amber screamed, "Jump, Stuart! Quick!"

Stuart backed up, sprinted toward the canyon wall, and leaped off a bushel-basket size boulder. Grunting as his body slammed into the canyon wall, he hung on to the ledge and pulled himself upward.

Amber continued to scramble higher onto fragile ledges. She turned to see that Colton had climbed up to a sturdy overhang.

Stuart, seeing that Amber and Colton were now safe, grabbed the branches of young canyon maple and leaned outward, straining to locate Tavaci, hoping to see him somewhere on another ledge. Instead, he was horrified to see his dear friend standing in the middle of the dry streambed pointing up-canyon toward the sound of the approaching thunder.

"Tavaci!" Stuart yelled. "Are you crazy? Climb up here, now!"

But, resembling a statue, Tavaci maintained his focused stare and simply lowered his arm. "Whether we called them or not, the evil ones are coming," he said quietly. "I have mocked Wainopits and Kinesava. They have come for me."

"Don't be ridiculous," Stuart yelled, "climb up that tree over there!"

The source of the *thunder* now came roaring around the bend. A ten-foot wall of murderous brown water was pushing a tumbling army of trees and boulders.

Stuart yelled at Tavaci again and started to climb down to reach out to him, but his friend stared at his watery demons, raised his arms high above his head, and yelled, "Be-Wa!" In the next instant, the coffee-brown mass pummeled him and he was swept away.

Stuart, wide-eyed, leaned forward and reached out in desperation, even while realizing it was hopeless.

The shift in his weight fractured a cracked section of the ledge, plunging Amber screaming into the flood.

Before Stuart could react, he heard Colton yell out Amber's name and leap after her into the roiling torrent. Stuart was stunned. He clung to the branches, mouth agape in wonder. Less than a minute ago there were four of them. Now, he was alone.

He stared down at the liquid killer, staggered back a step, and bumped into the canyon wall. He had never seen a flood like this; never even imagined one. Although it had seemed like an hour, the waters were reduced to a depth of two feet in a matter of minutes. Stuart blinked his eyes as if to awaken from a nightmare.

"What the hell just happened?" he swore to himself, scanning the water. "Amber? Colton? Tavaci?"

The roar proceeded down the canyon, leaving him in an unnerving silence. Stuart grabbed the branches again to lower himself to the boulder he used earlier as a springboard, but it was gone. Seeing no alternative, he too jumped into the now knee-deep, passive water.

As he picked his way around trees and boulders, he noticed that the water had receded to about ankle depth in just another minute. This confused him and prompted him to look skyward again. It was still a glorious shade of blue. "I don't understand," was all he could think to say. He shook his head as he pondered his reaction to finding his friend's bodies mangled and lifeless. Scattered thoughts shot through his mind: *What will I tell Emma? What will I tell Be-Wa? How will my three friends look now? Maybe I won't even find their bodies. Going home alone will be* . . . He put both hands on his head and squeezed, trying to kill the thoughts and bring sanity back to his mind.

As he sloshed through wet sand, he rounded a bend, leaned forward, and squinted his eyes to better focus on the grisly scene. In a small hollow carved by ancient floods, the blue color of Colton's shirt was a sharp contrast to the red sandstone walls. Stuart snapped erect, not wanting to witness the site but unable to turn away. Boots heavy with wet sand, he staggered toward his partner. *Dear God, why . . .*

Still fifty feet from Colton, Stuart saw that the blue sleeve of Colton's shirt was a poor attempt to use his arm to shield Amber from the direction of the flood. The rest of Colton's body was covered by red sand. Tears welled up in Stuart's eyes as he slumped to the ground.

"He tried to save her even then," Stuart moaned, "What am I going to do? God, help me. What am I going to do?"

The familiar sound of his voice somehow prompted a loud cough. Colton gasped, swayed as he sat up, then stroked his hand along Amber's motionless back.

"Hang on man, hang on," Stuart yelled. "I'm coming!"

Stuart hadn't reached him yet before Colton staggered to his knees, not caring that his clothes were torn and covered with sand and mud. His total attention was focused on Amber. He swept the debris off of her and strained to lift her upright to a sitting position. Wiping wet sand from her face, he instinctively placed his mouth over hers and blew air into her lungs. Miraculously, she coughed and sputtered as she shook her head back into consciousness.

"Amber," Colton moaned as he held her close and tears dropped onto her shirt. "Thank God that you're alive. Can you stand?"

"I . . . don't . . . know," she gasped as she fell back onto the sand.

By that time Stuart was there to help Colton lift her to her feet. The two survivors bent over with hands on their knees to catch their breath. In unison, they asked, "Tavaci?"

Stuart shook his head. "He was hit full force with that wall of water. I have no idea where he . . ." His emotions overwhelmed him as he placed his face in his hands and sobbed.

Colton and Amber embraced him as the three of them had their emotions rock between gratitude for their survival and grief for the probable loss of their dear friend. Guilt for coaxing Tavaci into the canyon eventually overcame each of them.

"We have to find him," said Colton.

They stumbled along toward the canyon entrance and checked behind every boulder and sand bar.

After two hundred yards, Colton cried out, "There he is. Straight ahead of us, lying face down in the mud."

They rushed to him, knowing that this would not be good news. "Tavaci, Tavaci," they mourned as they pulled his body out from between several huge trees that had been carried by the floodwaters. Colton sat on one of the tree trunks, held Tavaci in his arms, and wept like a small child.

"My brother, my brother, my brother," Colton cried until he ran out of tears. Then he wiped his eyes and glanced at the pile of trees. "Stuart, Amber, look. These aren't *trees* that were ripped up by floodwaters."

Amber glared. "They're cut *logs*. Look at the ends. These went through a sawmill."

"And look at the sky," Colton said. "As blue as ever."

"*Ethan*," Amber growled. "So help me, I'll—"

"No, you won't," Colton said. "I'll take care of this."

"Not without me," Stuart said.

Colton nodded, then turned back to Tavaci's body. "Help me carry . . ." he began to say but started to weep again.

Stuart soon joined him, "I haven't lost a close friend like him since Emma's husband drowned in the Columbia River. We've got to kill this Ethan beast."

Colton exhaled, then picked Tavaci up in his arms. Stuart ran over to help him. They trudged along for over a mile through mud and sand, carrying the body of a man they all loved.

"You know," Colton sighed, "*Tavaci* means Sun in the Ute language. And he certainly was that for all of us. I feel terrible for badgering him to join us to—"

"Don't you dare," scolded Amber. "All of us pushed him to join us. And it wasn't wrong. The only *wrong* here is Ethan. He separated you and me years ago, killed my parents, killed farmer Harold, and now . . ." Her voice broke. "Who knows how many others he has eliminated from his greedy ways. I'm telling you, if I ever see him again I'll—"

"I won't have that memory haunting us later. Stuart and I will find Ethan. Dealing with him won't bother me at all." Colton took a deep breath. "Tying Tavaci onto his horse and taking him back to Be-Wa will be the most difficult thing I have ever done." He shook his head, trying not to think of it. "Then the three of us will go up on the mesa. You go to the sawmill and wait there to make sure it's locked up and you are safe. Stuart and I will go up to Ethan's place and bring him back to justice . . . or give him some justice of our own."

51
Hunting Ethan

WHILE AMBER STARTED her ride up to the sawmill, Colton and Stuart took Tavaci's body home to Be-Wa. She was heartbroken and, after weeping loudly, complained that he was not supposed to go into those canyons. Colton apologized many times, but it felt hollow. He was crushed again when he was leaving and saw Tavaci's two sons playing at a neighbor's home. "Look Stuart, what do we tell them? Who is going to take care of them? How will they get enough money now for food and clothes?"

Stuart stared at the boys. "You're going to stay here now, aren't you Colton?"

It took Colton a minute to reply. "I can't turn my back on them."

"Amber would be happier too."

"Another reason I can't leave. It's a good thing I wrote up those contracts before I left." Colton smiled wryly. "Who knows, I might be following Tavaci's path soon."

"You didn't need to do that. You'll be fine. Let's go back to Portland and keep things going strong. We can both send money to Be-Wa."

"My first job is getting Ethan in jail."

"*Our* first job. Let's ride."

AMBER REACHED THE sawmill and went inside to clean up and to find one of the operators. "Hello?" she called, "Is anyone still here?"

"Yes, Miss Duncan," a man replied as he walked in from the loading yard. "We just finished cutting, and loading, the last pile of logs into good two by fours about an hour ago, so the other men went home already. The folks down below need this lumber real bad."

"Thanks, I know they do." Amber smiled, then her expression grew serious. "I don't want to alarm you, but there's been a flood from Cougar Creek Canyon that went toward town."

"A flood? But that creek has been bone dry."

"It appears it was dry because of Ethan Morley. And the flood's because of him too. I suspect he and his men dammed it up, then suddenly destroyed the dam," she explained. "I want you to go down to your family now and make certain they are all right. I'm sure they are fine, but we will both feel better if you check on them. I'm sure you can return to work here on Monday morning."

"Yes, Ma'am," he said, "are you staying here?"

"I'll lock things up for you. Mr. Grey and Mr. Stuart will be along here very soon."

"All right," he said as he ran outside to his horse.

COLTON AND STUART reached the top of the mesa on the horse trail and spurred their horses on to Ethan's ranch. As they neared his home, they read the sign posted over the road:

TUO YATS.

"Is that Paiute?" Stuart asked.

"No . . . it's not Paiute." Colton paused. "Wait a minute, it's *stay out* spelled backward," he scoffed. "It's just like him to name a ranch with backward lettering. That way he can say he warned people."

"He is a sick man," said Stuart.

"Yeah, that's part of it. I'm going in."

"So am I. Have you got a gun?"

Colton patted his hip. "Do you?

Stuart did the same. "What have you been thinking about doing in here?"

"I was thinking about something that Gandhi fellow in India said, 'Throughout history, there have been tyrants and murderers, and for a time, they can seem invincible, but in the end, they always fall. Think of it . . . always.' That's what keeps me going after this guy. But I'm not taking any chances. The trick is to be polite while our hand is on our hidden gun, just in case."

They rode up to Ethan's cabin slowly, trying to be alert in every direction. Within fifty yards they could see a few of his men sitting around on his porch. "We are looking at the physics of darkness," Colton said to Stuart, who tipped his hat politely to the men.

"Is Ethan here?" Colton asked the men, his hand under his jacket and on his gun.

"No, he ain't," the tallest one answered. "Whatcha wanna know for?"

"Seems there was a dam up here that nobody knew about," Colton said. "And now that dam's been destroyed and people have lost their lives down below. I'm talking about men with children. We want to see where that dam was."

The men were silent but stared at each other.

"So now we find out what kind of men *you* are," Colton pushed. "All we need is the truth. And I know that telling the truth can be tough, especially if you think it can harm you. But that's what really shows what kind of men you are."

"I TOLD you that was gonna happen!" the tall man yelled at the others. "Ethan done lost his mind! That's why the other men quit days ago and headed down to Arizona lookin' for work."

"Unless you men had something to do with that dam, you've got no worries about us," Colton promised.

"We shoulda done what Tom did and got outta here instead of helpin' build that damn dam," the tall man said to the other men.

Now the shortest of the group sprang out of his chair. "Yeah?" he asked. "Well, ain't nobody seen or heard of Tom for a long time. I'm thinkin' he ain't around here, or *anywhere else* alive no more."

The group grew silent and stared at each other.

The tall one turned back to Colton and Stuart. "Sorry about that dam, Mr.," he said. "I can take ya over there if ya want, but Ethan ain't here."

"Yes," said Colton. "We want to see it."

The tall man got on his horse and led them slowly trotting toward the dam site. But a small disturbance made all three of them turn back to look at the cabin again. The other men had mounted their horses and were riding off Ethan's land. "Reckon they be done here," the tall man said.

In ten minutes, they arrived at the upper mesa over the canyon and looked at the small stream trickling over the cliff's edge. Colton and Stuart climbed down to examine the remnants of the now obliterated dam. Only a few of the corner logs remained; one end cut by saw blades, the other end blown apart by dynamite. Colton glared at the logs, then put his hand on his gun and turned to the tall man.

"Wait a minute!" the man yelled. "I ain't got nothin' to do with blowin' this thing up. We just did like we was told, but we was feedin' horses when we heard an explosion. We came ridin' over here and seen that water gushin' over the edge. Some of the men quit Ethan right there, but they didn't know nuthin' about nobody getting' killed below. They just left. A few of us stuck around cuz we needed the work. But I think you seen everybody but me has just quit, and I'm outta here as soon as you two leave."

Stuart put his hand on Colton's arm to relax his grip on his pistol, but Colton wasn't quite finished yet. He pulled his pistol out and said, "I'm going to give you one chance, and only one, to tell me where Ethan is." He pulled the hammer back and pointed the gun at the man's head.

"All right, all right!" the man yelled. "He said him and Stitch was gonna finish business for good at the sawmill, take care of that Amber lady, and bust up that cable riggin' you guys use. They've been gone fer a while. Don't know which place they went first, and they could be anywhere by now. Just let me go and you'll never see me no more. I swear."

Colton looked at Stuart and gasped, "Amber." His eyes grew wide with fear. "Those places are in opposite directions from here. She could be at either place with that beast. We'll have to split up and ride like the wind."

"I don't like heights," Stuart said, "I'll take the sawmill."

Colton nodded but was already leaping onto the Wichanpi's saddle.

52

Water, Now Fire

ETHAN PULLED HIS buckboard up a hundred yards short of the sawmill. Stitch was right behind him riding his horse. When they saw only Amber's Buckskin tied to the post by the front door, they smiled at each other. Everything was going their way.

"Stitch, you stay here and watch to see if anybody else comes ridin' up here," Ethan commanded. "I don't want nobody interruptin' me and Miss Duncan. You understand?"

"Completely," Stitch nodded as he glanced at the sawmill.

Ethan walked to the large doors where the lumber was loaded, but they were locked. Walking quietly now, he went to the front door and lifted it slightly so it would not squeak when he entered. The mill was fairly dark inside, but he soon saw Amber in the office room putting papers in a box. He squared his shoulders, took a deep breath, and walked directly toward her.

Amber glanced up and saw Ethan fifty feet from her door. She quickly grabbed a lock and clamped on the hasp to keep him out.

Ethan simply smiled, leaned back, and kicked the door open. "Hello Missy," he snarled.

"Morley, you get out of here right now!" she yelled.

"Someone here gonna *make* me?" he laughed. "I think it's just you and me."

She glanced quickly at the desk and ran to open its top drawer, but Ethan slid across the desktop and grabbed her hand just as she reached inside for a pistol. He wrenched the gun out of her hand.

"You know, Queen Duncan, if people saw you reaching for

that gun they might think that you don't like me. And we know that ain't true." He grabbed her hair and pulled her head back with his right hand and pulled her in tight with his left arm. "Why, I remember them good old days way back at the Cotton Festival when you was sweet on me. You were quite a kisser. Remember?"

"You're crazy!" she yelled, struggling to free a hand.

"Yep, crazy about you," he sneered as he pulled her in closer and kissed her hard.

She struggled and groaned, then freed her left hand, reached up, and scratched him hard.

He threw her to the floor as blood dripped down the side of his face. Putting his hand on his cheek to stop the bleeding, he pointed at her and yelled, "You witch! I'm going to have you whether you like it or not." He looked at his bloody hand, then glared at her. "But I think the best way will be to do that right in front of Mr. Grey, just like at that stupid festival. Only this time, after teaching you a lesson, it will be the end of Mr. Grey. And I know right where to have this all happen."

He reached down and yanked her up off the floor. She went to scratch him again, but he held both her wrists in his left hand while making a threatening fist with his right. "Missy, you're gonna do what I tell you, or that pretty face of yours will be a mess when I finish pounding on you. And don't think I won't do it."

He shook his fist in front of her face, causing her to blink in fear. He grabbed a rope hanging on the wall and tied her hands behind her back. "You can walk, or I can drag you. Don't matter none to me." He started pulling her out of the office as she tearfully glanced back at the pistol in the desk drawer. She struggled to break free, but he was too strong. "Having a few bruises on you won't stop me from enjoying you later, but you might want to look good for the last time you're gonna see Colton Grey." Grabbing her elbow, he forced her over to the buckboard and tossed her into the back.

Amber's eyes widened as she saw boxes of dynamite, cans of kerosene, and several coils of long fuses. "Have you lost your mind, Ethan? As dry as it is around here that stuff would create a fire that could . . ." She paused, gasping. "Wait a minute. The explosion we heard before the flood was *your* dynamite."

"Maybe," Ethan admitted with a smile.

"Do you realize you killed Tavaci when the four of us were in that canyon? And who knows what damage you may have caused downstream from there."

"One less Injun ain't gonna hurt my feelings." Ethan shrugged. "But I was hoping that little water project would take out Colton and his buddy. Didn't know you was in there too. I don't want nuthin to happen to you . . . 'til I'm ready for it to happen. And that should be real soon now, or maybe not 'til we go to Colorado." He paused to look at her. "Hmmm, I can't have you yellin' as we move along." He took off her scarf and gagged her. "Stitch, you need to stay back here for a half hour or so to make sure nobody follows us to that cable mess. I mean *nobody*."

Stitch leered at Amber, then nodded, "No problem, Boss."

"Time to go set the trap for Colton Grey. But first . . ." He grabbed a can of kerosene and ran back to the sawmill. In a few minutes he returned, jumped onto the buckboard, and snapped the reins. That's when Amber saw the smoke rising up from the mill's rooftop.

STUART HAD PUSHED his horse as hard as he could, but as he approached the sawmill he saw the disaster Ethan had created. It did not take the flames long to devour the wooden building. The yard area was free of dry grasses and trees, and a few log piles were far enough away that the fire was contained to the building.

"Ethan," he grumbled as he shook his head. "Amber?" Looking at the raging flames he knew that if she was inside, she would have perished long ago. But he had to at least make the attempt to locate her.

ETHAN'S BUCKBOARD KICKED up a lot of dust as it stopped at the cables. He was in a hurry, and for good reasons. If his plan worked, he would kill Colton Grey, take Amber for himself, ruin the forest for the farmers below, and escape to Colorado.

"Out ya go, Missy," he snarled as he pulled Amber off the back of the buckboard. Shaking his fist in her face he added, "I ain't remindin' you again that you'd best behave or things will turn sour a lot quicker than you think." He grabbed a rope from the back of the wagon and drug her over to the edge of the cliff. "You wait right there Queen Duncan," he said as he tied her to the front cable timbers. "I got a little chore to do, then I'll be back and we'll see if Grey comes around as I expect he will. And the wind seems to be workin' just right for this whole party we're gonna have." He leaped onto the buckboard, whipped the horse, and yelled, "Run you fool, run!"

A quarter-mile into the forest, he pulled the horse to a stop and jumped out of the buckboard. He grabbed dynamite sticks and cans of kerosene from the back and began placing them about one hundred feet apart in four places of down and dead trees that were surrounded by tall, dry grass. He attached fuses between all four dynamite piles and ran back to the buckboard. Then he paused to make sure everything was in place. "This should do it," he muttered. "A nice line of fireworks facing that stupid cable setup. Plenty of trees for fuel, the wind is blowin' to the West right at Queen Duncan, and I've left a small escape route for me ridin' South just before the fire eats up everything right to the edge of the cliff. It's the perfect time to say *perfect*."

COLTON HAD WICHANPI running at full speed as he rode over the crest of the ridge overlooking the Cable System from the South. In the distance, he saw Amber tied to the Cable timbers. He leaned forward to race to her, but then pulled back on the reins and paused. *Where is Ethan?* he thought. *This might be a setup. If I go sprinting down to her, he might be hiding somewhere to kill us both.*

He scanned the hillsides but couldn't see Ethan anywhere. He saw only a swirl of dust coming off the ridge and heading toward the cables. "All right Wichanpi, we've got to go quick and quiet. Somebody is riding fast toward Amber right now." He pulled the reins to the left and rode hidden among the trees close to the edge of the cliff until he was about a hundred yards from Amber. Dismounting there, he decided not to tie the Appaloosa to a tree limb. "I don't know why, my friend, but I'm going to let you stay loose and free."

As Colton neared the Cable rigging, he paused and hid behind the last tree on the cliff's edge. He spied an empty buckboard near the cable rigging. *If that was Ethan coming over the ridge, he could be hiding anywhere by now. I can't mess this up and get her killed.*

Ethan was on the other side of the buckboard making sure his rifle was loaded. Satisfied, he walked over to Amber. Leaning his rifle against the bottom timbers, he went over to her and pulled the scarf off her mouth.

"Well, Queen Duncan, it's just you and me until we hear Grey ride up to rescue you," he said. "And that's what my rifle is for. Then you and me are gonna make some fireworks and head to Colorado. Hey, why don't we have some fireworks right now?" He grabbed her hair, pressed her head against the upper timbers of the rigging, and kissed her hard. "Maybe you should get used to bein' tied up. I can get some sweet stuff outta you when rope is involved." He grinned and went to kiss her again, but she spit in his face. He slapped her and yelled, "I told you before I ain't puttin' up with stuff like that." He wiped his face dry, grabbed her collar, and began to tear her shirt.

"Colton!" she screamed as she looked past Ethan.

Ethan grinned again, but then he heard running footsteps coming behind him. He turned just as Colton's fist hit him in the jaw. As he fell, he reached for his rifle leaning on the lower beam.

Colton saw the rifle too. He wrestled it away from Ethan and pointed it at his chest.

"Whatcha gonna do, Grey," Ethan laughed. "Shoot an unarmed man? If so, you ain't no better than me. Go ahead. Seems like my rifle's come into good use on the tops of cliffs."

Colton glared at him. "You've had worse ideas Morley, but you're right." He turned sideways and threw the rifle over the cliff.

"Colton." Amber sighed with relief.

Colton glared at Ethan and went to Amber to untie her.

In that instant, Ethan jumped up, leaped onto his buckboard, and raced toward the piles of dynamite. In a minute, he was lighting the fuses.

STUART REALIZED THAT fighting the fire in the sawmill would be futile. He shook his head, and wondered, *What else could go wrong?* Dismounting, he pulled his gun from its holster and ran as close to the fire as he could bear. *If she's in there, it's too late. But, maybe she escaped and rode to Colton. I've got to get to the Cable Works as fast as possible.* Holstering his gun, he ran back to his horse but was met by Stitch riding toward him. Stuart raised his hands in surrender.

Stitch had no plans for a prisoner. He stopped his horse, pulled his rifle from its scabbard, pointed it at Stuart, and pulled the hammer back. "You're *half* our problems," Stitch said, smiling. "And you're the half that's going to be gone the quickest." He aimed at Stuart's head just as a series of distant explosions thundered through the air and startled his horse. The horse reared up, flinging Stitch off and backward into a tree. His neck broke instantly.

Stuart shook as he reached for his pistol and aimed at the still body of Stitch. The gun wobbled in his hand and he breathed heavily as he realized how close he had come to death. He took one deep breath, exhaled, and looked in the direction of the explosions. "Colton and Amber," he gasped. He quickly mounted his horse and raced toward the Cable Works and, hopefully, his two friends.

The wall of fire that rose from the explosions looked like a volcanic eruption. Dead conifers and dry grass reacted as though they had been soaked in gasoline. The wind coming from the East increased the flames until they covered the crowns of all the trees, save a narrow passage to the South. That was Ethan's escape route.

Ethan raced the buckboard back toward the stranded couple, and yelled, "See you in Hell, Grey. Looks like you'll be there soon! That fire ain't gonna give me time to tie you up again Missy. You're gonna roast just like Grey." Laughing, he cracked a whip over his horse's head and bolted toward freedom.

Wichanpi, smelling the smoke and seeing the buckboard race by, dashed after it at full speed. He easily overtook Ethan and sprinted through the last of the dead trees just as they caught fire. By the time the buckboard reached that same passage, the trees were fully engulfed in a roaring inferno. Ethan's horse reared up in fear just as a huge, flaming branch crashed down on the tongue of the buckboard. The horse, now free, raced after Wichanpi, dragging its reins and harness.

Ethan, having knocked into the back of the wagon, barely sat up to escape when the main trunk of the huge tree crashed directly on top of him. The searing flames muffled his cries of agony as his prophecy to Colton instead came true for him.

Colton's eyes grew wide as he saw the wall of flames roaring toward them. Amber frantically looked for an escape route, but now there was none. She ran and embraced Colton. She was about to speak, but he picked her up over his shoulder and ran to the end of the cable system. He looked over the cliff's edge at the three thousand feet of cable extending to the bottom of the canyon.

"We've got no time to argue about this, Amber. Get into the cable box!" he yelled over the roar of the approaching flames.

"What are you talking about?" she screamed.

"You're going down on the cable. It's your only chance."

She peered over the edge and shuddered. "There's no way I'm going down on that, and I will *not* leave you here."

"You *must* leave! Don't you see? Ethan will win if you stay here and die. Get down there and take care of the Duncan and Grey ranches. Just promise that you won't forget me."

"How can you say—"

"No time left, sweetheart." He placed her into the cable box, ran back to the brake, and released her slowly into a gentle downhill glide.

She hung on to the cable but turned to look for him. He was at the back of the rigging and out of sight. "I love you, Colton Grey . . ." she sobbed.

The fire was close enough now that Colton could feel the heat on his back. He eased off on the brake and prayed that Amber would survive the terrifying two-minute ride.

STUART WATCHED THE black clouds of smoke and the orange-colored sky as he raced toward the Cable System. As he reached the crest of the small hill just East of the Cable, he was stopped by a solid wall of flames. He galloped to the North end of the mesa, but the fire was already there.

"Their only chance is to the South," he whispered. He patted the horse's neck. "Have you got a few more miles of running left inside?"

He pulled reins to the side and kicked the horse's flanks, but by the time he reached the Southern edge of the flames he realized there was no way he could break through that wall of fire.

Something in the flames caught his eye. He leaned forward and tried to shade his eyes with his hands. In the distance, he could barely make out the crushed form of a buckboard with its rear wheels now engulfed in the inferno.

"Colton didn't have a buckboard, and I don't think Amber did either. At least I hope not," he muttered. A shiver ran down his spine despite the incredible heat.

He decided his only option was to wait for the fire to continue blowing eastward until it eventually reached the edge of the cliff and run out of fuel. *Tavaci killed by water. Colton and Amber killed by fire.* Stuart shook his head. *It's just like he said it would be.*

53

Cable Rescue

AMBER CLUNG TO the cable with all her strength. As she approached the stanchions at the canyon floor, she leapt off the cable box and turned to look up at the cliff's edge. The sky was ablaze. It looked like the sun was setting, but in the east. What appeared to be black clouds were billows of smoke floating upward. She clenched her fists and held them tight to her heart. When the cable finally stopped moving, she knew that Colton was gone. Staring up at the tiny skeletal shape of the Cable timbers on the cliff's edge, she again sobbed, "I love you, Colton Grey." She closed her eyes, bowed her head, and dropped to her knees.

COLTON REALIZED A painful death was inevitable. His eyes scanned the wall of fire, looking for even a remote path of escape. There was none. He backed up against the Cable timbers and inched his way to the edge of the cliff. He trusted that Amber had made it safely to the valley floor, but he could not see her below. "I love you, Amber Duncan," he yelled in despair. He remembered Tavaci's final, brave stand against the rushing floodwaters. "See you soon, Tavaci," he said as he clutched the vertical timber on the cliff's edge. He turned to face his fiery nemesis and then squinted at a form he saw coming through the flames.

Have I died and gone to the next world already? He thought. *Who or what is that?*

A female figure walked through the flames and stopped at the
far end of the Cable rigging. Her long black braid swayed in an
invisible breeze. "Beware of the water and the fire," she said. She
pointed at a huge coil of rope lying on the ground in the center of
the Cable timbers and added, "Find my family." She blew a kiss to
him and said, "Puhnekay' vawsoom. Tooveets' ow' suhntuheun,
Colton Grey." Then she vanished.

"Mother," Colton choked, but he couldn't afford the time to
stand in astonishment. Star was gone. He jumped into the middle
of the cable timbers, grabbed the rope, and quickly tied an end
to the timber at the cliff's edge. He tied the other end around his
waist and tossed the rest of the coil over the edge. Standing at the
edge of the cliff, he grabbed the taught rope, took a step backward,
and descended slowly down the steep face of the mesa.

This rope is maybe only a hundred yards long . . . and it's a rope!
Colton's panicked thoughts raced. *It won't be good when the flames
reach the Cable system and start the timbers, and this rope, on fire.* He
glanced down and noticed he was nearing a narrow, hidden canyon he had never seen before. Estimating the remaining length of
rope, and the distance to the floor of that small canyon, he realized he would never reach it, but then he spied a tall tree. *I've got
only one chance. And that tall Ponderosa Pine is it.*

Hanging from the bottom of the rope, Colton pushed off the
sandstone wall and swung himself along the cliff face toward the
top of the tree, but saw that the rope was still fifteen feet short. He
looked upward and saw flames engulfing the Cable timbers. *I've
got no choice,* he thought as he reached for his knife.

He put the knife to the rope and started slicing, pausing only
once to make certain he was still hovering directly over the top of
the tree. His final cut sent him plummeting through what seemed
like countless needle-covered branches. Adrenaline prevented him
from feeling pain . . . until he crashed onto the canyon's sandy floor.

Colton lay dazed for ten minutes, trying to catch his breath. Brushing needles and branches off his body, he groaned as he staggered to his feet.

"I must have broken some ribs," he moaned as he grabbed his side and tried to stretch. Limping over to the pine, he touched its trunk. "Thank you for catching me, my friend," he said.

At that moment, the top end of the rope burned through and was freed from the cable timber. The burning end drifted down within fifty feet of where he stood.

I can't let those embers start a fire down here, he thought as he ran to the end of the rope. He stomped on the glowing fibers. When he bent down to pick up the rope, he glanced through a hedge of Manzanita shrubs and noticed a narrow chasm about fifty feet deep that paralleled the ravine where he stood.

I've never seen this before, he thought. *I've never even heard about this. If Tavaci had known about this he would have told me. We could have explored for days down there.* Then he noticed how steep the walls were. *Maybe not. The walls are totally smooth. We would have needed ropes to lower ourselves and*—His mouth dropped open as he leaned forward to get a better look. *What the . . . ?*

He lay down on his stomach and crawled to the edge of the chasm. Far below were the skeletal remains of four bodies, partially covered by sand. He could tell by their clothing that they were Southern Paiutes. Next to each body were the remnants of a broken basket with straps for carrying over the shoulders. *Those must be Star's fam—*

His thoughts were stopped when he heard the crackling sounds of a huge, burning pine bouncing off the walls above him as it fell from the cliff above. He dashed over to the cliff base to flatten himself against the wall to prevent being crushed. Although he was showered with sparks, the tree bounced over him and plummeted into the narrow chasm, completely covering the four bodies.

Rushing water must have pushed them into that deep hole. And there was no way out for them. I hate to think it, but I hope they were killed in the fall and didn't have to starve to death down there.

He looked up to the mesa top. The flames were nearly exhausted and the sky had cleared of smoke. *Amber,* was all he could think about now as he scanned the canyon floor. *If I walk north I should be able to find that trail the Paiutes used to climb this mesa. The one Wichanpi helped me find.* He looked up at the cliffs edge again, his thoughts drifting to the fates of Stuart and his horse. *Time to head down and find the answers.*

As Colton carefully picked his way along precarious sandstone ledges, he noticed a three-foot-by-three-foot entrance to a dark cavern, nearly masked by thick clusters of the prickly leaves of several Live-Oak trees. Boyhood curiosity overwhelmed him. He looped his rope and threw it over the branches of sharp leaves to help spread them apart so he could squeeze into the small passage on his knees. After crawling for ten feet, the cavern opened up until he could easily stand. There was now a slanted, narrow fissure above him that let the sunlight illuminate the main room of the cavern. To his astonishment, there were willow baskets, rabbit-skin blankets, deer-hide moccasins, a cradleboard, several arrows made from dried reeds and serviceberry shrubs, cottonwood bows, two elderberry flutes, and four sandals made from bark and yucca.

"Their Treasure Cave," he marveled aloud. "No gold or silver. Just the things that were part of Paiute life, and that would have meant so much to them."

Maybe not worth any money, but to The People it would be of great value, he thought. *I think Be-Wa is the only person I will tell about this, although she would never come up here.* He smiled at the contents of the *Treasure Cave,* then crawled back outside.

His smile turned sober when he again realized that Star's parents and grandparents had been found and their riddle solved. But the two people he hoped to solve the riddle for were no longer with him. He blinked tears away.

"Back to the trail, and Amber," Colton said aloud. He started searching for the trail again.

After several hundred yards of teetering on small ledges and grabbing branches for balance, Colton smiled when he saw a pile of four rocks. He knew that was the Paiute Trail Sign to turn left or right. He went to the left and within another hundred yards was a pile of three rocks, meaning the trail went downhill.

"Man, I love the Paiutes." He grinned when he finally saw another pile of three rocks, indicating the trail went straight ahead. He fought the urge to run down the hill toward Amber, knowing that a fall at this height would tear him to pieces.

When he finally reached the canyon floor and the cable stanchions, he called out Amber's name, but there was no response. *Where could she be?* he thought. He looked down at the sandy ground and saw her footprints leading toward the Virgin River. "Of course," he chuckled to himself as he followed her trail as fast as he could.

Then he stopped.

There she was, sitting on a rock along the bank, just staring at the river current. He didn't want to startle her, so he came up to her and quietly called, "Amber, I'm here."

She turned and blinked several times. Then she shook her head as to escape a dream, or nightmare. "Colton!" she yelled as she realized he was really there.

Their embrace felt as though they melted into each other's bodies.

"Oh, Colton, I was sure that you had—" she began to cry, but his kiss interrupted her. It was a matchless kiss that left her breathless and faint.

They held each other for an hour, but it seemed like only minutes had gone by when he finally spoke.

"Amber, I'm never leaving you again, no matter what happens," Colton said softly. "Take my hand."

"What about Ethan?" she asked, wide-eyed.

"He's finished."

"Did you—" She didn't want to finish the sentence.

He shook his head. "His own fire."

"What about Stuart?"

"I don't know. He went to the sawmill, I went to the Cable Works. We were both looking for you."

"Oh, Colton. Stitch was there waiting for him when Ethan and I rode away. I don't have any tears left. What should we do?"

"We can't hide under a rock," Colton said. "Let's start walking to your ranch. You have some rifles there, don't you?"

"Yes, but it will take us hours to get there."

"And just as long for Stitch to ride down from the sawmill. Let's go."

54
Only Some Dreams Come True

COLTON AND AMBER were exhausted as they reached the inside of her ranch house. "I can't run another step," she gasped as they both collapsed onto chairs.

"Same here," Colton wheezed. "I think we're getting too used to having all the running done by horses."

"Shh, you mentioned horses. Listen." Amber motioned for him to be quiet. "I hear several of them riding up here right now. It must be Stitch and some of his gang."

They each grabbed a rifle and went to the windows by the front porch. Just as they were about to break glass and prepare to fire, Colton yelled, "It's Stuart! And he's got Wichanpi!"

"And Banner," Amber added happily.

Amber and Colton ran out to meet Stuart as he was dismounting. They nearly tackled him when his boot hit the ground.

"Man, are we glad to see you," Colton said. "We figured that maybe Stitch—"

"Yeah, things didn't work out too well for Stitch," Stuart said. "He couldn't keep his head on straight."

"What?" Colton quirked an eyebrow.

"Doesn't matter." Stuart shook his head. "He had an accident and won't be bothering anyone anymore. Banner was still in the area near the sawmill, and he came to me as I was riding toward the Cable. Guess he recognized my horse."

"And Wichanpi?" Colton asked.

"I saw this wall of flames near the Cables and the only place

I could see an opening was a narrow path on the South edge of the cliff. By the time I got there, I saw Wichanpi racing my way like a lightning bolt. He came to me when I called him, but I think it was mostly because he saw Banner. By that time the fire had made a complete line across and I couldn't get through to you, so I waited until it burned out so I could, you know, find you both and do what needed to be done. I figured I had another Tavaci incident. When the fire burned its way to the cliff's edge and the fuel was basically gone, I rode in toward the Cables. I passed what looked like the remains of a wagon or buckboard. Not much left but the metal wheel rims."

"Ethan's under that," Colton said softly.

"Wish I had known that." Stuart sighed. "When I got to the Cable Works, I couldn't find a trace of either one of you. How did you get to this ranch?"

"Amber rode the cables down, and—"

Stuart gasped at Amber, "You *rode* the cables down two thousand feet? What was that like?"

"I don't remember." She laughed. "Most of the time I had my eyes closed, unless I glanced up to watch the fire close in on Colton. Then I couldn't watch anymore. And *no*, I would never do that again. Nobody should."

Stuart turned back to Colton. "And how did you get down here, Colt?"

"I saw Star again and she saved my life. She told me what to do, and then spoke in Paiute and told me, 'I'll see you again. I love you, Colton Grey.' I think she means in another life. And then she vanished."

Both Stuart and Amber looked at Colton in astonishment.

"I am so grateful we are alive and together again," Stuart remarked.

Colton nodded. "I just wish Tavaci was with us . . . It's not the same unless all of us are together."

"Yeah, I had some time to be thinking about that," Stuart said.

Colton and Amber became somber. "And . . . ?"

"I'm heading back to Portland," Stuart replied. "This area just isn't me. It's beautiful here, and I love you both, but I miss green, and Emma and Todd, and my auto, and . . ."

"Elizabeth?" Colton asked.

"Yes, believe it or not," Stuart agreed. "I'm figuring three days' rest, seeing sites, saying goodbyes, then I'll be getting on that train again." He looked at Colton and Amber. "I'm guessing you'll be staying here with this beautiful, young lady."

"I never should have left here in the first place," Colton said, taking Amber by the hand. "Plus there's Be-Wa and her children to care for. I need to stay, and I want to stay."

"You'll come visit us, won't you? There's Multnomah Falls, and forests, and the Columbia, and the ocean, and ships . . . you probably didn't need to hear that last one."

"I'd like to see those places," Amber said.

"Of course, we'll visit," Colton promised. "Those sites are wonderful, but we would mostly be coming to see you."

Stuart nodded. "Three days then. I assume a wedding will be happening here soon."

"Absolutely," Colton replied, "but I haven't even asked—"

"Yes," Amber interrupted.

"Well, here are your horses," Stuart laughed. "I'm heading to the Big Rock Cabin for a good night's sleep. And, believe it or not, I'm going to miss that place." He glanced around the canyon and added, "I'll miss most everything here." He looked at Colton. "Look here, brother, you'll be spending the rest of your life with Amber and—"

"Longer than that," Amber corrected, smiling.

"Okay . . . forever then," Stuart conceded. "So how about you and I spending some relaxation time at your Thinking Place, and then a final camp killing spiders at the Cabin?"

"Of course." Colton grinned. "That's a great idea." He turned to Amber. "Amber, I—"

"I'll be fine here tonight," she reassured him. "The bad guys are gone, and I'm home."

55

The Three Stars, Again

A S USUAL, COLTON woke up very early that morning. He picked up his boots, looked across the cabin at sleeping Stuart, and tiptoed out of the Big Rock Cabin so he wouldn't wake him. He had a surprise project to finish for Amber. It was something he had built when he was a young man and still had dreams about the Grey and Duncan Ranches joining together one day.

Sun will be up soon. Stuart will wake, and Amber will be here too. I've got to hurry. He rode fast to his Thinking Place along the Virgin River. He dismounted and went to a tall but narrow gap between two large boulders. "It's still here," he wondered aloud as he pulled out a four-foot-by-four-foot piece of wood with a three-foot long piece of chain attached to each end. *It's not as heavy as when I hid it in there,* he thought. *Of course, I am somewhat older.* He picked up the wood and carried it over to one of the ten-foot posts he put in the ground so many years ago.

"Wichanpi, come here boy," he called to his horse, who eagerly obeyed.

Colton stood on Wichanpi's saddle, leaned against one pole, and pulled the board up until he could attach one chain link onto a bolt at the top of the pole. With a light touch on the reins, he moved the horse to the other pole, where he pulled the board up and attached the other chain. The board was now perfectly suspended between the two posts, wide enough for a wagon to pass through. *All right, that's as good as it can be for now. They can come anytime now.*

At the sun rose over the mountain crest, Stuart and Amber rode up to the river and found Colton relaxing there. They dismounted and each of them gave him a warm embrace.

Stuart began, "I know the two of you have a lot to do, so there's no need to take me to the train. I know how to get there," he said as he rubbed his behind. They all laughed, but he wasn't finished. "Colton, we've been through a lot together. And I hope we have a lot more to do."

"You'll do well, Stuart," Colton said. "You, and that lucky girl."

"And the auto," Amber added with a laugh.

"I just want you to understand, Stuart," Colton said, his tone serious. "That I could never become what I needed to be, by staying the *way* I was, or *where* I was."

"I understand completely. My best wishes to you both," Stuart said. Then he winked at Amber and added, "Forever." He mounted his horse, tipped his hat, and rode west toward Saint George.

As Stuart went over the hill and out of sight, Colton turned to look at the river and entered into deep thought.

Amber approached him from the side and leaned on his arm, but Colton didn't stir. He was focused on a wave rolling over a particular rock. "Where's your mind at, Colton?" she asked.

"I just remembered a wave that I watched going over the bow of my ship."

"Your ship. Did it have a name?"

"It was called The Orion." He pointed over at the poles and the sign hanging between them. On the sign, the letters C & A were painted inside a large diamond. And above the diamond was the Orion constellation.

Their kiss was soft and sincere. It was one that meant *forever*.